JENSON

MELISSA BELLE

ALSO BY MELISSA BELLE

Boston Boys Series

BOSTON BILLIONAIRE

BOSTON LOVE

BOSTON ESCAPE

BOSTON ROOMIE

WILD MEN Series

WILD MAN

COLTON

DYLAN

AYDEN

JENSON

BRAYDEN

CAMERON

Sign up for Melissa's Newsletter to receive alerts and updates on upcoming book releases.

ABOUT

It's been years, but they never got over each other ... A SECOND CHANCE OFF-LIMITS ROMANCE

Olivia

Jenson's not just a former star quarterback turned brilliant football coach. He's not only an amazing father to twin sons.

He's also...mine.

The problem? He's always been off-limits.

But we always planned to be together one day. Except sometimes plans change. So we both moved on, or we tried to.

But now, after all these years, Jenson's back in town. We're both single. And we can't keep our hands off each other.

Jenson

When Olivia was born, I was told to look out for her, and she was the girl who made me smile when nothing else could.

When we got older, I fell in love with her. And then we broke each other's hearts.

I'm a single father now, with two boys who look up to me. And I'm about to show them how to get the win when the clock's running down and the defense is stacked against you. I'm going to fight for the one thing, outside of them, that's meant the most to me in my life.

I've come back to town on a mission:

To make Olivia mine. Because she and I are meant to be.

But for Olivia and me, meant to be has never been easy...

STAY UP TO DATE WITH MELISSA

Do you want to stay up to date on awesome sales, upcoming hot releases, and giveaways? Sign up for my VIP List and get access to frequent freebies!

For anyone who's ever felt wrong to love who you love.

CHAPTER ONE

Jenson

In five hours and two left turns, I'll be pulling into the town I left years ago, the same place I left my heart. I tuck my two sons into their car seats and buckle them in before I climb into the driver's seat and start the truck. We pull out of my townhouse complex in Pittsburgh, and I head for the highway.

"Daddy, how long before we get there?"

As we pull up at a stoplight, I look at Kyle in the rearview mirror. "A little while. But before you know it, we'll be home. To the home where I grew up," I clarify. "You boys remember the town. You always love visiting Liberty Falls."

"Will we get to play football with your new team like we do here? What if they don't let us?" Connor asks me, as he pulls his blankie tighter around him.

They may be identical twins, but my two boys couldn't be more different in temperament: Kyle's always running three steps away from me, and Connor makes his decisions more cautiously. I'm trying to take a page from each of them and follow my heart without ignoring all sense of logic. Like this move I'm making across the state of Pennsylvania—I've wanted to do it for a while, but I didn't make the leap. Not until right now. My heart pounds at the risk I'm taking, but the woman at the finish line is worth it. She's always been worth it, and she always will be.

"I've already told the head coach how much you love coming to practice. He's looking forward to meeting you both," I assure Connor.

"Will we see Grandma?" Kyle asks.

"We're going to stay with her and Grandpa, like always," I say.

"What about Livia?" Connor asks, staring at me in the mirror with those serious green eyes that match mine in color and intensity. "Will we see her too?"

"Yeah, I want to see Livia!" Kyle chimes in, nodding his blond head vigorously.

My chest tightens. "I hope so boys. I certainly plan on it."

As the light turns green, I put my focus back on the road. But my thoughts are only on one woman.

Olivia Graham, I'm coming back for you, babe. I hope you're ready because I'm not giving up this time without one hell of a fight.

———

Olivia

#JustDivorcedGoals

1) Keep well-meaning but pushy relatives off my back so I can figure out my love life on my own.

2) Date a man who makes my palms sweat and my heart pound. A man I trust and who accepts me for the somewhat neurotic, numbers-obsessed, good-hearted, quirky-humored woman that I am. Someone like...

I suck in a deep breath as hot sensations flood my mind. And my body. And...intimate parts of me.

I spin around in my office chair, squirming in my seat and pressing my feet into the carpet to try to shake the memory of Jenson Beau. Before I can force myself to concentrate on my work, the phone rings at my desk.

I whip my chair back around and grab the phone. "Hello and welcome to Liberty Falls Union Bank. This is Olivia. How may I help you?"

"Olivia, I have some bad news," Hayley says in a nervous tone.

"What is it?" I say in alarm. "Are you okay?"

"Oh, I'm fine. It's just...don't kill me, but I have to work this Sunday."

"What?!" Panic fills my chest. "You can't go to my great-aunt's birthday party with me?"

"This huge editing project due Monday literally just came up, and my boss is insisting I'm the only one who can do it. And I would start in on it early so that maybe I'd be done by Sunday, but the client isn't even sending the proposal over until Saturday. They're paying double for the quick turn-around, so it will be a nice paycheck for me."

"Well, that part is great," I say. "But you were going to be my friend-date. My sidekick to help me stave off my pushy relatives, who will no doubt be pestering me all day about what went so wrong to drive me to divorce. Not to mention everyone trying to set me up."

"I know. And I swear I will be there for you for the next shindig. When is the next Graham family event?"

"In a week. But this one will be the worst because it's first. No one's seen me since my divorce was finalized, and they're going to be lying in wait like a pack of lions."

"I have a plan for my replacement. I'll meet you at your house tonight. With a bottle of wine."

"Make it two," I say as I hang up the phone.

———

"No way in hell." I nearly drop my half-empty glass of wine onto my living room floor as I vigorously slash an emphatic "no" through the air with my hand. "I can't."

"But why not?" Hayley asks only in the way a person who knows why I'm saying no can. Her auburn hair is piled messily on top of her head, and her pale blue eyes light up as she carries on explaining her crazy-ass plan to me. "I know your backstory with Jenson Beau, Olivia."

"So then you understand why Jenson can't, under any circumstances, be my date to a family event. We were raised like cousins."

"But you aren't cousins."

"That's a technicality our families refuse to acknowledge."

Hayley's clearly not listening because she's already pulled Jenson's Facebook page up on my laptop. "Message him."

"No."

"If you're saying no, then you're simply not drunk enough."

"What do you want me to say to him—'my divorce was just finalized, and I'm single for the first time since forever, and I'm hoping you are too so we can pick up where we left off when we were kids? Oh, and before you had children with another woman?'"

"It sounded better inside my head, but yes! Do it!"

"I can't. Jenson and I are...friends now. That's it. His mom said something about a new woman he was seeing." A comment Cindy made off-handedly but that I filed away in my mind. "She said it a while ago, but I never heard about any break-up. So they're probably still together."

"So ask him to be your friend-date. You know, to replace me. Nothing romantic."

Friend-date.

My drunken fingers hover over the keyboard. Jenson Beau was always there for me. And even though we went our separate ways when he left for college clear across the country, we kept in touch. And we see each other sporadically on holidays and at family gatherings. I love his two sons. And they love me. But the way I feel about their father...that was never quite as easy to define.

Hayley taps the screen as she refills my wine glass.

I chug down the alcohol faster than I probably should, but between that and the first bottle Hayley and I already finished, it's more than enough to get a full-on buzz going.

I stare at Jenson's handsome face on his social media page. For a moment, I feel like those bottomless green eyes are staring right at me. Begging me to act.

And I start typing.

Thanks to the wine coursing through my veins, I write quickly and with no filter. When I finish, I lean back and let out a big breath.

Before I can even reread what I wrote, Hayley, with those lightning-quick editor fingers of hers, reaches around me and hits Send.

No, no, no, no, no.

What have I just done?

———

Jenson

I carry Connor into my mom's house and put him to bed in the guest room she has set up with twin beds. Kyle always needs time to wind down after one of our trips, so I set us up in the den and fire up the iPad.

"How about we watch a wildlife video?" I ask him as he snuggles into my chest.

His emerald green eyes that look so much like mine get big. "With lions?"

I rub his head and chuckle. "Definitely with lions."

I look back at the screen in front of me, but before I can click on the video, my social media app lights up with a message.

"Daddy!" Kyle jabs his chubby finger at the alert. "You have a message."

"I know, but I can check it later," I say. "Let's get to the video."

Before I can stop him, he clicks on the alert.

"Kyle, we've been over this, remember? My messages are for me to open, not you or Conn..." The message on the screen shuts me up cold.

"Daddy? Is it your new football team?"

"Not exactly."

One.

Two.

Three.

Four.

That's how many times I read Olivia's message.

Kyle, who at five wants to believe he's mastered reading but in reality he's still getting there, leans in and looks right along with me. And I'm too floored to stop him.

"I can't read what it says," he says as he gives up and lays his head on my lap. "Can we watch the video now?"

"In a second."

Olivia's message is brief and to the point, exactly like her.

J, I'm sure you've heard about my separation, so I'll be quick. My divorce was finalized today, and I'm sure you can imagine what tomorrow will be like at Auntie Sue's birthday party. I was hoping to see a friendly face amongst the room of lions. If you're otherwise engaged and not planning to attend, no worries, and I apologize in advance for embarrassing myself.

Shit. My heart feels like it's going to come out of my chest. Because this news is...fucking huge. I knew Olivia was going through a separation with her dick of a husband, but I hadn't heard anything concrete about it in weeks. And I didn't want to push her like I'm sure everyone else in her family's been doing. So I didn't reach out. Instead, I held my breath and...hoped for the best for her.

I click off the message and open up the video for Kyle. Before we're two seconds in, Connor appears in the doorway. He settles in on my other side, and the three of us watch a pack of lions search for food on the savanna. But I'm barely paying attention.

Divorced.

She's officially divorced.

Like me.

And for the first fucking time in a long time, Olivia Graham and I are in the same place at the same time.

When the path opened up for me to finally move back home to Liberty Falls, I held onto the near-impossible dream that somehow the stars would align for us. But I didn't allow myself to truly believe things would have a shot in hell of working. But just now...Olivia sent me a ray of hope.

A smile crosses my face.

Happy homecoming.

CHAPTER TWO

Olivia

I pull into the back of the parking lot outside Liberty Falls banquet hall and turn off the car. My windows are down, and the scent hits my nose immediately.

Lilacs in bloom.

And the nostalgia...it's so strong my throat aches.

I was sixteen, caught between being the baby of my family and studying my ass off to be the first one to go to an Ivy League business school.

Jenson was gorgeous, three years older, and my best friend in the world. I used to sneak out at night and meet him underneath the covered bridge in the center of town. The lilac bushes grew on either side of the bridge, and while Jenson was giving me my first kiss, the incredible aroma of the flowers in bloom was overwhelming my senses.

Then he was taking me to second base, and I was giving him my heart.

But before I could give him everything, we stopped. And we waited.

We waited for me to turn eighteen and legal. He was

always three steps ahead of me, so when I was sixteen, he was already legally too old to date a minor in Pennsylvania. Add to that the fact that our families would have highly disapproved and tried to do anything to avoid the judgment and scandal of the mayor's youngest daughter falling for her "cousin." Even though Jenson isn't actually my cousin, nobody seems to remember that little fact.

None of that could stop us from feeling the way we did about each other.

But we found love young, too young to know just how rare and precious it was. Jenson waited for me to catch up to him, but when I did...

Life got in the way.

I swallow down the pressure building in my throat and force myself to exit the car.

It's time. Time for the party where everyone will ask me about my failed marriage and remark on how I'm not getting any younger. No matter that I'm still in my twenties; to my family-oriented relatives, I was halfway to finished when I didn't have a baby on my hip by twenty-four.

I tried to keep my divorce under wraps until Auntie Sue's party was over, but word spread within minutes of me receiving the papers. I don't even know how, or who, spilled the news.

But that's what it's like living in a small town with a large family where everybody knows everything about everyone. There are no secrets except for those truths buried so deep no one seems to think they exist anymore.

I've taken two steps through the parking lot when I run straight into my aunt.

"There you are! You poor thing!" Aunt Edna rushes me with two arms outstretched and grips me hard.

"I'm fine, Edna," I say. "I really am."

Mom is right behind her. "She's strong like steel," she says to her sister-in-law. "But I'm telling you, Olivia, thank goodness you didn't get that job you applied for in New York. Imagine if you'd moved there with"—Mom shudders—"that awful ex-husband of yours? And then you found out he was sleeping with his colleague? You would have been a victim of circumstance and stuck in the Big Apple all alone!"

I pat her arm. "Mom, please relax. I'm okay. I really am. And honestly, I'm glad I went to New York for that interview. Otherwise, I may not have caught Nate cheating."

Aunt Edna's eyes grow round as saucers.

"I'm fine," I say quickly.

"But you must be so lonely," Aunt Edna opines as the three of us finally turn and start walking toward the banquet hall. "To not even get kids out of the deal—now you're in your mid-twenties with a ticking clock!"

"A time bomb, I call it," Mom says in a hushed tone as we step underneath the awning and head for the door. "When you were married and taking your time, Olivia, things were fine. But now you have to start over completely! Finding the right man could take years all on its own. Then, you have to plan the wedding and hope his sperm are fast swimmers so you can start your family by thirty."

I think I'm going to throw up.

I turn away from my mom and Aunt Edna and catch my bright blue eyes reflected in the window next to the heavy wooden door leading into the banquet hall. Jenson would stare into my eyes for hours by the moonlight during the cold Pennsylvania winters of our youth. I clench my teeth, wishing for the millionth time that we had thrown the rulebook out the window and just played for keeps. But that's all wishful thinking. Jenson's in Pittsburgh, I'm here, and sixteen and innocent has come and gone.

Mom opens the door to the building. "Showtime, ladies."

As the flash from the cameras hits us, I tug at the

spaghetti strap on my silky silver dress and walk into the large open room filled with people already seated at tables. This is a simple birthday party for the matriarch of our family, but because my father's the town mayor, the local paper has sent a crew of photographers like they do for every family event we hold. Harold Graham has been involved in the political landscape of Liberty Falls my entire life, and I've grown to expect that every choice I make will be examined and judged under the harsh, but well-meaning, light of my small, conservative town.

I go kiss Auntie Sue, who's seated at the table of honor in her gold-trimmed wheelchair decorated with pink ribbons and a Happy Birthday sign tied to the back. Her daughter, Matilda, spoons a bite of applesauce into Auntie Sue's mouth and wipes her face with those fancy cloth napkins the hall puts out. Auntie Sue's son, Jeff, sits on her other side, pretending to look helpful but not really doing much of anything.

"Hey, Auntie Sue." I kneel down next to her and whisper into her ear, "Today's going to be one of those long ones, isn't it? You're the birthday girl, but I'm not so sure you wouldn't rather be somewhere else."

Auntie Sue turns to me and gives a twitch of her eyebrow. She doesn't speak in words, not anymore. But we've always been close, from when she tried in vain to teach me how to knit to when we went swimming together in the town lake when I was little. She worked at Union Bank too, as a teller, years ago before she became a wife and a mother. She spoke of her job with such affection and enthusiasm, and she's part of the reason I went into the financial industry. She's our family leader, and just because she can't talk doesn't mean I understand her any less.

"It's Purgatory," my cousin Stacey whispers to me as I leave Auntie Sue and pass her table. "Today is Auntie Sue's ninetieth birthday party. We're all here, her closest relatives, about to stuff our faces with her cake and dance to her songs, and she can't even feed herself anymore. Purgatory, I'm telling you, Olivia. She'd be better off deciding to die."

"It's not her time yet," I say softly as I walk toward my parents' table. "Timing is in God's hands, after all."

"Hey, baby sis. How's it going?" My brother, Sheldon, older than me by a year and a half, greets me as he cuddles with his fiancée, Cara, at the table.

"Couldn't be better," I say as I take a seat across from him.

He chuckles. "It'll be okay."

Never knowing when one of the milling cameramen will be snapping a photo, I try to keep my expression neutral. "Right. Tell me that in about a month when all the gossip has died down."

My oldest sibling, Daphne, calls out a hello to me as she urges her husband, Todd, into his chair. She wants him at the far corner so he can tend to their five-year-old, Alec, and Daphne can then sit across from him with their two-year-old, Amy. As a camera bulb flashes in her face, Daphne grits her teeth into a pained smile as Todd teases her about being uptight while he tosses a pretzel up in the air and Alec runs to catch it with a screech. Daphne slides into her seat, dragging a screaming Amy onto her lap. I smile at her sympathetically, wondering as I look at her worn face when my sister stopped looking happy.

Cybil, Auntie Sue's only living sibling, dashes up to our table nimbly, not looking close to her eighty-eight years. Her daughter, Patsy, follows her wearily. Patsy nearly looks as old as Cybil, certainly as worn. She looks tired like Daphne, I realize as I take a closer look at my own sister, who's now fighting Amy for her plastic drinking cup so she can refill it with juice.

"Olivia!" Patsy says as she and Cybil head straight for me. "How brave of you to come today."

I nod, hearing Sheldon's muffled laughter across the table. "Nice to see you both."

"That's what family's all about, isn't it?" Patsy says. "They always have your back even when you're lying flat on the ground."

"I'm sitting up and feeling fine," I say cheerfully, giving her the thumbs up as a photographer's flash blinds me temporarily.

My father, God bless him, rises from his chair to give a birthday toast to Auntie Sue, and Cybil and Patsy hurry off to their seats.

I let out a breath of relief. For the next five minutes, no one will be talking to me or about me.

God, this party is already never-ending.

"Olive."

One word, spoken quietly in my ear, is all it takes to change my entire mood. My body lights up at the sound of the voice I'd know in my dreams. Low, sexy, and unmistakably his.

Jenson's here.

"J," I say softly, without turning around.

"God, it's been so long, Olive. Since I even saw you..."

"The holiday party last year."

"Right."

His warm breath tickling my neck sets my pulse racing. He must be at the table behind me. Did he slip in once Dad started talking? No way was he in the room when I sat down because I wouldn't have missed the telltale shivers that always run through me when he's around.

"I got your message."

"Crap."

A low, sexy chuckle hits my ears. "It was to the point."

"I was drunk," I say.

"I guessed that."

Knowing we can't attract unwanted attention, I continue to watch my father. I don't turn around the way I want to so I can look into Jenson's brilliant green eyes and tell him how much I've missed him.

"I'm sorry about your...divorce."

"Huh." I start tapping my foot on the tiled floor, the only sign of my unease as I pretend to be deeply engrossed in Dad's never-ending words of wisdom and cheer for Auntie Sue.

His voice goes so low I have to strain to hear him. "Honestly, in terms of the divorce, I'm sorry only if you're hurting. I never liked that asshole. You were way too good for him."

I stop tapping my foot as the tension leaves my body. "Thank you."

Jenson touches my back lightly. I start to lean into him without thought, but he removes his hand just as fast. "I wanted to call you when my mom mentioned your separation —you have no idea how much—but I didn't think it would help."

No, it probably wouldn't have. To be wondering about us, about him, about his current love life, would probably not have helped while I was in the process of finalizing my divorce.

I tug at the strap on my silver dress, wondering what he's wearing and if his hairstyle's still the same. The curiosity is killing me.

Like he can read my mind, Jenson lets out a long exhale.

His hot breath hits my bare neck, and I shiver.

"I'd like to see you later," he says. "In private."

Eight words that hit me like an arrow to the gut.

Before I can answer him, I hear him shift and then... silence. I know he's gone. My heart is pounding, and my palms are sweating because I haven't been this single—and this close—to Jenson Beau in a long time.

———

Kyle races over to me after dinner where I'm sitting on the couch next to Mom at the back of the hall. I invite him into my lap and give him a hug.

"I missed you, Livia." He twists around so he can look up into my face.

"I missed you too, sweetie."

Between Kyle's blond hair, green eyes, and trusting gaze, it's like looking at a miniature version of his father. Jenson has an extra wickedness to his gaze, though, a sexy mischievousness that always drove me wild with need.

My breath catches in my throat.

"And they say that tomorrow's supposed to be even hotter than today," Mom continues her rambling about the weather forecast.

Talking about the weather is something my mother likes to do, especially at public events with roving cameramen. Weather is safe that way, comforting.

"July heat is just so muggy, you know?"

"I know." Kyle snuggles further onto my lap, and I kiss his head.

My searching gaze locates Jenson, and I finally get to check him out like I've been craving to do.

God, he looks good.

So good.

Those green eyes and blond hair, combined with a mouth that always takes me back to our first kiss...

He turns his head, and his gaze shifts around the room. I know he's looking for me, but I'm still out of view of his line of sight. I enjoy ogling him secretly—admiring his chiseled jaw with its trademark sexy stubble, his muscular ass in those black dress pants, and the way his chest fills out his green striped dress shirt. He was a star quarterback in high school, and he may work behind the scenes now rather than playing, but his body still screams athlete. He looks fit like always, and I swallow down my lust. His body never seems to suffer the way his heart does.

"There's nothing like humidity," Mom says next to me. "Gets under your skin."

I nod distractedly. Jenson's blond hair has gotten longer since the last time I saw him. It's a little shaggy, nearly the length it was when he was a teenager, the last time I got to touch him. I always liked his hair shaggy. I liked running my fingers through it over and over again.

I reach back to pull my shoulder-length black hair up off my neck. I'm sweaty all of a sudden, and with this type of material, the sweat's going to show through my dress any second.

"Although it may rain," Mom chatters on, "which hope-fully would cool everything off."

I hear her voice like background noise. I hug Kyle closer to me, wondering how long Jenson's in town for.

"Livia!" Connor nearly trips in his haste to jump up on the couch in between Mom and me. "Aunt Nora!"

Mom hugs him tightly. "Hi, sweetheart. Aren't you boys growing up quickly?"

I lean in to give Connor a kiss. "Hey, little man. You get taller every time I see you."

"Daddy drove really fast to get here." Connor's green eyes match his identical twin brother's, and they shine with excite-ment. "He said we made excellent time."

I smile at him. "Good for you guys. We're all happy to see you."

No one more than me.

Jenson

I can't find her. I've got my head on a damn swivel as I glance around the room while trying to keep up with the conversation in front of me. My stepdad, Dee, is talking my ear off, but my attention is elsewhere. It's where it's always been—on Olivia Graham. Like always, Olivia is the best part of coming home. She *is* home to me.

Our relationship's always been complicated, but she's been my closest friend since we were kids and, outside of my mom, one of only two people in the world who knows the entire truth about my family.

Once I grew old enough to like girls, I can't remember a time when I didn't want to be with Olivia. I can't remember a moment I didn't crave her. No matter how challenging things got, I never stopped believing we had a chance and that somehow, fate would find a way to step in and make this right.

But before I knew it, nearly eight years had passed from that summer night when Olivia was sixteen and innocent, too innocent for me to feel right taking things to a level we couldn't come back from. Eight years I can't get back, but I'm not about to let another day slip by.

Olivia Graham and I deserve to be together for real. And this time, I'm going to lay all my cards on the table with her. This time, I'm going to give her everything. I just hope she still wants it.

I finally locate her crossing the room at a brisk pace. Her long legs are as toned as ever, and her body looks like heaven and sin in that dress. Her shiny black hair hangs perfectly down her back. She's in pain, though—if the narrowing of her eyes isn't enough evidence, the way she's scrunching up her nose makes it crystal clear.

I move toward her without thinking. Olivia doesn't need saving; she never did. She detests the very concept. But one thing she's always loved? Disappearing with me to a place where no one else can find us.

That I can do.

CHAPTER THREE

Olivia

When I first arrived at the party, comments about my divorce were direct and to the point. And to my face. And while that was bad, the furtive looks and whispers sting even more.

Glenn, the good-hearted reporter my family's known for years and the only one I trust at Auntie Sue's party, pulls me aside and asks if I want to say anything on the record.

"Nate and I remain friends," I say, lying through my fixed smile. "But marriage is something we both agree we're better off doing with other people."

He puts down his notes. "Between you and me, I never liked him, Ms. Graham."

I wink at him. "And that's why you're my favorite reporter in Liberty Falls."

Calvin, my least-favorite reporter in town and someone I would rather avoid on a good day, pushes his way through the crowd and follows me as I try to find some privacy.

"Olivia." His slicked black hair glistens under the hall lights, and his beady blue eyes are hard as he stares at me.

"Care to tell me some details about your divorce or about future dating plans?"

"Nope," I say with a breezy smile. "Not even a little. Excuse me."

I make my way across the room, hearing the whispers like a buzzing around my head. They follow me as I walk to the restroom. They're still around when I return to my mother's side on the couch. They get louder when I walk alone to the bar for a much-needed beverage.

But once I reach the bar, where the alcohol has made everyone's tongue loose, the whispers return to direct questions.

"I'm so sorry about your divorce, Olivia," Aunt Eleanor says to me. "What a pity. You're single again."

"Yes, well, it *was* a pity when I found Nate on top of someone else," I say to her.

She gives me a hug. "It will get better."

"Do you think children just aren't in the cards for you, dear?" Cybil says to me. "Those eggs of yours aren't getting any younger, you know. Although you could try freezing the suckers; worked wonders for my neighbor's daughter. She was forty and just birthed triplets!"

"I never trusted your husband," Kathy, Dee's daughter from a previous marriage, pipes in.

"Ex-husband," I say quickly.

She flips her hand in the air like this information is irrelevant. "He's quite the shark on Wall Street now, huh? Thank God you didn't land that job in New York. You're better off staying in Liberty Falls. Who wants to leave home?"

Right now, New York—or Mars—looks pretty damn good.

"Honestly?" I say, my temper rising as I forget about the cameras, "I don't care about..."

Before I can continue with my less-than-civil response, a

warm hand touches my lower back, immediately guiding me away from the crowd of staring women and toward the exit.

"My mom's got the kids. Come away with me." Jenson's low voice buzzes in my ear. "I think you've suffered enough for one day."

I shiver, refusing to make eye contact with him.

But he knows what I need. He always has.

He continues gently leading me toward the door, not stopping until he's put me safely in his truck. No cameras follow us out, and for the first time in three hours, nobody's judging me.

Jenson shuts the passenger door, walks around to the driver's side, and we leave the banquet hall—and our family—behind at last.

Jenson drives around the corner to the nature preserve a block away. The lot is empty, and he pulls into a corner space and puts the truck into park. When he turns to face me, I raise my eyes to meet his brilliant green ones.

Just like it always has, his piercing gaze looks right through me. I swear Jenson Beau can read my heart better than I can sometimes.

"Hey." His voice is rough, and that one word is enough to make me melt.

"Hey."

"You doing okay?"

I nod. "I was prepared for the questions. The stares and whispers were a bit of a surprise, but nothing I can't handle."

His gaze on me gets more intense, and everything else disappears. It's just Jenson and me sitting in his truck, and for this moment at least, nothing else matters. I catch my breath at the same time he does, and he lets out a ragged exhale.

"Olive." He cups my face with both of his large hands. "Shit, I've missed you."

I stare into his eyes, trying to read them. "Are you...your

mom said something about a new woman..." Cindy called her a potential stepmother to her two grandsons.

"I'm single." The words tumble out fast like he couldn't wait to tell me. "I went on a few casual dates to pass the time. Waiting to hear..."

He cuts off.

"Waiting to hear..." I prompt him.

"Isn't it obvious?" His hand on my cheek drifts to my neck, and my eyes nearly close from the sensation. "Waiting to hear about you."

"If we'd ever be in the same place at the same time."

"Exactly." His green eyes flare with emotion. "It's been a long fucking time since I've kissed you, Olive. I've pictured it."

"How often?"

His hand goes to my shoulder where he lightly fingers the thin strap of my dress. "All the time. Plenty of times when I shouldn't have. I've got a lot of fantasies built up in my head."

A bolt of lust shoots through me, and I let out a soft moan.

Screech!

The sound is followed by the annoying honking of a truck as it weaves into the parking lot toward us.

I jerk back from Jenson, who glances over at the intruders.

"Kids," he says in a tone clearly meant to reassure. "No reporters. Or family."

But the moment is broken.

"I should get back to the banquet hall," I say. "I'm not going back to the party. But I need my car."

"Sure." He puts his hands on the steering wheel. "I'll take you."

We drive the short return trip to the hall in silence.

I glance out the window at the small crowd of people just

leaving the banquet hall. A cameraman and reporter from the paper, plus Jenson's mom, Kyle, and Connor, are all making their way through the parking lot.

"Where's Dee?" I say.

"He'll be on his way. My mom's probably just trying to get a good word in about the mayoral campaign to the reporter."

Jenson's mom has worked for my dad for years now, and she's deeply invested in making sure he gets re-elected next year for another term.

Jenson pulls up next to my parked car.

"I should go," I murmur even though I don't move.

"We're going to sort this out, Olive." A wicked gleam flashes through his eyes. "In all kinds of ways."

I flush with heat as I open the passenger door and start to step out backward, my eyes never leaving his.

Jenson glances out the window past my head. "By the way," he says in a low tone. "I need to tell you something. I don't want you to hear it from someone else."

Those words.

I freeze, my leg halfway to the ground. The last time Jenson said those words to me, they were followed by "shocked" and "unexpectedly pregnant."

"Olive." He says my name so quietly I almost don't hear it. "It's okay." His eyes fix on mine.

"Oh. What is it?"

"I'm moving back home. To Liberty Falls."

I lose my grip on the handle, and my leg, which is still hanging out the open door of the truck, buckles underneath me. I go tumbling to the ground, and suddenly I'm staring up at the sky.

Jenson's around to my side in a flash.

But so are the cameraman, Cindy, Kyle, and Connor.

"Oh, it's the stress from your divorce!" Cindy cries out. "Jenson, pick up your cousin!"

Jenson's hands are on my waist, helping me to a standing position while the cameraman shamelessly photographs the scene.

"Let me drive you home," Jenson says as I brush myself off.

"I swear, I'm fine." I fake a smile for the camera and Cindy, and then say to Jenson in a whisper, "I'll talk to you later."

"You'll be okay, Livia." Kyle puts his chubby hand on my arm. "Maybe you need a hug from Daddy. He gives good boo-boo hugs."

Jenson's hand tightens on my back, and I make sure to keep my expression smooth in front of the cameraman who's still capturing every moment.

I lean down and kiss Kyle's cheek. "I'm sure he does. But I'm really okay, sweetie. I'm just going to go home and get some rest."

I step toward my car and unlock it. Jenson holds the door open for me until I'm in the driver's seat, and then he leans in close as I start the engine. "I'll call you."

I shake the entire drive home.

Jenson. And me. Both single. After so many long-ass years.

———

I pull into my driveway and step out of the car.

Everything about Jenson Beau—what I know and what I was told—rushes through my mind.

When Cindy got pregnant with Jenson, she was alone and young. In our rural hometown, being unmarried and pregnant wasn't exactly accepted. She was criticized, and she was shamed.

Cindy and Dee used to date, and even though they'd since

broken up, my dad and Dee were best friends, and Dad knew Cindy like a sister. My father's always been a saver, and as a rising politician in town, he wanted to make Cindy feel included again in Liberty Falls, a part of something "bigger than herself." So he unofficially made her part of the Graham family.

The Grahams go back six generations in Liberty Falls, and being made a part of our large extended family meant instant approval in town. So when Jenson was born, he was thought of as one of us, and my father's hopes were realized. Jenson was able to grow up like every kid should be allowed to—with love and acceptance.

When Jenson was two and half, Mom found out she was pregnant with me. From the moment I was born, Jenson was a part of my life. Three years older than me, and a million years wiser, he became my everything. My best friend, my comrade, my hero. He was at every family birthday party and every holiday.

Meanwhile, Cindy and Dee were dating again, and by the time Jenson turned five, they married. Dee was an orphan and had been an unofficial member of the Graham family since he and Dad became friends as teenagers. With that marriage, any line between the Grahams and Cindy and Jenson disappeared.

I learned Jenson's backstory when I was young, but my parents were careful to explain that while he may not be blood, he was just like a cousin to Daphne, Sheldon, and me. He had been born into our family as an unofficial Graham, and Dad never wanted him to feel like an outsider. Eventually, a lot of people in Liberty Falls seemed to forget that Jenson isn't actually related to us.

When I got to be a teenager, Dad sat us down.

"You two may not be biologically related," he said, "But you're family all the same. That means, Jenson, you need to watch out for Olivia like a big brother would—take care of her. And Olivia, remember how much Liberty Falls needs to see that Jenson is part of our family. He's no different than Sheldon."

His point was clear—don't cross the romantic line. To do so would be a betrayal to everything my father and his mother had worked so hard to forge—a safe life and new family for a single mother and most importantly, for her little boy.

So Jenson couldn't be a romantic option. That didn't stop me from falling in love with him.

I let myself into my house, remembering Jenson's rough, strong hands on my face earlier. I still want him. He still wants me. I wonder if we could possibly make it work...

I shut off the thought as I shake my head at myself. I vowed to never pin my hopes on Jenson and me. Not again. Not after the way he broke my heart the last time. He didn't break it on purpose, but I'm still picking up the pieces. And I can't take a second heartbreak like that in one lifetime.

CHAPTER FOUR

"Oh, wow." The cheerful young woman standing at the teller window smiles at me bright and early the next morning. "Senior Branch Manager and Vice-President. You must be the right person to talk to here."

Being vice-president in a small-town bank is nothing like working for a big bank in New York City, but I'll take the compliment. "I hope so. What can I do for you?"

"We're interested in opening a joint account." She hugs the man next to her and nearly squeals with enthusiasm. "We're moving in together this weekend!"

They both have smooth skin and clear eyes. And they're beaming. Clearly naïve to the perils of love. But then the guy grins back at me, suddenly looking less naïve and more like a young college grad who's in way over his head with this commitment and joint account business. He looks far too much like Nate for me not to notice. This could be a hard sell. But this is why I still love to run the teller window for a few hours each day; I enjoy the customer contact, and I love the challenge of converting non-customers into customers.

From her teller station next to me, Cassandra glances at

the guy, and then scribbles "you got this" on her pad, shoving it close enough so I can read it.

I lock the cash drawer as I straighten the nametag on my blazer and grab my favorite pen.

"You're the best deal closer at Union," Cassandra whispers to me. "This should be a walk in the park for you."

I smile at her and step around the teller station. "If you would please follow me," I say to the couple.

When we arrive at my desk in the corner of the platform section, I direct the couple into chairs and then take a seat across from them behind the desk.

"Oh," the woman says, sounding disappointed. "No private office for the vice-president?"

"Only the president has a private office at Union Bank," I say. Vivian has been the president for over twenty years, and she doesn't believe in offices for anyone but her. She says it leads to laziness and chit-chat behind closed doors.

I pick up a brochure that highlights the different checking accounts. "Shall we begin?"

Despite my lack of a private office, being a bank manager has its benefits. I like money. I like being around money, and I like making money. Getting the reputation as the branch's deal closer was easy for me. I focus on the end result, visualize it in my mind, and I've been able to convert a ridiculously high percentage of non-customers to new customers.

So yes, my financial health is great. I am gainfully employed, fiscally stable, and my money is in good hands, all the way from a strong 401K and several stable stock funds to a savings account I hardly touch. But having all of that economic security didn't fix my personal problems. With Jenson off-limits, I got engaged to a guy I didn't love, and even though I managed to come to my senses enough to break it off, I then married another man impulsively. I tried to rectify all of it by reaching for a killer job on Wall Street.

But the man kind of came with the job, and when I filed for divorce, there went Manhattan.

I guess I thought being inside a bank all day would help to insulate me from the outer world, the world of relationships. But not always.

Right now, for example, a relationship is sitting right in front of me. I exhale behind the paperwork I'm riffling through as a means of stalling. When I finally hand the pamphlets to the couple, they barely notice. They're too busy kissing, being all mushy and lovey-dovey.

I clear my throat.

"Oh, I'm sorry!" The woman giggles. "I almost forgot where we were!"

"Love can do that to you," I say, remembering being in Jenson's truck with him last night.

My desk phone rings as I'm reviewing the options with them. "The basic checking account is no charge," I say. "But if you're willing and able to pay a small monthly fee for the premier account, the benefits can really be worth it." The phone stops ringing as it goes to voicemail, but then it begins again insistently. It's too distracting to ignore. "Excuse me while I take this call," I say to them.

"Hello and welcome to Liberty Falls Union Bank," I say. "This is Olivia. How may I help you?"

"Let me think." Jenson's voice comes through the phone in a flirty tone, and I turn toward the windows so the couple I'm working with won't see me blush. "Um..." He draws out the next four words. "I have an idea."

"J, I'm working."

"Me too."

Loud voices on the other end of the line get my attention. "Wait. Where are you?"

"On a football field."

"Really?"

I remember how hot Jenson always looked when I watched him play quarterback for state, and I smile. "What are you doing on a football field?"

"I'll tell you tonight. Let me take you to dinner," he says to me.

"I'm not sure..."

"I missed you, Olive." His voice is soft.

"J. Are you seriously moving back here?"

"Tonight," is all he says. "I'll tell you everything. You walked to work, right? I'll come pick you up."

"I did walk, but I can't do it tonight. I have to meet my mom."

"Let's meet at the bridge later then," he says.

I knew he was going to suggest that. It's July, and it's hot, and it's light out until about eight p.m. And while my body is fully on board with this plan, I'm still reeling from our near-kiss last night in his truck; and the idea of being alone with Jenson in the place where we last kissed—it's a lot to take in.

But I detect the slight hint of tension in his voice, and it soothes me just enough, knowing I'm not the only one who's overwhelmed by what's always been between us.

I pause before saying, "Okay."

"How about ten o'clock?" he says. "The boys will hope-fully be asleep, and my mom will be home with them."

"It's dark at ten," I say.

"I know." I can feel him smiling through the phone. "I'll see you then."

I swallow hard as I hang up and turn back to my customers.

———

Jenson

"So what you want to do here is go through your progressions like always, but pay extra attention to the left side of the field," I say as I address my new team for the first time. "The first two games we're in this year—the left side will be our opponents' weak side."

I'm in my element, standing out here in the middle of a football field. And being able to come home and coach at a local college—it's a dream come true.

As practice picks up, the quarterback throws three straight incompletions. And they're all his fault.

"Hey!" Head Coach Hughes calls out. "Focus, Smith!"

Coach Hughes comes over to me, shaking his head. "Don't know what's up with him today."

"He's not into it," I say as I watch Smith throw another high ball. "What I saw of him on tape looked great. This— not so much."

"Coach Beau, are you replacing the quarterbacks coach?" one player asks me as he jogs by.

I shake my head. "I'm more behind the scenes than that. I'll be here every day at practice, but Coach Hughes hired me to study film and design plays. That's my main job."

The kid nods and returns his attention to the scrimmage.

"You look good in our school colors." Coach Hughes nods approvingly at the gold and maroon team sweatshirt I'm wearing.

I grin. "Thanks. Fits perfectly."

We chat for the next few minutes about protocol and what plays I'm thinking of drawing up for our next practice.

But when the quarterback throws an interception, and Coach Hughes curses next to me, I step onto the field.

"Hey, Smith!" I call out.

The quarterback looks past the huddle at me.

"Give me the ball." I hold out my hand.

He smirks. "I think I've got it. *Coach*," he adds bitingly.

"Smith," I say warningly, "give me the damn ball and step back."

He mumbles something about me not being a player, but he hands me the football.

But that's where he's wrong. I may not have played in college, but it wasn't for lack of talent.

I give the ball to the gaping center guard standing in front of me.

"On three," I tell him as I position myself behind him.

He immediately turns and hikes me the ball. I take it in my hand and drop back. I scan the field, nimbly stepping around a flying lineman trying to sack me. I find an open receiver downfield, and I bring my arm back and let the ball go. It zips through the air in a perfect spiral, hitting the receiver right in the hands. He catches it, turns, and bang—easy touchdown.

"Fuck." The center turns to stare at me like I'm an alien who just dropped onto the field.

Smith's scowl has disappeared. "Nice throw," he says to me.

I tap his helmet. "You can do that too, if you quit zoning out."

Coach Hughes steps forward, his dark beard not quite covering his smiling mouth. "Jenson Beau was all-state in Pennsylvania. Could have gone pro if he hadn't thrown out his knee. You'd do best to listen to his advice, Smith."

Smith gives a quick nod, and I walk back to the sidelines with Coach Hughes.

"Good to have you back home, Jenson," he says to me. "We're gonna have one hell of a fall."

I think of Olivia and how close I was to her mouth yesterday. My pulse picks up, and I answer, "I sure hope so. I'm really glad to be back."

Olivia

At six on the dot, I leave the bank and step outside. Mom's already at the curb, waving at me wildly from her truck even though nobody else is parked within a block of the building.

I open the passenger door and step inside the cab. "Hi, Mom."

"How are you, honey?" She puts the truck into drive and presses on the accelerator so fast I jerk forward. "I didn't want to miss the green light," she explains as I grab for my seatbelt.

We drive three streets over to the Liberty Falls Senior Center. As soon as we step inside the front doors, Bea's walking toward us. Her long gray hair is tied up in a pretty bun on the top of her head, and she's dressed casually in blue jeans and a "Getting Old Sucks" t-shirt.

Bea is a first cousin of Mom's mother. Grandma and Bea were super close their whole lives, and when Grandma passed away last winter, Mom was afraid Bea would take it too hard, so she set up weekly get-togethers for the three of us.

"If Bea keeps busy," she said to me. "She'll live longer."

Bea leads Mom and me over to the sign-up table for the Adult Education sculpting class, and then we head into the classroom down the hall. The Senior Center holds Adult Ed classes every Wednesday, and this week, it's sculpture. Usually, more people Bea's age than mine show up for these classes, but thankfully tonight, I'm not the only lonely twenty-four year old in Liberty Falls. There are eight people in the class, and as I look around the room, I notice a man and woman about my age. The man's wearing sunglasses, even though we're indoors. The woman has her arms crossed over her stomach and she's staring down at her feet. I glance down, suddenly self-conscious of my navy blue blazer and matching skirt suit. *I just came from work.* At least I'm making good money doing something I enjoy. So what if the majority of my closet is filled with suits just like this? Not everybody is fashion-conscious.

The teacher introduces herself as Denice, and then tells us the model's almost ready. I glance over at the back corner of the room, which is partitioned off by a dark curtain.

I flick my gaze over to Mom. "We're going to sculpt a live person?"

She shrugs, looking as confused as I am.

When an older naked man steps out from behind the curtain, I suppress my scream. Mom doesn't quite succeed. A noise escapes her mouth, but she sucks it back just as fast, so it ends up sounding almost like she choked on air.

"I find it best if we sculpt a real live body," Denice explains with a glance at my mother. "Clothing tends to distract."

From the look on Mom's face, I'd say the no-clothing idea is a hell of a lot more distracting. But Denice isn't asking what I think.

Bea giggles as we follow Denice to the plastic bags of clay at the front.

"Well, this is something new, Nora," she whispers to Mom.

Mom smiles weakly. "Something to tell Dad about when I get home, I guess," she says to me. "I saw a naked man tonight, and it wasn't you, honey."

"Mom, please." I reach into the bag and wrestle with the clay until I've successfully broken off a large piece.

But once we're all back at our desks, with the naked man perched on a table in front of us, I feel weird sculpting him. I pretend to be sculpting, but really I'm stalling. My cell phone saves me with a beep.

I drape my clay-covered hand with a paper towel in order to pull the phone out of my bag.

No moon tonight. Bring a flashlight.

Butterflies explode in my stomach at Jenson's text, and shit...I can't wait to see him. I exhale and pull the bottom of my shirt in and out a few times to cool off. Now I've got clay all over it, but I don't mind.

I look again at the model's pale skin and frail frame. I take my desk and turn it away from him, so he's no longer in my line of sight. Bea looks over at me, her eyes bright with interest. I smile at her and get to work.

———

An hour later, Denice walks around to take a look at everyone's progress. She stops short when she sees what I've done with my clay.

"Oh...my." She pauses for breath as she sees the quite obvious male anatomy sitting on top of my desk.

That's right. I sculpted Jenson's package. It wouldn't have looked so bad if there had been something else to my sculpture, but there isn't. It's just a penis and balls. While I was actually working the clay, I was immersed in my own lust and didn't much care who saw what I did, but now that the entire class—not to mention my mother and Bea—are all staring at my work of art, I want to disappear into the floor. God, why did Jenson have to text me? It's like he gets so under my skin that I can't help myself.

"Well," Denice says. She looks at the old man and then down at my piece of art like she can tell the two do not go together. I guess the fact that I'm facing away from the model gives me away, so I quickly turn my desk back to the correct position. But my "work" looks too...thick, I suppose, to be a match to the model looking in our direction.

Bea smiles at me. "It's...an original, yes?"

I hope not. I hope it's an exact replica of Jenson's goods. As a teenager, I touched him there once, but it was brief and over jeans, so I really needed to let my imagination do the sculpting for me. I've certainly felt his hardness desperately pressing against my body, but we were always clothed.

Mom clears her throat and mumbles something about how the three of us are definitely *not* taking that papier-mâché class she saw on the Adult Ed bulletin board earlier.

———

After class, I seek to put an end to my humiliation and ask Mom to drop me off around the block at Bernie's Coffee Haus. Bernie's is the quaint German coffee shop on Main Street where we all hang out—Sheldon and Cara, my best friend, Hayley and her boyfriend, Max, and me. Daphne used to join us too, but once she married Todd and they had kids, they stopped hanging out at Bernie's years ago.

Tonight, only Hayley's going to be here. Thank God, because she's the only one in my life who knows about Jenson and me. Everyone else just thinks I have serious relationship issues.

But as soon as I reach Bernie's, Sheldon meets me in the doorway and immediately stares down at what's in my arms.

It's my sculpture, surreptitiously hidden inside a cardboard box Mom anxiously found for me in her trunk. "You don't want to parade that all around town, Olivia," Mom said as she handed me the box and practically threw the sculpture into it. "Now, I'm all for sexual expression, but that artwork is very intimate, and it could give the people in this town the wrong idea."

I hold the box tightly with both hands as I stare Sheldon

down. "Back off," I say to him. "I'm not talking to you tonight."

"What'd I do?" he says as he tries to follow me inside. His light brown hair is falling in his eyes, and I resist the urge to tell him to get a haircut because I know he's just an easy target for how vulnerable I'm feeling. Sheldon and I are there for each other in all the important ways, and sometimes that means being a punching bag.

"I need to talk to Hayley alone," I say. "So go. I thought you and Cara had date night or something."

"Cara and I have wedding planning night," he corrects me. "I needed a caffeine fix first." He holds up his to-go coffee cup and grabs his keys out of his jeans pocket. "I'm on my way out."

I smile at him. "Well, good luck. I can't give you a pep talk because I cancelled one wedding and then the one I didn't cancel ended in divorce."

Sheldon grins as he waves goodbye. "You really do need to start dating again. I'm going to find you someone."

I brush past him. "Don't even think about it!" I call back.

As I step further into the coffee shop, I spot Hayley waving to me from our usual couch at the far back.

Hayley and I met at Bernie's one Saturday morning when I was home from college on Christmas break. It was a snowy day in January, and she and I were both in line to buy coffee. Hayley complimented me on my wool hat, we started talking, and we haven't stopped since.

I smile and head over to take a seat next to her on the couch. When I show her what I made in class before quickly putting it back in the cardboard box, she doesn't say anything at first.

She just stares at me. I stare back at her.

"You sculpted his junk?" Hayley sounds incredulous.

"What the hell is the big deal?" I lean back against the

couch cushions and curl my legs under me. "Up until now, my imagination has been the only thing I had."

"But now?" She raises a perfectly-manicured eyebrow, the one part of her she fusses over.

I bite my lip. "Your guess is as good as mine."

"He's here. For you." She points to the box next to me. "You don't need to make up fantasies anymore."

"It's so surreal I don't really believe it yet. That he's going to stay."

Hayley studies my face. "So you two have been pining away for each other all these years, and you don't even know what his dick feels like? Olivia, you better find out."

I break into an anxious laugh. "Let's shift this conversation to something less...sex-focused."

We chat about her day at work for a bit, until the topic returns to Jenson.

"It's surreal that he's here," I admit. "I guess I never imagined he would move back."

"Do you think he's going to..." Hayley lowers her voice to a whisper, "ever look for his biological father?"

"I don't know. There are things about it that..." I cut off. "That nobody knows."

Cindy always tells everyone that Jenson was the result of a drunken one night stand with a man she never caught the name of, a man she slept with right after she and Dee broke up the first time they were together. But then Jenson found his original birth certificate hidden in the back of her closet. And instead of "unknown" in the father box, this one said Donald Waverly.

We figured out pretty quickly why his mom had covered up the truth. Donald Waverly was Dee's good friend, along with my dad's, and when Jenson confronted her about the birth certificate, Cindy admitted that she slept with Donald right *before* she and Dee broke up. They were all young and

Dee and Cindy had been fighting a lot, and Cindy said it was a moment of weakness that brought her a precious gift—her only child.

She always wanted Dee back, though, and once they reconnected and then married, she vowed to never share the truth.

So Dee still doesn't know that Cindy cheated on him with his friend. Donald and his parents moved out of town shortly after he was with Cindy. He was unaware he had conceived a child, and Donald didn't keep in touch with anyone in Liberty Falls. For almost two years before he left for college, I helped Jenson investigate, but we were never able to track Donald down. It was like he'd disappeared into thin air.

"Maybe someday." I shrug at Hayley. "All of it will be sorted out."

CHAPTER FIVE

When I reach the covered bridge, I turn my flashlight on to light my way. Jenson's there waiting for me. He picks me up and hugs me tightly.

"It's so good to see you again," he says in a low tone.

We just saw each other last night, but I know what he means. In a way, we haven't really seen each other since I was seventeen.

Jenson puts his arm around my shoulders, and we sit down together on the pavement, our backs against the bridge wall and our legs stretched out into the empty road. I look around at the tiny one-lane road that passes underneath the bridge. Hardly any cars take this bridge in the daylight; this late, we shouldn't even see one. I turn off the flashlight, and we're immediately surrounded by the safety and escape of total darkness. Under the covering of the bridge, it's like there's nobody else in town. Nobody but us.

"I remember how we came here when we were kids," Jenson says quietly.

"You kissed me for the first time here and the last time

too." I swallow hard. "If I'd known it would be our last time, I'd have asked you not to stop."

He turns to face me, and my eyes, now adjusted to the dark, can make out his strong jaw and blond hair. His expression is somber.

"I've gone over that moment a million times since things ended between us. I wish eight years hadn't passed since then."

I exhale. "I know what you mean."

"This whole thing's been torture." His voice is rough.

He's never said it outright like that.

I inhale. "It has." Reaching for an easier topic, I say, "Both the boys seem good."

"They are."

I smile at the pride in his voice.

"They've been enjoying coming to work with me lately."

"Really?" I laugh. "That is so cute—do they know all the players?"

"Pretty much."

I hear him suck in a breath. And then—

"I've been hired as an assistant football coach for Randolph College."

"Wait..." I stumble. "What?"

"I'm working for Randolph's football team."

"But that's where Dad teaches—Randolph is just outside Liberty Falls!"

"I know. I told you I'm moving back home, Olive."

"You—" I drop the flashlight and then scramble to grab it before it rolls away. "How did I not know this? Randolph always announces their new coaching staff, and I don't remember seeing your name on the website."

And God knows I would have noticed.

"It was a last-minute opening, and they haven't made the

announcement yet. The coach called me up a month ago; I've known him since high school, but he wasn't sure they had room in their budget for me. I'm going to work with the offense, study game tape and design plays. Today was my first day on the field; the announcement should be coming out tomorrow."

"Congratulations. But isn't that...a big step down from the Division I program you were coaching at out in Pittsburgh?"

He brushes my cheek softly with his hand. "Coming back to Liberty Falls is a million steps up, Olive. It can't be quantified."

I drop my jaw as I stare at him. "You're willing to give up that coaching position for..."

"Yes." He kisses my forehead. "A million times over. Yes. It feels perfect."

My heart lodges somewhere in my throat. He's right. It does feel perfect. Too perfect. Because the last time I thought Jenson Beau and I were finally going to be together, our fairytale ending was ripped apart.

"What about Kyle and Connor?" I ask him.

"They're coming with me," he says.

"What about Meghan? You guys share custody."

"She and her boyfriend, Andy, are going to move in together, and Andy's from out this way. They've decided to move to Philly, and they're driving out here this week to look around for housing. So she and I will split the time with the boys while she's in the area, and then they'll go back with her to Pittsburgh until she packs up next month."

"So you're moving in the fall? How will that work with football season?"

"I've already moved." His tone softens. "I have my townhouse in Pittsburgh until the end of the month, and I'll have to go back to deal with that. But I'm officially on staff with the football team as of today, so...I'm here."

"That's..." I swallow hard. "Wow. A lot of changes."

"I hope it can be a fresh start," he says, his meaning clear. *A fresh start for us.*

I still remember Jenson's last words to me before he left for college in Seattle for what turned out to be one of the many unplanned chapters in his life. "Ask me to wait for you, Olive." His eyes were pleading. "Ask me."

Because he would. I was all he wanted. He was all I wanted. But I was young and naïve, and in my heart, I knew I wasn't ready for everything we deserved.

Plus, we had two years to fill—I was sixteen, and Jenson was nineteen—before we could be together in any real sense, and I wanted Jenson to enjoy his college experience, his first time away from home. We talked it through, with Jenson adamant that if we were going to do this, he wanted to make sure it went both ways so that I would experience high school like a normal sixteen-year-old deserves to. We tried to look on the bright side—if we didn't take this time apart, even if we did end up together, one or the other of us would end up resentful.

After much tearful discussion, we made a promise that for the next two years, we would date "age-appropriate" people and not discuss our love lives with one another.

"No holding back," Jenson said to me. "Okay? Whoever you want to date, or..." He cleared his throat and trailed off. "Don't censor yourself. We'll still see each other when I come home, and it will be like old times. But this is your time, Olive. You're only sixteen years old once. I don't ever want to be the one who held you back from anything. Promise me you'll take the time to focus on yourself."

"You too." I held his hand tightly in mine, fighting back the tears that were already sliding down my cheeks. "Promise you'll enjoy college, J. Date, have girlfriends, and party. Do whatever you want to do. Okay? We'll meet up again soon."

"Two years." His voice dropped so low I had to strain to

hear him. "It will fly by. And then you'll be mine. And I'll be yours. Forever."

"Forever," I repeated.

We held to our promise. I went to Prom, to Homecoming, and to the movies on the weekends. I let boys kiss me and tried to feel a spark even if there wasn't one. I had a few boyfriends, and I know Jenson had his share of dates in college. We did our best to be "normal," knowing that this was our time to explore and grow on our own.

And whenever Jenson came home, we were as inseparable as ever. "Cousins" to our family and to everyone in town and so much more in private. Never more than stolen kisses; our clothes never came off. Because Jenson was serious about waiting until I turned eighteen. He wanted to do things "the right way."

At the edge of seventeen, I was exhausted from trying to maintain a line my heart and body were desperate to rebel against. I was one day away from starting my freshman year at UPenn and one month from turning eighteen. I was so looking forward to crossing that finish line so Jenson and I could finally be a real couple.

I only had one month to kill at college before my big birthday. One more month of going on dates with boys who couldn't hold a candle to the only boy I'd ever really wanted.

But the night before I left for school, Jenson found out the piece of news that would unequivocally change the course of his life. And the course of mine. He was going to be a father. And the mother of his children wasn't me.

The memories flood my brain while we sit together underneath the safety of the bridge, and I clench my hands together on my lap. "Looking back," I admit, "I feel like I got married just to try to numb the pain of losing you."

"Being married never helped me, Olive," Jenson says in a ragged tone. "I know my marriage was...unplanned. And I love my sons. Wouldn't change that part of it at all. But Meghan and I never should have forced the marriage through because she got pregnant. We always used protection, were always so careful. We both knew what we were doing was temporary. And yet, Kyle and Connor came along anyway."

"And you wanted to be a full-time father, to be there for your sons every single day from the moment they were born, the way your biological father wasn't," I say softly. "I got it then, and I get it now, J."

"And yet, I know how it crushed you."

Yes, going to Jenson's wedding was deadly. I couldn't even make it through the ceremony. Hearing about his divorce was less so. Of course, he and Meghan had their two boys by then, so she's a permanent part of his life. She's very nice; I always liked her. She was in the impossible position of marrying a man who couldn't love her back, whose heart was already with somebody else. She never knew about me, and Jenson was never unfaithful to her. But we'd already given our hearts to each other, and no matter how hard we tried to move on, it didn't seem to work.

"I thought I was taking responsibility as a father. Doing right by my sons." His tone sounds strangled. "By everyone."

My throat goes tight, but I finally say the words I've always wanted to say to him. "I'm sorry I told you I wanted to forget about us. I was seventeen, stupid, and heartbroken."

His eyes find mine in the dark. "Can you tell me the whole story?"

I choke back the emotion filling my throat. "My father..."

"Your father?" Jenson's tone is hard. "What'd he say to you?"

"He had no clue about us," I assure him. "None of them did."

We were always experts at hiding our attraction to each

other. Because we had always been close, everyone in our family accepted that we were simply best friends.

"So if he didn't suspect anything, what did he say?"

"He came to see me a couple weeks after I'd moved to school in Philly. And he talked about you. About how we had all learned you were going to become a father."

"And..."

"And he kind of told me to take a step back in my friendship with you. He said it was important for us to remain close, like cousins, but that you and Meghan needed time to sort things out. He said with all the big changes, you becoming parents together, you needed private time to get to know each other and go through her pregnancy."

"He had no right to do that. You were so young—you needed me."

"I did, but the thing is he was right in a way. I would have never forgiven myself if you and Meghan hadn't had the space to really give your marriage a shot. And..."

"There's more?"

"And I knew how badly you'd always wanted your own family, and I didn't want you to lose the one you had because of me being selfish and wanting you for myself."

"Shit, Olive." Jenson runs his hand through his hair.

"I know. It was so hard, but I cared about you too much to tell you why I was pulling back. If I'd told you, you would have lost focus on Meghan. And you needed to know for sure if she was the one for you or not. In my screwed-up teenage mind, I thought it would be my fault if you had all that ripped away from you. But I hated myself for not telling you my reasons."

He wipes at his eyes. "Please don't hate yourself. We felt like the world was against us. I'm just glad you finally told me the truth."

I brush a single tear off his cheek. "I just want to make

clear—I never doubted the way I felt for you, J. I always wanted you. That hasn't changed. Ever."

"For me, neither." His hand finds mine.

"Honestly," I say in nearly a whisper. "I was in so much pain. And I didn't know how to feel better. I guess part of me thought that if we just stopped being so close, we'd grow apart and maybe Meghan would help you forget about me."

"Forget this?" His hand squeezes mine. "Forget us? Olive, it was never possible for me to forget you. Meghan and I—we weren't ever in love."

I squeeze his hand back. "It was a long time ago."

"It was." He shifts closer to me. "But the insane way that I want you has never diminished."

My heart rises into my throat as I stare into his eyes.

He squeezes my shoulder. "Even though you'd pulled away from me, remember how I called you up the night Kyle and Connor were born?"

"Of course."

We hadn't had a real conversation since he told me his baby news. Then, Jenson called out of the blue and asked me to drive out to Pittsburgh the night his twin sons entered the world. I skipped my last two classes of the day and jumped in the car. I met him at the hospital where he took me to the maternity wing and pointed out Connor and Kyle among all the other babies lying behind the glass wall. I said I would have recognized them anyway because they were the most beautiful babies in the room. When I left the hospital that night, I felt what was left of my heart shatter into a million pieces.

"I can't imagine what that was like for you." He laces his strong fingers through my soft ones. "The fact that you came all the way out there, just for me, when it must have hurt like hell for you to be a part of something so..."

"Something that was so beautiful," I say so quietly he has

to dip his head to hear me. "Seeing you as a father for the first time is a sight I'd never take back."

We stop talking, and silence hits the bridge. Soon, all I can hear are our heavy breaths filling the air.

"Our story's not over, Olive." Jenson's lips brush my cheek. "That last kiss we had here all those years ago? Turns out it doesn't have to be our last."

"Really?" My voice comes out raw as I turn to face him.

"Really." His tone dips into red-hot sexy territory. "So. What do you say?"

"Jenson." My tone is raw. "Come here."

His mouth reaches mine at the same time that I wrap my arms around his neck. He seeks my lips desperately and threads his fingers through my hair as his mouth melds to mine. He smells like mint and tastes like him. His lips urge mine to open to him, and I'm lost.

No one kisses like Jenson Beau. He gives me every ounce of himself like he'll never enjoy anything in his life as much as making love to my mouth.

His kiss is rough and insistent, and he breaks the kiss just long enough to mutter how much he missed me. His hand cups my ass, and he urgently pulls me onto his lap. Every single thing about him turns me on as much as it always did, and I let out little gasps with each touch of his hand on my burning-hot skin. He trails kisses down my neck and collarbone, not stopping until his hot tongue finds my breast. He pulls aside my bra cup and draws my aroused nipple into his mouth, and I run my hands through his blond shaggy hair and hold him close to me.

The thick strands feel just as good as I'd thought they would when I saw him yesterday.

Abruptly, he shifts so that he's on his back, pulling me on top of him. His hands go to my head, and he pulls the elastic out of my ponytail so my hair hangs loose.

"Come closer," he murmurs. "I need you closer."

I moan as his erection hits me in just the right spot, and I move my hips while his hands hold onto my waist tightly.

"Hayley said I need to touch your dick," I say into his mouth.

He lets out a gruff laugh. "She did, did she? Is that what you want?"

"More than anything." I grind into him harder.

"I can help you with that," he says as he holds me firmly by the hips and pushes hard against me.

"Oh God, J." I'm so close to coming already, and we're fully clothed.

And his tongue in my mouth has me completely dizzy and distracted, so much so that I hardly notice the headlights coming toward us.

But the brightness gets my attention. I jerk up and stare at the opening of the bridge. The lights are closing in on us; they're not at the bridge just yet, but I can tell from where they are that there's no turning back now. That vehicle would have to go into reverse and back up to avoid coming through here, and even that wouldn't be an easy decision. The steep hill leading down into the bridge makes it nearly impossible to back up once you've started down the road.

Jenson grabs my hand and we jump up. We run as fast as we can through the bridge and toward the opening at the other side. We reach the open air, and Jenson leads me down the stone steps toward the river below. He turns on his flashlight when we're below eyesight from the road above, and we look up to see a truck driving out of the bridge. It keeps driving like it doesn't have a care in the world or a clue that it nearly collided with us.

As I start to walk back up the steps to the street, Jenson touches my butt from behind. I keep climbing the stairs, and he keeps his hand on my ass as he follows.

I turn around and push his hand away as soon as I reach the top step. "We're out in public again."

He nuzzles my neck. "What if I said I don't care?"

"I would say I'm not sure we should be making life-changing decisions like that tonight." I stop abruptly in the middle of the road. "This is a lot to take in. You moving back here, us both single for the first time since we were teenagers. And I'm not sure how we'll possibly make things work. My dad's still mayor of this town, and all eyes are on my family as you well know. And with your mom working for him, she could lose her job if things go wrong and he loses the election because of our relationship..."

"Leave all of that to me," he says. "I'm not going to put us last this time, Olive. We'll figure things out slowly so we know what's ahead of us, but I'm not going to give up on us ever again."

"What about Kyle and Connor?" I say, breaking the silence between us. "Will this confuse them? I don't want the town to judge them..."

But Jenson interjects. "I try to teach Kyle and Connor to follow their hearts, and how can they listen to me if I'm not doing the same?"

Good point.

I fidget in front of him. "Can we go slow?"

Jenson's eyes find mine under the street lights. "As slow as you want. We'll do things right this time, in a way that lasts. I know we tried to do things right last time, but we were worrying about everyone else but us. This time, we'll make sure we don't ignore our own hearts in the process."

I squeeze his hand. "Sounds like a plan."

CHAPTER SIX

"We'll finish up our walk by your house," Mom says to me the next morning, her breathing heavy from the exercise. "That way you won't have any extra travel."

Mom came up with the idea for our mother-daughter walks after her doctor told her she had high blood pressure. Dad teaches a class at Randolph College, and he leaves at six a.m. to do research or grade papers, and after that, he's non-stop tied up with his mayoral duties for the rest of the day. Sheldon doesn't exercise—says he's morally against it, and Daphne is busy taking care of her kids, so that leaves me.

"Thanks, Mom." It's muggy out already, and I'll definitely have to shower before I leave for work.

"So I've been thinking," Mom begins.

Oh no.

"How open are you to a blind date?"

"Mom. NOT." I pick up the pace even more, and Mom has to double her steps to keep up with me. "OPEN. At all."

"But honey..."

"Subject closed. Kind of the way I am to a blind date.

That's my level of openness on the matter." I hustle along, desperate for this walk to end.

We're about a block from my house when Mom stops short.

"Oh, look!" She blinks like she's seeing a mirage. "It's Jenson!"

I turn to where she's pointing. Jenson's dressed up in a collared white shirt, black dress pants, and green tie that matches his eyes. And he's clean-shaven. I feel momentarily self-conscious at how sweaty I am, not to mention my ratty gray sweatpants and skimpy white tank top that barely covers my stomach, but it's too late to turn away. He's clearly already seen us.

"Hi." Jenson smiles as he reaches us and raises his to-go coffee cup in a salute. "You two are making me feel lazy."

"Hi, honey." Mom leans over to hug him. Her long black hair, that's now going gray but tastefully dyed, nearly hits him in the face when she kisses his cheek. "Don't you look handsome?"

I try to subtly wipe the sweat off my forehead, but Jenson's watching me. He grins as my cheeks heat. Mom's oblivious.

"And congratulations on the coaching position!" Mom says with enthusiasm. "Harold told me it hit the campus already. He didn't have a clue; they really kept it quiet."

Jenson nods. "They usually do until it's one hundred percent certain. I'm headed there now for the formal announcement."

"Thus the suit?" I say with a smile.

"Exactly. I'm more comfortable running around a football field, but today, I have to stand at a podium and answer questions. And I'm looking at house rentals after that, trying to find the right neighborhood for Kyle and Connor."

"I'm sure the boys would love Olivia's neighborhood,"

Mom says. "And you'd be close to your cousin that way, Olivia. Wouldn't that be nice?"

My voice comes out in a bare whisper. "It would."

"It's a great neighborhood, Nora." Jenson glances at me.

His shirt hugs his biceps, and my eyes travel down his torso to his crotch. Realizing I'm staring, I raise my gaze to his face, and he winks at me like he knows where my mind is. In a lust-filled gutter is where.

"This neighborhood is within walking distance to everything," Mom says. "I rather wish Harold and I had raised our kids here. Would have saved us some gas."

I breathe out heavily. Mom notices and looks over at me. "Something wrong, honey?" she says. "You still out of breath from our workout?"

"No, Mom," I say. "I'm good."

"Jenson, we're about done here. I have to give myself plenty of time to get ready for today's luncheon with Harold. You should walk Olivia back to her house," Mom suggests. "While she showers, you can go into her backyard and get a feel for her area from behind."

Oh no, she did not just string that sentence together. Jenson turns his head away but not fast enough to hide his smirk.

"It's hard sometimes to always be in the front," Mom continues. "You can't get a full view of everything." Jenson's smile is huge now. "Take advantage of Olivia's backside, Jenson," Mom says. "Get a look from that angle. I highly encourage it."

"Mom, I beg you to stop," I burst out, my face nearly nuclear with heat.

Jenson raises his eyebrows at me.

"Why?" Mom asks innocently. "Whatever's the matter?"

"I just...Jenson's kids won't be here full-time. This may not be the best neighborhood for a part-time situation."

"Well, even if it's part-time right now, eventually Jenson will remarry and have more children. And this time, it will be full-time." A smile crosses Mom's face as she looks at Jenson expectantly. "Won't it, honey?"

The only way to stop my mother in these situations is to separate from her, so I spring into action. I kiss her good-bye and promise I'll let Jenson into my backyard. I swear he almost drops his coffee.

But Mom finally relaxes and lets us go.

Jenson and I don't touch each other at all as we walk away from her. He waits until we reach my driveway before he glances back casually.

"She's turned the corner," he says as he reaches for my hand.

I head quickly for the front door, feeling like my mother is still with us.

"You guys go quick, huh?" Jenson says as we reach the top step.

"We try to," I say. "Mom needs to stay in good cardio shape."

As we walk inside and Jenson shuts the door behind us, I know I'm not going to be able to shower with him in such close proximity. I'll want to drag him in with me, and that's something I'm not quite ready for. Well, my body's more than ready; it's my heart that's throwing out the red warning flag.

"It's great you guys can walk together," he says.

I nod. "I've learned that being twenty-four and single gives you a lot of spare time to spend as your mother's companion whether it be walking or taking classes through Adult Ed."

He laughs even though he knows it's not really funny. But my joke breaks the ice. It's nice to have him back in town. Nobody ever understood me like he does.

"So this introduction with the school board is pretty fancy, huh? Your sexy stubble's gone."

"You like the stubble?" he asks me.

"You know I do."

He grins and rubs his clean-shaven jaw. "Yeah, I shaved to hopefully give a good impression to all the board members. You know I tend to veer on the side of naughty more than nice."

"One of the things I've always liked about you. So what time is the big event?"

"Not till just after lunchtime. I left the house to grab a quick coffee, and then I'm heading back to have breakfast with Kyle and Connor before Meghan picks them up right before I leave for the college."

"You look hot." My gaze travels the length of his body.

His face flushes, and he steps closer to me, but I back up. "I'm all sweaty."

"I know." His eyes darken. "I've been wanting to kiss you since I saw you. And maybe take that sexy little tank top off of you."

I back up another step. "Not now. I'll be late for work."

"From one kiss?"

"I'll want more than that right now. Trust me."

He licks his lips and groans. "You're killing me, Olive." He backs up but keeps his gaze on me when he says, slowly and with purpose, "I want to date you, Olive. I just want to make that clear up front."

I bite my lip. "I'm not sure how to do that with you. Dating like normal people. You were right last night. This has been torture."

"It's been torture because we've been trying to pretend we can live without each other. I want this to work between us. Like a second chance."

"You mean a last chance," I say without meaning to.

Jenson's intense gaze holds mine. "Yeah. I guess you're right. This does feel like a last chance for us. And I'm going to make sure we get what we want this time."

———

Jenson

"Daddy!!!" Connor's earsplitting scream sounds like the world just exploded around him.

I drop the bread knife and jar of peanut butter on the kitchen counter and race down the hallway and into the guest room where the boys sleep when we're at Mom and Dee's house.

"What's wrong?"

Connor has Kyle in a headlock, and Kyle's face is bright red.

"Hey!" I push in between my sons and force them apart, grabbing each one by an arm. "What are you two fighting about?"

"Kyle stole my Superman bathing suit! Mommy said we'd go swimming today!" Connor points at Kyle whose face color is slowly returning to normal.

"Why?" I say to him. "You've got your Batman suit."

"I know."

"So why take your brother's?"

Kyle grins devilishly. "I wanted to hear him scream. He sounds like he's in a horror movie."

Connor screams again, dropping a choice swear word in the process.

I spin on him. "Where did you learn that word? From one of the players on the team?"

"Nope. Uncle Colton said it to Uncle Dylan once." Connor giggles, and Kyle joins him.

"Well, you don't say it. Got it? Kyle, on three—give your

brother back his bathing suit. And Connor, no more using the f-word. Especially not with mother thrown in there."

"No mother f-word," Connor says solemnly as Kyle reaches underneath his pillow and hands Connor back his bathing suit.

My cell phone buzzes in my pocket, and I pull it out.

"Who is it, Daddy?" Connor says.

"Your uncle." I swipe the screen to answer. "Hey, Colt."

"J. What's up?" My best friend's always-casual tone is missing. Yesterday was his first day back at training camp, and the exhaustion and hint of stress in his voice is his first giveaway.

As the star tight end of the defending Super Bowl champion California Cougars football team, Colton Wild may be a famous professional football player, but to me, he's still the same down-to-earth guy I met when I was nine years old. I recognize pretty much all his tells, the subtle and the obvious, and he can do the same with me. Colton and I were both sent to football camp for boys under fourteen one summer. We were the youngest kids there—him a year older than me, and we bonded right away.

We were both only children who loved football. I wanted to play quarterback, and I ended up the starter on the Liberty Falls high school squad while Colton dreamed of being a tight end or wide receiver. His dad was his best friend while I called my biological father a sperm donor. Dee was a great stepfather, but he and my mom fought constantly. So I spent a lot of time at the Graham house where Olivia's dad did his best to fill in any gaps, something I'm forever grateful for.

Even so, I often felt lonely. Olivia was my touchstone and my closest confidante, but she couldn't replace the hole in my heart for male companionship. And her brother and I never really clicked; I love Sheldon, but he and I never had much in common.

But when we were at football camp that summer, Colton talked nonstop about his cousins—Dylan, Brayden, Ayden, and Cameron—and he promised he was going to make me a Wild boy too. He said they would unofficially adopt me into the fold. At the end of camp, Colton went home to Montana, and I returned to Pennsylvania. But we stayed in touch, and Colton kept true to his word. Once a year, he invited me to visit him in Montana. I met Dylan and Brayden right away, and Ayden and Cam flew out the second time I was in town.

Despite the miles in between, the six of us became inseparable, and nothing—not high school, college, big football contracts, or women—ever tore us apart. Being part of the Wild pack changed my life. I love Colton like a brother. Other than Olivia, he's the only one who knows my family secret, the whole story about my biological father. He's also the one person in my inner circle who knows my true feelings for Olivia.

"How was the first day of training camp?" I ask him as I help Kyle and Connor finish packing.

"Man, it was brutal." He exhales. "I loved getting back out there, but shit. I thought I'd kept in decent shape this off-season, but the body doesn't lie. I'm fucking sore. And I'm on my way to do it all over again today."

"It will get easier," I tell him. I still remember the two-a-days of practice, and how much my body ached. "You know, you adjust."

"Speaking of—how's the new team? You started coaching already, right?"

"Just day one. It was awesome."

"That's great, J. You remember how you used to diagram plays for all of us when we'd practice together in Montana? You were always a genius at that shit."

"Genius is a stretch," I say.

"Not a stretch," he insists. "You could work in the NFL if

you wanted to. Start at the bottom and work your way up. Dyl and I would put in a word for you here if you ever wanted to move to L.A."

"You know I can't do that. I can't move that far away. Plus, coaching in the pros tends to be a twenty-four-seven job. And I'm not interested in being a workaholic."

"I know. Being a father comes first for you." His tone is proud.

It's not only my sons that keep me in Pennsylvania. It's the woman I just left a Division I football program for to coach at a Division III school. Most would call that a step down. I call coming home to Olivia the best decision I ever made.

"I just want you to know the chance is always here for you if you want it."

"Thanks, Colt. I appreciate that. You know I'd love to boss you and Dylan around on the field."

"And the way you handled taking off the jersey...you were always a stud about dealing with the unexpected..." He trails off.

I tried to get through the major derailment in my football plans gracefully, tried to insist that I wanted to walk away from the sport so I could major in sports psychology.

And partially, that was true. I had won a full scholarship to college based on my 4.0 GPA and SAT scores; the football was a bonus. When I started at college, I hadn't even known if I'd make the team.

As it turned out, I played so well that I was tapped to be the starting quarterback even though I was only a freshman. But in the first game, a quarter and a half in, my career was over with one missed block on my blind side.

Colton knows how much it stung when I blew out my knee. He knows the scar on my leg from the three surgeries I had to try to repair the damage doesn't really fade with time.

But I managed to convince him and his cousins that I was okay making the choice to stop playing. I never told him about the heartbreak I felt that last day at the doctor's office when he told me I'd never again be able to stand behind center and risk taking another hit to my leg.

I took the semester off and came home to Liberty Falls.

For one reason—Olivia was there.

I had two of my surgeries, plus hours of rehab, while living back with my mom and Dee.

And Olivia was my sanctuary.

She was still in high school, but she came over every day after school, and we spent hours talking and hanging out. She made me realize that Jenson the person was far more important to her than Jenson the football star. And I don't know if she'll ever realize how much that meant to me.

I spent the entire fall rehabbing my knee in hopes of getting back on the football field, but it wasn't meant to be. It hurt like hell to lose the ability to play competitively, but as I returned to school and got into the coaching side of football, I realized I enjoyed that nearly as much.

"I always loved to dissect plays," I say to Colton. "I'm looking forward to doing it with this new team."

"Cool. I'm excited to follow your season. So." He pauses. "How else goes it in P.A.?" His question is casual, but his meaning anything but.

"Going well."

"Yeah? Have you seen her?"

"J, I went to a family party on night one." I walk out of the room and away from little ears. "Of course I saw her."

"And? How was it?"

"Same as always. Fantastic."

"All right," he says with enthusiasm. "So did you tell her you're moving there?"

"Yes."

"And? Jesus, J, do I have to drag the story out of you? It's not even daylight here, and I'm on my way to put my body through hell—help a guy out."

I roll my shoulders and take a seat at the kitchen table. "I don't think Olivia trusts yet that this can work."

"She'll come around once she realizes you're dead serious."

"I hope so." Done talking about Olivia and me, I don't elaborate.

Colton takes the cue. "How are the boys?"

"One of them just said 'motherfucker.' Guess where he claims he learned it?"

Long chuckle. "Sorry about that. I told him not to use it."

I laugh. "Any other news before you have to go?"

"Yeah. Dylan's charity has a meeting in Philly tomorrow on our one off-day this week. I'd go with him so I could hang with you, but Sky's mom is in town. And Jasalie has a big meeting with an art gallery she can't reschedule. So Dyl, because he hates doing these things alone, has convinced Brayden to go with him. He's actually having his private plane make an extra stop in Montana to pick Bray up."

I grin. "Christ."

"I know. He's so damn spoiled. Jasalie can't stop teasing him for it." Even as he jokes, Colton's tone is filled with pride and affection.

"Will they have time to meet me for lunch?"

"Definitely. Dylan's going to text you when he arrives; he wants to meet in Liberty Falls. He's going to have a car service take him and Bray. And remember the Cougars are playing Philly in preseason. So we'll see you in August. I'll get tickets for you, Olivia, and the boys."

"That's awesome, Colt. Thanks."

"Oh, by the way...something's a little different with Dylan since you saw him last."

"Since Maine and the memorial for Ayden's father? That was only a month ago."

"Yeah, well—" He trails off. "Look closely. That's all I'll say."

As soon as we hang up, Meghan texts that she's stuck in a staff meeting at work, and she can't pick up the boys. Is it okay if they stay with me until tomorrow afternoon?

I run my hand down my face. Not the news I want to hear today, especially so last-minute. Mom and Dee have left to visit his daughter, and they're at least an hour away. Olivia's dad has that luncheon with the neighboring town's mayor, and her mom's going also. Daphne's probably home but...well, she and I have never been close. And Sheldon and Olivia are both at work.

But I have about thirty minutes to pack up the boys and get to my board meeting on time. Missing the school's announcement of my hiring would not be a good look.

Not knowing what else to do, I reach for the phone.

Olivia answers on the second ring. "Good morning and welcome to Union Bank. My name is Olivia. How can I help you?"

"Olive." I try to keep the panic out of my voice. "I hate to bother you at work. I didn't know who else to call."

CHAPTER SEVEN

Olivia

Jenson hustles through the front doors of Union Bank with Kyle and Connor in tow. Both boys are wearing t-shirts and shorts and have adorable little backpacks over their shoulders.

"Hi." Jenson flashes me a quick grin, and my toes curl. His whole face lights up with gratitude, and he looks so sexy in that suit. His hair's combed back neatly, and his green eyes sparkle. "Can't tell you how much I appreciate this, Olive."

"It's no problem. I gave Vivian a heads-up, so she's expecting my little banking helpers to be here for the afternoon." I hold out my arms and both boys let me envelop them in a hug.

"Livia!" Kyle says, his eyes shining with joy. "I stole Connor's bathing suit, and he screamed like he was being murdered! It was awesome!"

"Wow. That sounds...intense." I glance up at Jenson, who mouths "little troublemaker" at me.

He ruffles Kyle's hair. "But he won't be doing anything like that in here, will you, Kyle?"

Kyle shakes his head. "Nope. We'll be good. We want to learn how to make money!"

I point to the two extra chairs I've set up at my desk. "Okay—why don't you both take a seat? You'll each be on either side of me, and I'll show you what I do here every day."

Connor's already sitting down. He tosses his backpack onto my desk. "Ready, Livia!"

Jenson's gaze slides to mine. "Are you sure you can handle them and get anything done at the same time?"

I put my hand on his arm. "Don't worry! We'll be fine. Good luck this afternoon. I'm so excited to hear about how it all goes."

He leans in close and whispers in my ear, "I'll make it up to you."

My heart melts as he kisses Kyle and Connor on their heads. "Be good for Olivia, boys."

He shoots me a half-grin, and he's gone.

I turn to Kyle and Connor. "Who wants to find out the best ways to save up money for something you really want?"

Two arms fly up in the air and wave at me excitedly.

I smile as I sit down in between the two boys and open up my laptop.

Keeping the attention of two very energetic five-year-olds is pretty much impossible. They sit politely for about ten minutes, and I give each of them a wallet. But Connor's still mad about Kyle stealing his bathing suit, and he pokes Kyle behind my back, until finally, they end up chasing each other around my desk. I put a stop to the fun when Connor body-slides across my desk on his stomach in order to "take a short cut to get to Kyle."

I've given up on getting any work done until I discover

the magic of markers. I set up Kyle and Connor with paper and a multitude of colored markers. They immediately quiet and start coloring.

By the time Jenson returns to the bank later that afternoon, both boys are asleep with their heads in my lap and their exhausted bodies curled up in their chairs.

Jenson takes in the scene and runs his hand through his hair. "That bad, huh?"

"I admired you before for being an amazing father," I say. "But now I think you and Meghan must be saints. I don't know how you manage as single parents."

He kneels down next to me. "It's a challenge," he admits, his eyes shifting to his sons both peacefully asleep. "It changes your entire life. But it's all good—okay, most of it's good," he adds with a grin.

"How did everything go at the college?"

"Great." He pulls at his tie. "I'm ready to change out of this suit. But I like the people I met. I have to admit, though, I'm looking forward to getting back to the football part of my job tomorrow."

"I'm glad it went well."

He tilts his head in the direction of his sons. "These little animals must have worn you out. How can I repay you?"

"I've actually got an idea. It's silly, but we'll have fun."

———

"I can't believe that's all you want," Jenson says as we step inside my house. "Hang out with you at Bernie's coffee house? That's too easy."

I bump him with my hip. "We never hang out with Sheldon and Cara. Not in ages, anyway."

As Kyle and Connor run across my living room and over to the sliding glass door, I whisper into Jenson's ear, "I

thought by going to Bernie's, we could start easing our relatives into the idea of...us. It could be like our first public date.
Except only we'll know."

Jenson's eyes search mine like he's looking to make sure
I'm serious. He must be okay with what he finds because he
gives me a thumbs up. "Bernie's it is. And I found out this
morning that Dylan and Brayden will be in town tomorrow."

"Gosh," I say wistfully. "I haven't seen those guys in so
long. Except for the television screen on Sundays," I add with
a laugh.

"I know. I wish you'd been at the Super Bowl with us."

"The Super Bowl!" Kyle rushes back over to us and jumps
up and down. "Livia, did you watch the Super Bowl?"

"I did, honey," I say. What I don't say is that I spent the
aftermath of the win meticulously scanning the crowd for
Jenson as the cameras panned the box where Dylan and
Colton's family and friends were gathered. "I thought maybe
I'd see my two favorite boys on TV!"

Connor's eyes get big. "Did you see us, Livia? On
the TV?"

I glance over at Jenson, who winks. "Unfortunately, I
didn't," I say, and Connor frowns. "But it was so hard to see
everyone. I could have missed you."

"I bet maybe you did!" Kyle says. "We could have been on
TV, right Daddy?"

Jenson holds out the football he brought in from his
truck. "Maybe. But remember, that's not why Uncle Colt and
Dylan play football. They do it because they love it. That's
what matters."

Kyle takes the football out of Jenson's hands. "I love football too. Can we play before dinner?"

"Not right now. I'm going to help Olivia cook."

But I shake my head. "I'm totally fine to do it. I'm just
making grilled cheese."

"Grilled cheese is my favorite!" Connor says.

"I know." I pick him up and set him on my kitchen counter. "That's why you're going to help me make it."

"Cool."

Jenson heads into my backyard with Kyle to try and burn off some of the excess energy he swears Kyle was born with. I watch them through the bay window, feeling a sense of home I haven't felt in my house before. It's nice. It's better than nice—it's something I want all the time.

―――――

I change out of my work suit and into a tank top and cut-offs before the four of us sit down and eat grilled cheese and hash browns.

After dinner, we walk over to Cindy and Dee's, and I read Kyle and Connor a bedtime story while Jenson changes out of his suit and into jeans and a fitted green t-shirt that matches his eyes. Both boys fall asleep in the middle of the book, and Jenson and I kiss them goodnight before tiptoeing out the door. Cindy and Dee are in the living room watching a movie, and they urge us to go out and have some fun.

When Jenson and I arrive at Bernie's, Sheldon and Cara are already there, and Hayley and Max walk in right behind us. Jenson takes a seat next to me on the couch and puts his arm up on the back of it. Nobody thinks anything of it. We're family, after all.

I introduce Hayley and Max to Jenson.

"So nice to meet you, Jenson. Olivia's told me a lot about you," Hayley says to him. "A lot, a lot."

I give her a hard stare, and she bats her long dark lashes at me innocently before she starts to ramble about her long day at work. "I mean, I'm a proofreader. That doesn't sound stressful, right?"

Jenson opens his mouth to answer her, but Hayley's always been a talker, and she keeps right on going.

"But it is. I get paid to make things right. Remember that if you ever need help with a problem." Another look from me, and her blue eyes sparkle mischievously. "But it's stressful because of the deadlines. And the clients don't give a shit. They just want their crap. Well, except they don't want it to be crap; they want it to be perfect."

"Do you freelance?" Jenson asks her.

"Sometimes," Hayley says. "But I also work full-time for a consulting company, because it's steady work and I know what my paycheck's going to look like every two weeks, you know?"

Jenson concurs and then asks Max what he does for work. Max has just barely gotten out that he's an illustrator when Sheldon interrupts. "So are you guys ready to party after Cara and I exchange vows?"

"I'll be at the bar," Hayley says. "Same place I'll be when Max and I finally tie the knot."

Max kisses Hayley's cheek and tells her he can't wait. I want to ask what they're waiting for, but I don't want to pry. Hayley's always been very private about her wedding plans. I wouldn't be surprised if she and Max went off one weekend and came back with rings on their fingers.

"What about you, Jenson?" Sheldon turns to him. "It's awesome you're moving back home. Will you be able to make it to my wedding?"

Jenson nods. "Wouldn't miss it."

Sheldon turns to me next. "Hey, Olive," he says in that irritating, teasing tone I recognize so well. My brother's in a mood, and he knows just where to go with that: his little sister.

I fix a blank expression on my face. I've found that if I

appear nonplussed, Sheldon won't always be able to get what he wants, which is to get a rise out of me.

"As you know, Cara and I decided to have an adult-only reception after our wedding."

I freeze. "The invitation didn't say that."

"It said 'adults only' at the bottom," Cara says. "See, I knew I didn't make the writing big enough!" she says to Sheldon.

"I'm sure I was just distracted and missed it," I assure her.

"You should bring a date," Sheldon says. "I insist. The men you've been with so far have been shit." Sheldon pauses and then points to a blond woman at a nearby table. "Maybe she's more to your liking."

I roll my eyes. "Stop meddling in my love life, Sheldon. I'm not interested in anyone you pick out for me."

But he's not finished. He points out a dark-haired older guy over in the corner.

"What about him?" he says. "I'll go invite him over."

Cara pokes Sheldon in the ribs. "That's a little obvious, baby, don't you think?" she says, turning to me with pity in her eyes.

My face goes hot. Sheldon hated my ex-husband, and he was relieved I filed for divorce. But because of that fiasco, he's convinced I don't know how to pick the right partner.

"Oh, so you do like him!" Sheldon says. "You're blushing!"

"I don't, no," I get out.

"Jenson," Sheldon says to him. "What do you think? You think he's good enough for Olivia?"

"No," Jenson says in a hard tone. "I think Olivia can do better than that."

"Who then?" Sheldon says. "Who in this room would you pick? Olivia needs a date for my wedding. If she doesn't get one, Mom has a line-up in mind."

"Seriously?" I lean forward. "She mentioned something

about a blind date to me on our walk, but I thought I success-fully dissuaded her."

Sheldon wags his finger at me. "You know our mother. She's going to keep going until you're dating again."

"What a nightmare," Hayley says as I groan into my hands that are now covering my face.

"I'll be Olivia's date."

Jenson's statement is so certain that, for a moment, I think I must have imagined it. I unpeel my hands from my face.

Sheldon and Cara are staring at Jenson like he's going to take back his offer any second and say he's joking. But his expression is blank.

"What do you mean?" Sheldon finally gets out. "You two are cousins. You can't be her date."

Dead silence hits our group as Jenson says nothing to break the awkwardness, and I freeze up completely.

"He means her friend-date," Hayley says finally with a quick glance at me. "Duh, Sheldon. Haven't you ever heard of it? It's called helping a friend out of a jam. Which clearly Olivia needs."

"That is so sweet," Cara says, her eyes softening. "My mom told me her brother was her date to the prom because her boyfriend dumped her last-minute."

Super.

"You're really going to look out for her?" Sheldon asks Jenson in a serious tone. "You'll protect Olivia from the sea of men our relatives will no doubt send her way at her brother's wedding?"

Jenson rubs my shoulder briefly but purposefully. "I'll always protect her."

"Cool." Sheldon reaches out to shake Jenson's hand. "All joking aside, that's a weight off my mind then. Our mom is bad on a good day with this set-up crap, but I know that at my wedding, she's bound to be downright nuts."

Before Jenson can respond, I interrupt to mention I'm worried about Daphne.

My attempt at distraction does the trick.

"So am I, but I can't get her to come out anymore," Sheldon says. "And I hate going to her house. She's always so moody."

I say that maybe it's because of the stress of having to take care of a family.

Cara agrees with me. "The first two to three years of your child's life are really stressful. Her husband's gone all day, and she's home alone with the kids."

"I can understand that," Sheldon says. "But there's a difference between stress and misery." He waxes into a long soliloquy on why Daphne's unhappy, ending with the theory that her marriage wasn't on solid footing from the beginning. "And if you're not solid before the kids," he says as he raps his knuckle on the oak coffee table in front of us. "What chance do you have?"

Jenson nods slowly. "I have to agree with you there."

I lean back against the couch the same time Jenson does, and our arms accidentally touch. Heat scorches my side like I'm on fire. I resist the urge to lean into him, nearly biting down on my lip to stay still. This is ridiculous—I sound like I'm in junior high school talking about my first crush.

When Sheldon and Cara start kissing, Jenson says to me in a low voice, "You want to get out of here?"

My gaze drops to his lips and then shifts back up to his eyes. "How?" I mouth.

"Let's hang out a little longer," he says in a low voice. "And then you say you're tired. I'll meet you at the corner of Oak."

We spend the rest of the time flirting with each other but pretending not to. Hayley gives me a look, or several looks, but Sheldon seems clueless. Jenson snaps my bra when I lean forward to pick up my drink, and I curse out loud.

"What happened?" Sheldon says.

"Oh," I stammer. "Nothing. I just...Jenson flicked my back."

"Still teasing your cousin, huh?" Sheldon says. "Well, you'll be able to do that as much as you want to now that you're moving home."

"Hey, Olivia," Hayley says abruptly, "come with me while I get a muffin."

She stands up, and I follow her as she walks toward the counter but then veers at the last second and walks over to the corner table, where no one ever sits because it's so dimly lit, and you have to practically step over the garbage can to reach it. She takes a seat and gestures I do the same.

"I remember the night you told me about him," Hayley says without taking time for a lead-in.

I can't blame her for her lack of a preamble. We probably have about two minutes of peace before Sheldon barges over.

I smile. "You're the only person in my life who knows the whole story. Of course, I didn't remember I told you because I was drunk."

"I came by the bank with coffee in the morning and said something about your cousin, and you turned white as a sheet. It was like you thought I'd pulled your deepest secret out of you while you were sleeping." Hayley reaches over to give me a hug. "I'm so happy to finally meet him. He's super hot. And nice. He's one of the good ones, Olive."

I nod. "He is. And I owe you for the save. Friend-date? You made it all okay. Thank you so much, Hayl."

She waves this off. "What are friends for? But I'm telling you, the sparks between you two are off-the-charts. I can't believe no one's said anything."

I bite my lip. "They don't want to see."

Hayley's eyes fill with sympathy. "It's almost weird to meet him in person. It's like this guy you've heard about for so long, and then suddenly, he's part of your group of friends. And you can't stop staring at him, trying to match him up to all the stories."

I stare down at the table. "He wants us to try. You know, dating. Even if we don't tell our families yet."

"Yay!" Hayley claps. "Reality is much more grey than the simplistic concepts of wrong and right. I think it's sweet what your family did for him. I really do. But you two need to get together already."

I pull my hair up into a high ponytail, immediately feeling the relief of having it off my sweaty neck. It really is hot as blazes outside. "Our relatives—and this whole town—act like we're really and truly cousins. It makes things weird. And this weekend at the fair—you know how the paper takes a million photos, and my dad rings the liberty bell to start things off. I always feel ogled at the fair on a normal year. This year, with Dad's re-election coming up—it's going to be that times ten."

Hayley waves her hand. "You'll figure it out. It may take all summer, but mark my words: by the time the weather turns, you and the love of your life will be a full-fledged, official couple."

Sounds too good to be true, but I smile at her and try to feed off her optimism.

———

Soon after Hayley and I return to the group, I start yawning before standing up and saying good night. I leave Bernie's quickly and cross the intersection to Oak Street. There's a bookstore on the corner, and I duck inside it to wait.

I have my nose buried in *Pride & Prejudice* when Jenson touches my hip. I raise my eyes to meet his curious green ones. He rests his chin on my shoulder as he stands beside me.

"That was always your favorite," he says, pointing at the novel in my hands.

I close the book and return it to its rightful place on the shelf. "I so love this story. But we can't linger here. Sheldon has freakishly good radar."

"Really?" Jenson catches up to me at the door and holds it open for us as we leave the store. "He seems pretty lost about all of it if you ask me."

"Well, my brother tends to surprise me when I least expect it," I say as we head down Oak toward my house.

"He asked you if you wanted to date a woman," he says. "And, he completely missed me flirting my ass off with you. Clueless, I'm telling you. And you have to bring a date to his wedding?"

"Requiring a date to anything is not what I need right now." I frown. "But I appreciate you stepping in like that."

Jenson takes my hand.

"You do know that everyone in the family will look at us like we're pathetic, though," I say.

"And we'll be the only ones who know the truth," Jenson says. "That we're not pathetic at all. We're two of the lucky ones who found something so rare that we didn't give up on it."

Not a soul is out in Liberty Falls at midnight in the middle of the week, and my heart is happy as we make our way to my house.

"Come on in," I say as we reach my front door.

As soon as we step inside, Jenson backs me up against the door.

"Olive." His voice is rough. "I've been waiting to kiss you for hours."

I slide my hands up his muscular chest. "You have been?"

"Actually, scratch that." He takes my bottom lip in his teeth before releasing it. "I've been waiting to kiss you for years."

And then his mouth is hard on mine. Every inch of me comes alive as I part my lips and his tongue slides inside my mouth.

"Remember last night at the bridge?" He murmurs into my lips. "You seemed close."

I flush with heat as I fist his shirt and press my breasts against his chest. "Close how?"

He shifts his lips to my neck. "Close to coming. Tell me I'm wrong."

"I can't do that," I get out on a half-moan. "I'm halfway to coming now, too."

Immediately, he lifts up my tank top. "You're going to go more than halfway tonight, babe."

Within seconds, my top and bra are on the ground. Jenson's large hands gently wrap around my waist as our eyes catch. His gaze runs the length of my body before he brings his eyes back up to meet mine.

"Olive." His voice is hoarse. "Christ, you're beautiful."

He palms one of my bare breasts. "It's been so long since I've touched you."

I whisper, "You've never touched me like this. Not...bare."

His teeth lightly graze the hard bud of my nipple, and I let out a moan.

"No, I haven't. That's a fucking shame." He sucks harder, and I grab at his hair and pull him even closer.

The sensation between my legs is so intense I can hardly stay standing. He unbuttons my cut-offs and slides his hand inside the band of my underwear.

I don't know who's shaking more as he touches me between my legs for the first time. He curses into my breast as his finger presses inside me.

"Olive." His voice is a harsh whisper. "Fuck. You're so wet."

I clutch at his shoulders, needing his strength to keep myself upright.

Three thrusts of his finger, and I come hard on his hand.

A half-sob leaves my throat. Jenson scoops me up into his arms and carries me over to the couch where he wraps an afghan around me.

I snuggle into his chest and look up at him. His green eyes scan my face like he's trying to understand everything I'm feeling.

"Remember your request? To take things slow?" he asks me.

I nod.

"We're going to hold to that. Because it's what we need. But I just want you to know—I want to do everything with you, Olive." He leans in to kiss me softly. "Everything."

I kiss his strong jawline. "Me too."

———

Jenson kisses me goodbye on my top step, right outside the front door. I wave as he leaves, walking down my driveway backward so he can watch me until he reaches the street.

Tonight felt like a real date, something we've never had.

I always wanted to be with the love of my life. I wanted that choice to be one I could make. But that hasn't been the way fate has worked out for me so far. And even though I know I shouldn't be, even though I know I shouldn't count on things between us lasting, tonight I'm ridiculously happy.

CHAPTER EIGHT

Jenson

The next morning, I sit in my new office in the athletic wing of the college and rub my eyes as I stare at the screen of my laptop. I've been here since before seven a.m., going over film of the team's games from last year. I can't get Olivia out of my head. Her curves, the way she melted into me last night. I'm lucky I'm sitting behind my desk because every time I think of her, I get hard. Being able to take our time like this is a luxury, but my dick doesn't appreciate luxury. Or patience. My dick has a pretty one-track mind when it comes to Olivia, and that's to see her again as soon as possible with even fewer clothes on than last night.

"Jenson." Coach Hughes steps into the room. "You want to show me what you've found?"

"Sure." I gesture him over. "I've been staring at this one game all morning."

He looks at my screen.

"The Saints." He shakes his head. "That game damn near ruined us. We lost two lineman to injury; our receivers couldn't fucking catch shit; and I swear, the punter forgot how to kick the damn ball. We had three special teams mistakes in the first half alone."

I know all of this, of course, but I let him vent.

Losing a football game, especially when you know you didn't put your best foot forward, can be downright demoralizing. You only get one game a week to make those brutal practices count for something. There is no game in a day or two to get out your frustrations; there's just five days of practice until the next weekend.

"So what do you think?" he says when he's done rehashing. "We play the Saints first this season. Can we fix what went wrong, at least on the offensive side of the ball? I've got Tucker dealing with special teams, and Bill and I are working on the defense."

I pull up the series I've been studying. "This play here— where the tight end goes on a slant route and the wide receiver goes deep—how about if we have the slot receiver curl back and the running back become the intended target? That way, the blind side is protected better, and the linemen don't have to block for as long."

Like I'm learning he likes to do, Coach Hughes repeats what I just said out loud. Then, he slaps my back.

"I like it. Let's try it at practice."

I stand up. "All right—I'm meeting some friends for lunch. I'll see you this afternoon."

———

"This coaching position sounds like a great fit," Dylan says as I sit at the restaurant table with him and Brayden and they ask me about my new job.

"Yeah, it seems to be so far...holy shit!" I stare at Dylan's left hand as he takes a sip of water. "You're married."

His smile is wide. "I am. To the most incredible woman in the world."

Jasalie and Dylan met the night the California Cougars won the Super Bowl. Jasalie had walls Dylan wasn't sure he'd ever get through, and vice versa. But they were so clearly meant for each other, and before long, they were inseparable. Now they're husband and wife.

Dylan has been a star quarterback since he was drafted right out of college, but his fame skyrocketed exponentially once the Cougars won the Super Bowl in February, and he was named MVP of the game. The three of us wanted privacy, somewhere Dylan wouldn't be asked for tons of pictures or autographs, so I reserved us a private room at Maria's Café, the low-key Italian restaurant at the edge of town.

The table is large, plenty big enough for us. Dylan's nearly six foot five and keeps his body in phenomenal shape. Brayden was Dylan's receiver in high school, and he and I are both well over six feet. Between the three of us, we need a lot of leg room.

"You're married? When the hell did that happen?" I ask him. We'd managed to order and chat for a good twenty minutes before I noticed Dylan's ring.

Brayden chuckles. "He and Jasalie eloped right after our weekend in Maine. I didn't know, either, not until he showed up in Montana in his private plane because he wouldn't let me fly coach."

Dylan's dark eyes sparkle as I continue to stare at the thick platinum wedding band on his ring finger. "It's real, Jenson."

I go silent as flashbacks of my own brief marriage hit me unexpectedly.

Meghan's eyes filled with doubt and fear as we exchanged vows.

My own churning stomach sent me a clear message to trust my gut and call the whole thing off. Of course, I didn't listen.

And Olivia was sitting in the very back pew by herself. I saw her when I was standing at the altar while I was supposed to be watching Meghan walk down the aisle, but my gaze got caught up in the blue dress Olivia was wearing, and my eyes traveled up her body to her face, which was etched in pain. To someone other than me, she probably just looked preoccupied, but the haunting emptiness in her eyes and the set line of her mouth are two things I wish I could wipe from my memory.

When the short ceremony ended, I looked for her again, but she was gone.

The empty space at the back of the church felt like a match to my heart.

I'd lost Olivia Graham. Once and for all, I'd lost her for good.

"Hey." Dylan waves a hand in front of my face. "You okay?"

I give one quick nod and turn the attention back to him. "That's awesome, man. Congratulations."

"Thanks. We're having a renewal ceremony and reception in Montana in the fall, during the Cougars' bye week. You, Bray, Cam, Ayden, and Colt will be groomsmen. Jasalie and I are going all in on the public renewal. And you should bring someone."

I blink. "Who?"

"A date. I told Bray the same thing."

Brayden shakes his head, his overgrown blond hair falling into his eyes. "Dylan wants those of us who are still single to find our soul mates. I'm not getting into a relationship again for a long time. If ever."

"You're a damn liar," Dylan says to Brayden. "Cam may want to stay single right now, and I get it. I hope he and Amy are still done. But you don't have an excuse."

"I don't need a damn excuse," Brayden mutters. "Relationships are hard, exhausting, and with little pay-off. I'm happily single and not looking to change that."

Dylan and I chuckle.

"Good luck with that," Dylan says to him. "That's usually when you get punched in the gut by love."

"No way," Brayden says. "I'm going solo to your wedding renewal, dude. Like it or not."

Undaunted, Dylan turns his attention back to me. "J, what about the mystery woman Colton was telling us about when we were in Maine, the supposed reason you moved back to Liberty Falls—can you bring her?"

I clench my jaw.

Colton was a dead man that night.

He's never come so close to spilling about Olivia. Later, he told me he was extra emotional because the memorial for Ayden's dad brought up memories of his late father, who passed away when Colton was a teenager. Colton was feeling off, and he was drinking, not a good combination.

He apologized because he knows I don't talk about Olivia with anyone but him.

Not because I don't trust the other Wilds, but I wanted to protect Olivia from any judgment or awkwardness, and I knew that the more people I told, the greater the chance of the story getting back to our families. She and I always had an "it's us against the world" mentality, and we rarely talked to anyone but each other about our relationship.

But life is short, and I'm beyond sick of pretending I'm single and looking when my heart has been with the same girl since I was a kid.

Dyl and Brayden are watching me.

"Are things going okay in that department?" Brayden asks me quietly.

"Yes."

Silence.

Then, "You know, you've never mentioned a specific woman from here before," Dylan says. "Meghan's from college, and I know it isn't her, anyway."

"Right." I pause, wanting to give them something other than a closed door. So I share a piece of the truth. "The mystery woman I came back for—she's someone I've wanted for a long time, but it's always been an off-limits sort of situation."

Brayden whistles. "That sounds rough."

"Understatement," I say. "But I'm fighting for her. For us."

Dylan nods in approval. "Good."

———

After lunch, we stop by Mom and Dee's house so Dylan and Brayden can visit with the boys.

"Uncle Dylan!"

"Uncle Bray!"

Kyle leaps into Dylan's arms at the same time that Connor hurls his little body against Brayden's legs.

Brayden picks him up and swings him around. "How you doing, buddy?"

"We want to play football with you!" Connor shouts.

Dylan rubs Connor's blond head. "I think that can be arranged. Your dad probably knows of a good place to play."

I don't want to take them to Randolph's football field and put Dylan in the spotlight where he'll have to take a bunch of photos with the multitude of athletes milling around campus. So we end up driving to the park in town. Dylan and Brayden each pair up with one of the boys, and I play coach for a two-on-two game of flag football.

Once Connor and Kyle start tackling each other and forgetting that a football even exists, I call the game a tie.

We pile back into my truck, and I turn onto Main Street.

"Livia!" Connor screams out.

I whip my head right and then left. "Where?" I say.

"There."

I slow down nearly to a stop and glance in the rearview mirror.

"Con." He's pointing at Union Bank. "Yes, that's where Olivia works. But she's busy."

"I want to say hi to her!"

"Me too!" Kyle chimes in.

"I haven't seen your cousin since you moved away from Liberty Falls," Dylan says. "I don't think she was at your wedding. Are you two still close then?"

At first I pretend not to hear his question. I focus on turning the truck into a parking space right outside the bank.

But when I glance over at Dylan, he's looking at me, waiting for an answer.

"Yes," I say finally. "We are."

"She was a sweet girl," Brayden says as I turn off the truck. "It will be fun to see her again."

Olivia

"Oh. My. God. Hot guy alert. Three hot guy alert." Cassandra freezes in place across from my desk where she'd popped by to drop off some papers for me.

Her shaky finger points toward the door, and I turn in that direction.

Jenson and his two sons, followed by Dylan and Brayden Wild.

Yes, they make quite the group. Dark-haired Dylan, who could just as easily pass for a model as a football star, is the tallest. Brayden and Jenson are both a few inches shorter,

blond, muscular, and fit. And Jenson's two sons are like miniature versions of him.

"You should see when the other three are with them," I
murmur. "The hotness meter just goes up." And I haven't
seen them all together in years. They've grown up, and from
the looks of it, only in good ways.

"Is that..." Cassandra keeps staring as the entourage heads
in our direction. "Dylan Wild?!!"

I jerk my chin at her. "Yes, but don't you have a customer
up at the teller window?"

She reluctantly turns toward the window. "Gosh, you have
all the fun around here," she grumbles as she leaves.

I hung out with the Wilds numerous times when Jenson
lived in Liberty Falls, but once he moved to Pittsburgh, he
would see them out there or at one of their places. I haven't
seen any of them since the night Jenson's sons were born. I
also saw them at Jenson's wedding, but they didn't see me
either time. At the wedding, I was hiding in the back pew of
the church, hoping to hide the tears I knew would come
when I heard Jenson officially become another woman's
husband. Another woman's forever.

The night I drove to Pittsburgh to meet Jenson's sons at
the hospital, Colton was there too. All five Wilds were there,
actually, but only Colton saw me.

After Jenson and I said good-bye to each other, I'd
returned to the hospital nursery to take one last look at Kyle
and Connor. The Wilds were at the other end of the hallway.
They were leaving and had their backs to me, but Colton
looked over his shoulder, and we caught eyes.

He waved his cousins on and walked back to me. His
blond hair was so similar to Jenson's, but where Jenson leans
toward the serious side, Colton's more of a jokester.

He wasn't joking that day, though. He was solemn as we

stood silently, side by side, staring through the glass at Jenson's sons.

"I can't imagine how you're feeling, Olive," Colton said, his attention still focused straight ahead. His hands were in his pockets, and his profile was etched with sympathy.

I couldn't speak. My throat was too raw.

Colton turned to face me then. "This is a detour for you two. Don't think of it as the final chapter."

I managed a nod.

"Your story with Jenson isn't over," he said, his tone fierce and certain.

My thoughts of the past disappear, and I return to the present as Kyle and Connor rush me.

"Livia!" they scream in unison.

Kyle grabs onto one of my legs and Connor the other. Kyle's got a smudge of dirt across one cheek, and Connor's entire shirt is covered in grass stains.

I laugh. "You two look like you've been playing outside."

"We played football with Uncle Dylan and Uncle Brayden. Daddy was the coach."

I lock eyes with Jenson whose attention is focused on me. "That sounds fun."

Dylan steps forward and manages to one-arm hug me, despite Kyle and Connor not letting go of my legs. "God, it's been ages, Olivia," he says, his smile as warm and genuine as I remember. "You're all grown up."

Brayden kisses my cheek. "It's great to see you again," he says, his blue eyes bright.

"It's so good to see you both," I say. I didn't realize just how much I've missed seeing them all until just now. "You both look as handsome as ever. Dylan, I've seen you on television a bunch—congratulations on winning the championship. And the MVP, of course."

Dylan flushes, clearly not wanting any extra attention. "Thank you. It was an amazing season."

"You should be really proud of yourself," I say.

Jenson, who's been holding back, steps closer. "Boys, give Olive a little room, okay?" He takes each of his sons by a shoulder and gently urges them to unpeel themselves from my thighs.

Once that's accomplished, he leans in close so he can speak only to me. "My mom told me about the last-minute speech your dad's giving tonight."

"Yes. Will you be joining us on stage?"

"Of course. Save me a seat," he says with a wink.

As I nod, I can't help the blush that I know stains my cheeks. Not wanting to see if Dylan or Brayden have noticed, I keep my gaze trained on Jenson's.

His green eyes study me. "I like your suit."

I smile. I'm in my favorite business suit, the one I bought with my Christmas bonus. It may be conservative blue in color, but it flatters my figure, and the pink top I'm wearing underneath the fitted blazer brightens the whole ensemble.

"Thank you."

"How's your day going?" he asks me softly.

"Good. Not as eventful as yesterday; that is until you all walked in."

Kyle and Connor are still standing in between us with Kyle now hugging Jenson's leg and Connor leaning into my side. I rub his head as I joke with Jenson.

Then I glance past him.

Dylan and Brayden are staring—I mean *staring*—at me.

Dylan blinks first.

"I was just...realizing something," he says with an embarrassed grin. "I wasn't leering or anything. Not that you're not beautiful, Olivia."

Jenson whips around. "What the hell—"

CHAPTER NINE

Jenson

Fuck. *They know.*

As soon as I turn toward Dylan and Brayden, I see their faces as the truth starts to crystallize: Olivia Graham is my mystery woman.

I tell Olivia I'll call her later, take Kyle and Connor by the hands, and practically run out of the bank.

"Jenson." Dylan's voice behind me is one of stunned awareness.

"Let me put the boys in the truck." I situate Kyle and Connor in their car seats and turn on the A/C.

Once I make sure both boys are preoccupied, singing to their favorite music and can't hear me, I close the truck door and turn to face Dylan and Brayden.

Arms crossed over my chest—okay, my heart—I say, "I couldn't tell you."

"But Colton knows." Dylan's question isn't judgmental or accusing in any way—it's simply stating a fact.

My expression must confirm this to be true because

Dylan and Brayden both cross their arms over their chests, mimicking my pose.

"You looked at her the way I look at Jasalie." Dylan's tone is so certain I blink.

I give a slow nod. "The way I feel about her is forever."

"Talk to us." Dylan leans against the side of my truck.

"Not here." I open the driver's door. "Let's drop the boys off at my mom's so they won't be late for Meghan picking them up. I'll drive you to your plane, and we'll talk on the way."

———

On the way to the small airport where Dylan's private plane is waiting for him and Brayden, I give them an overview of my relationship with Olivia.

"So it's always been her." Dylan glances over at me from the passenger seat.

"Always. Always will be."

"I knew you and Meghan were young and felt forced into marriage," he says. "But this adds a whole new layer of pain."

"Olivia was at my wedding," I say, remembering how he'd said he didn't see her there. "She left early."

"I don't blame her," Dylan murmurs. "Must have been pure hell."

"We're figuring this out one step at a time right now," I say. "It's been a lot of years and a lot of time apart. We're getting to know each other all over again this summer, and to bring in our families too soon—I'm afraid it would kill whatever momentum we have going for us. Plus, Olivia's dad's the town mayor; she's under a constant microscope. Most people here truly think we're actual cousins."

"I feel like an asshole that I've been calling her your cousin," Dylan says as he runs his hand through his hair.

"You shouldn't feel badly in the least," I say. "My mom introduced her to you that way. And I never corrected that with you."

"You were kids," Brayden says. "What were you supposed to do—fight two families at once over something that probably confused the hell out of you? Forbidden relationships are hard for a reason, J."

"I know." I grip the steering wheel so hard my hands hurt. "Plus, Olivia was underage. She's almost three years younger than me, and when you're teenagers, that's a big fucking deal."

"I didn't realize the age difference..." Dylan counts silently. "So when you were already eighteen, she was just fifteen?"

I nod. "Too young. She was only sixteen when I left for school, and I wanted her to have a normal high school experience. I didn't want her waiting around for me and not get to enjoy being a teenager. So we broke things off, as much as we could, and agreed to see where we ended up. But life takes hairpin turns sometimes."

"Kyle and Connor," Brayden says. "Wow."

"Olive was one month from turning eighteen when Meghan got pregnant."

"Shit, J." Dylan's eyes fill with sympathy. "I wish I'd known..."

"She and I never talk about it to other people. I only told Colt, and she's told only one person ever as well. If that." Olivia never told me that she shared our story with Hayley, but from the way Hayley was eyeing the two of us, I'd bet a lot of money that she knows.

"You can trust us," Dylan says. "Nothing said in here will ever leave this truck."

Brayden adds, "Not to Cam or Ayden, either, in case

you're worried. It's your story to tell, J—you'll tell it when you're ready."

My grip on the wheel relaxes a touch, and I nod my thanks. But I need a subject change—fast. "So anyone else got news?"

Brayden lets out a long breath. "The ranch owners want to sell."

I catch his gaze in the rearview mirror. "Whoa."

Brayden's been living on the same Montana ranch for years. Along with coaching high school football, it's what he loves most.

Dylan jerks his head around to face Brayden. "What? You never said anything about it."

"I know. I didn't want to worry you."

I get it. "So what are you going to do now?"

"Wait a minute." Dylan's now twisted completely around in his seat. "Does that mean you have to move?"

"Hopefully there's another solution," he says simply.

Brayden's always been more private than the other Wilds. He's someone you would trust with your life, and he's always been able to see multiple angles of a situation. But he doesn't share like the others do.

"Can I help?" Dylan presses. "I'm not asking to piss you off, Bray. I'm asking because I want to make sure you're okay. You know I can help if you need some time to figure things out."

"I know." Brayden's voice is quiet. "But I'm okay. I have some ideas I'm running over in my head but nothing I want to discuss yet. I just know it's time I finally jump off the deep end and force myself to learn to swim."

Olivia

I sit in a row with my family behind the looming podium where Dad will be speaking in a few minutes. I came straight from work and am still in my business suit.

The crowded town hall is buzzing with conversation between the residents chatting amongst each other as they sit in their metal chairs and wait for Dad to take the microphone.

Right now, he's standing just out of view with Cindy and his assistant while they go over tonight's agenda, which is really him making the official announcement that he's not retiring from his mayoral post. Not this election.

My phone buzzes, and I pull it out of my purse.

Sorry about the bank fiasco. I'm almost to the town hall.

Didn't bother me, I type back to him. *I kept the seat on my right empty.*

Daphne, who's never on time to these things, rushes up to the stage. Before I can stop her, she drops into the seat on my right.

"Daph, I was saving that for..."

"Olive, no one needs this seat more than I do right now." She gives me a pleading look, her eyes widening with emotion. "Please don't make me go sit next to our brother. Sheldon will send me into tears as soon as he takes one look at me."

Her hair is in braids, and her outfit consists of a pink blouse with a black A-line skirt that looks cute except...

"Is that spaghetti sauce?" I say as I point to the stain on her blouse collar.

"Can you believe it?" She blushes, and I have the urge to hug her. "I just got Alec off to bed, but Amy wouldn't settle, and Todd worked late again. He got home the second before I rushed out of the house. I look a mess, Olive."

"You look great." I reach into my purse and hand her a stain-stick remover. "Try this."

"YOU look fine," Daphne corrects me as she takes the stick out of my hand and tries to furtively dab at her collar. "Better than fine, in fact," she says as she looks at my face more closely. She lowers her voice. "Did you have sex recently?"

I smile but don't answer her.

"You did, didn't you?" she says, the tension in her jaw disappearing as she keeps rubbing her collar with the stick and the red stain diminishes significantly.

I let her continue to think what she wants as I take the stick back from her and return it to my purse. No, I haven't had actual intercourse yet, but whatever Jenson and I are doing together is so much better than any sex I've ever had. Being near him, around him, with him, makes me happy, and I know it shows. My skin is clearer, my eyes look brighter, and my mouth is...well, desperate for his lips. All the damn time.

"Oh, just wait till you get married, Olive," Daphne says bitterly. "I tell Amy this all the time. All that happiness will fade away. And when you have kids? Gone for good."

I put my hand on Daphne's arm in concern. "Why?" I say. "Why will it all go away? Getting married and having kids is supposed to be one of those fantasies come true, isn't it?"

Daphne shrugs. "I guess it is. But the fantasy ends at the honeymoon. There are bills to pay, and all that great sex leads to something once you're married—babies who have mouths to feed."

"So did you feel like you had to have kids as soon as you married?" I ask her.

"Todd wanted kids right away." Daphne shrugs. "And I guess part of me did too. I was naïve, though. It's so draining."

I exhale, feeling exhausted.

"Hey, you two."

I jerk my head up to the beautiful sight of Jenson Beau standing in front of me.

His green eyes are as bright and intense as ever, and he's wearing a white collared shirt and black dress pants. His slightly-long blond hair is combed back neatly. And he's smiling.

"What happened to my seat?" he says teasingly.

I gesture toward Daphne. "My oldest sibling snagged it."

Daphne giggles and pats the empty chair to her right. "Sit next to me, Jenson. We can catch up."

He shoots me an "I'd rather be catching up with you" look before taking the seat on the other side of my sister.

Daphne turns her back on me and starts laughing with Jenson right away. Darts of jealousy shoot through me. Which is absolutely crazy—to feel like I need to compete with my married sister for the attention of a man she thinks is off-limits and really has never been very close to, but I'm not feeling rational right now.

When Jenson's mom kneels down next to him, and they start talking, Daphne turns back around and whispers to me, "Jenson's really hot, don't you think?"

I spin and look at her. "What?"

"Oh, I know he's our cousin," she says. "I'm just saying he's incredibly good-looking. He always was, don't you remember? He was so hot on the football field, quarterbacking the team in high school. He was a star in town. Pity he couldn't pursue it in college."

"You know why," I say. "His knee."

"I know. But even though he doesn't play football anymore, he's still got an amazing body. Look at his biceps." Daphne shifts to look at Jenson like he's half-naked and posing. "God, he must look great naked."

"Daphne!" I elbow her. "Shh."

She giggles. "I know it's wrong of me to talk about him like that. But sweet Lord, is he fun to look at."

"He's not our cousin," I say without thinking.

Daphne stops and stares at me. "Why would you say that? Jenson's family. He's been family his whole life. I thought you two were close."

"We are." I feel my cheeks flushing with heat. "I just meant—he's not actually our blood cousin, so when you said he was cute, it's okay to feel that way."

"Oh." A thought passes across her face, and I freeze, but then she shakes her head, appearing to shake the thought away, too. "He is a hottie, isn't he?"

"He sure is," I say in a short tone.

Dad strides up to the podium and calls out a hello into the microphone, saving me from having to speak more to Daphne about Jenson's hot body.

"I'm thrilled to officially announce my intention to run again as mayor of Liberty Falls," Dad says to loud applause.

Once the clapping dies down, he clears his throat.

"I'd like to thank my wife, Nora, for all her love and support, along with my children," he says smoothly like he's rehearsed this a thousand times. "My daughter, Daphne, and her husband, Todd, who's at home right now with my two grandchildren; my son, Sheldon, and his bride-to-be, Cara; my daughter, Olivia, and her husba—"

Oh, no. He didn't. He couldn't have.

My father turns back to look at me, a pained apology written all over his face.

He did.

He whips back around to the crowd, who are tittering and murmuring.

"Excuse me. And...her cousin, Jenson, who's like my second son. I know Dee's his stepdad, but Jenson's part of the Graham family, and he always will be."

And the hits just keep on coming.

Now Dad practically just announced Jenson as my *step-brother?*

Luckily, my father steers the rest of his speech away from family and focuses instead on the issues he plans to focus on if he wins re-election—to end bullying in the schools; to get more business in the downtown area; and to continue to make Liberty Falls "one of the safest towns in the state of Pennsylvania." Then, he adds half-jokingly, "And another goal, I hope, is to bring a much-needed winning season to Randolph College's football program. The addition of Jenson to the coaching staff should be a big boost."

Football's huge in Liberty Falls, and the applause is louder for that part of Dad's speech than anything else he'd said. I turn and raise my eyebrows at Jenson, who mouths "no pressure, right?"

When Dad mercifully finishes talking, we all clap and cheer, and then we go out to dinner as a family to our favorite Mexican restaurant in town. Everyone except for Daphne, who says she's too tired to eat out.

My parents sit with Cindy and Dee at the big booth in the middle of the restaurant, and the hostess leads Sheldon, Cara, Jenson, and me to a separate space a few feet away.

Customers call out to us as we weave around the tables. One of them tells me he's pulling for my dad to be mayor forever.

I laugh. "I don't know if that's going to happen but hopefully he will be for a while."

Another customer asks Jenson if he's going to be at the fair's bell ringing.

"Wouldn't miss it," he says with a smile.

"Love seeing you and Jenson together, Olivia," the woman says. "I wish my cousin and I got on this well."

I clench my jaw and nod. "We're very lucky. Have a good evening."

By the time we reach our booth, I feel nauseous. Jenson slides in next to me, and Sheldon and Cara sit across from us.

"Are you two friend-dating to all events now?" Sheldon says in a teasing tone.

"That's right." Jenson plays it off with a grin. "All in preparation for your big day. We want to make sure we know each other well enough and don't act like strangers."

"You're cousins—you've been best friends your whole lives," Sheldon says. "What is there to get to know?"

Jenson shrugs casually. "I haven't been back much lately."

"Hi Olivia. Hello, Jenson. Welcome home." Calvin, the reporter for the Star, smirks at me as he walks by.

His comment is innocent enough, but there's something about his expression, like he's been listening...

"Was that weird?" I say to Jenson, barely moving my lips. As the daughter of a man constantly in the public eye, I learned how to smile and talk without changing my face a long time ago.

"We're family," Jenson says to me in a low tone. "Dinner together is expected. If he's angling for something else, that's his problem."

"You're right," I say, feeling sad for some reason. "But you know Calvin. He's always been an ass."

"I know." He catches my eye as the waitress hands out menus to the group of us. "Just ignore the noise," he murmurs to me as he opens his menu. "Let's get our favorite."

Chicken fajitas. We used to order this dish every year before the fair. Until Jenson moved away, he and I went to the fair together every year.

"You haven't been to the fair in so long," I say as I reach for my glass of water.

"I know. I might be late getting there because of team practice, but Kyle and Connor are stoked to go."

"I bet they are," Cara says. "They'll love some of the silly events."

"Silly?" Sheldon says in mock offense. "Baby, I live for those events. I'm going to win something this year. Mark my words."

The four of us chat casually throughout dinner, catching up on little things. Like how Jenson loves guacamole now.

"What?!" I say.

Jenson breaks into a laugh.

"You hated guacamole forever!" I say.

"I got started on it in Pittsburgh. The group of quarterbacks I was coaching were all obsessed with avocado, and one day at practice, I promised them that if none of them threw an interception, I'd take them out for Mexican, and I'd eat a dish of guacamole on my own. The fuckers played perfect football that day. I swear the defense helped them out by playing like shit, but I had to keep my word."

Sheldon chuckles. "And? You learned the joys of guacamole that Olivia's been telling you about since we were kids?"

Jenson points to his menu. "I did. You all want to share a bowl of it with some tortilla chips?"

"Count me in," Sheldon says as he and Cara excuse themselves for the restroom. "Be right back; order us more beers too."

Jenson turns to me. "What about you? You want to share a bowl of guacamole?"

"I'd love to." I'd love to share anything with this man. "I've missed this. Hanging out together."

The emerald of his eyes darkens. "Me too."

After dinner, Jenson and I say goodnight to everyone outside the restaurant.

"Make sure to walk Olivia to her door," Mom begs Jenson. "She always insists she's safe, but I prefer her to have a companion when it's this dark out."

"I will, Nora," Jenson says.

We wave goodbye and turn for my house.

Within minutes, we're completely alone.

"So I cracked and told Dylan and Brayden about us," he says immediately.

"I figured you wouldn't have much of a choice. Their expressions were pretty priceless when the realization seemed to hit them."

"No shit." He lets out a short laugh. "Not the way I pictured filling them in on the most important woman in my life."

I inhale sharply. "J..."

He leans down to see my face. "The. Most. Important," he repeats.

I chew on my lip anxiously.

"I haven't even been back here a week," he says. "We're going to figure this out, Olive. It may be messy, but we'll work through it."

"So you told them," I say, trying to return us to the topic he started with. "They never had a clue when we were younger. What was different when they saw us together this time?"

"I'd given them a couple of big clues they'd never had before." He fills me in on his trip to Maine and how Colton nearly spilled about us. "And I let them know it was a forbidden relationship. When he saw us together, Dylan said I looked at you the way he looks at his wife. And Brayden... I'm not sure. He said he just knew."

"Dylan's married?"

He laughs and fills me in on Dylan and Jasalie eloping.

"Good for him. That's awesome. And I wouldn't worry about them finding out. I never expressly told you, but Hayley knows too," I say quietly.

"I assumed."

Our eyes catch and hold.

I study his face, trying to see his expression in the dark. "What else is going on? You look like you have something else to tell me."

He reaches for my hand and pulls up to a stop. "Your radar's still intact, huh? Yeah, I have something to tell you. My realtor called. She has a great lead on a house rental."

I swallow. "In Liberty Falls?"

"Yes. About ten minutes from you on the other side of Main Street. By the old train station."

Holy crap.

"I love that area."

His eyes brighten. "I remember. We always said we'd like to live there together."

"Have you seen it?" I say.

"I'm going tomorrow. The house is empty, so if I like it, the owners want me to move in as soon as possible, which is fine with me."

"That would be..." *Amazing.* "A big change."

"A good change," he says as he leans in close.

The minty scent of his aftershave engulfs me, and his eyes burn with heat. His jaw clenches as he fixes his gaze on my mouth.

"Let's go," he says in a rough tone. "I need to be alone with you."

————

As we walk up the front steps, Jenson takes the key out of my outstretched hand and unlocks the door. "Is it okay if I come in?"

I don't think I would allow him to leave even if he tried. I need Jenson so badly right now it hurts. The ache between my thighs is painful as I nod yes and gesture him in ahead of me. I close the door slowly, wanting to give myself a moment to clear my head before I go forward. Because I'm opening up more and more with each moment we spend together, and I hope to Jesus I know what I'm doing.

"So if it feels right..." I say as I turn to face him.

"Then yes." Jenson's eyes are heavy with lust as he steps closer to me, unbuttons my suit jacket, and abruptly pulls it off my shoulders until it drops to the ground.

He unbuttons my blouse next, and doesn't stop until it too is on the floor.

My nipples immediately harden underneath my thin cotton bra, and a sexy sound escapes Jenson's throat.

"Olivia." His mouth goes to my neck, and one strong arm wraps around my waist, urging me closer.

My breath catches in my throat as he walks us back toward the couch. We fall onto it together, and Jenson pulls me on top of him. He grabs my ass and presses me against his growing bulge, and I let out a moan.

His mouth goes to my lips, and his tongue tangles with mine until I'm dizzy and not thinking at all.

I'm crazy with lust, so much that any hesitation and fear leave me. I don't slow down. I don't stop to think. I just move on instinct and feeling. I shift my head so I can lick Jenson's neck. As he groans, I move down so I can lift up his shirt and kiss his bare muscled chest, and then his stomach. His breathing gets heavier, and his hands tighten their grip on my hair. I unbuckle his jeans and keep going until I can wrap my lips around the soft tip of his hard length.

Oh, God.

My first time doing this with him, and I'm so turned on it hurts.

"Olive."

I raise my head and lock eyes with him. "You're beautiful," I tell him.

The green of his eyes flashes with emotion.

"I'm finally touching your dick, just like I said I wanted."

"You are definitely doing that." His voice is rough and sexy. "What do you think?"

"Perfect." Jenson's package was definitely worth the wait, and my imagination in sculpting him didn't do his impressive erection justice. "I want it in my mouth."

"You can have it wherever you want it, babe. I want to be inside you in every way."

Sex with Jenson Beau? My body screams yes, but my heart isn't quite ready to take that leap.

So if using my mouth is the only way to feel Jenson inside of me tonight, I will gladly make that compromise.

———

Jenson

When Olive takes me into her mouth, the sensations that hit me nearly knock me out. I slam my eyes shut, unable to focus on anything—literally anything—other than the mind-blowing feeling of her lips on me. I'm so hard it's nearly painful to drag this out, but with each lick and suck, I fall further and further into fucking bliss.

"Olive. Shit." I buck up into her soft, perfect mouth, my hands gripping her hair like a lifeline. "Oh, God, babe. So fucking good..."

When she slips her hand around the bottom of my length and starts stroking me without letting up with her tongue, I'm a goner. My orgasm takes over my body and my mind.

By the time I've stopped seeing stars and have opened my eyes, Olivia is lying next to me, her head on my shoulder.

I kiss her head. "You literally just blew my mind."

She giggles. "Pun intended?"

"Absolutely." I shift so I can see her eyes. "You okay?"

Her nod is quick—too quick.

"What's wrong?" I take her chin in my hand. "You're freaking out about what we just did? I am too a little bit— every step forward for us is a big deal, and I'm not making light of any of it."

"I know. And God, being able to finally touch you like that—I'm so happy, J." Her voice is soft, but a shadow crosses her face as she peeks up at me. "Do you think marriage is a prison sentence?"

"My marriage felt like prison for me," I say honestly.

"It is for Daphne, too."

"Why are you asking?" I keep my gaze firmly focused on hers, wanting to make sure I don't miss any clues she's giving off.

She bites her lip. "I guess Daphne scared me. She makes it sound like it all sucks. Marriage, kids, you know. Like it's just jail."

I take her bottom lip in my teeth and lightly bite it myself. "I think you're scared of something that has nothing to do with your sister."

She sighs into my mouth as I continue to nibble her lips. "You're probably right. It's just...this is all new to me. Being with you as an adult."

"So let's just keep enjoying ourselves and getting to know each other again."

"I want that. More than anything," she says.

I do too.

CHAPTER TEN

Olivia

The next morning, Mom surprises me at work.

"Everything all right?" I ask her in concern.

She hastens over to my desk. "Olivia, I'm sorry to surprise you like this," she begins as she takes a seat across from me. "Absolutely nothing is wrong."

Her cheeks flush the way they do when she feels guilty, and I know I'm not going to like whatever reason brought her here. "You know Cybil's daughter, Patsy?"

"Yes," I say suspiciously. "Of course I do."

"Well," Mom continues enthusiastically. "Patsy's dear friend, Maureen, has a son, and he just moved back to town..."

"No, no, no—a million times no!" I say as Cassandra looks over from the teller window.

"He's a nice boy, Olivia," Mom says in a low voice. "Patsy's known him since he was in diapers. He grew up in Bearport. You know the town over from here?"

"Yeah," I say with clenched teeth. "I'm familiar."

"The thing is, Dad feels just terrible about what he said

last night. About what he *almost* said, I should say. And he and I got to talking afterward about you and your single status. At your age, a woman likes to be at least on her way to a secure relationship."

"Mom, I swear to God. This is not 1950 anymore, or haven't you noticed?"

"Olivia, I know it's not 1950. But I want you to have a partner in life. Not a savior," she adds hastily when she sees my face. "A partner. Someone to share battle scars with, someone to share fairy tales with. I know you're not Sleeping Beauty who needs rescuing. That was always more Daphne, never you. Look at you now." She pauses to sweep her arm around the bank dramatically. "You could be running this place in ten years. You've done very well, sweetheart, and Dad and I are so proud of you. We really are. But I want you to love, too. Not just money but another person."

I drop my head into my hands. "Mom, I tried marriage. It didn't work."

"You mean Nate didn't work. You obviously married the wrong man. But I haven't given up on you finding the right one."

I raise my head and look at her face filled with hope.

I don't have a clue what to say to her. Not being able to tell my mother about my first and only love has been more than painful; it's created a distance between us that I know she doesn't understand. Because Mom and I are close, we really are. But because I can't share what's in my heart with her...well, it's made things confusing. "I—"

"Would you at least meet Will Saturday at the fair?" she asks. "He's expecting you."

As much as I want to, now isn't the time to fill her in on Jenson. So I stall.

"I—can't. I'm not looking to meet anyone new yet. I can't

explain it to you more clearly than that right now. Just trust me."

Mom nods and changes the subject to the weather, something I take as a good sign that we're on the same page and moving on. "It's supposed to be a beautiful sunny day on Saturday. Even Auntie Sue's going to make it."

"That's great. Hopefully, she'll enjoy herself."

"Sheldon and Cara will both be there, of course. But Daphne's busy—they're visiting Todd's family. Do you know if Jenson's planning on coming? Dad would really appreciate having him there."

I swallow and don't look at her as I answer. "I know the Hawks have practice that morning. But he mentioned something about taking Kyle and Connor afterward."

"Good," Mom says. "It's too bad he broke it off with that woman out in Pittsburgh, but I guess she wasn't the one for him after all."

Pain hits my chest, and I just barely get out, "Guess not."

Before I have to chat more about Jenson, Vivian approaches my desk, and Mom leaves with a whispered, "I'll meet you at six. I've got great plans for tonight's Adult Ed class."

Good Lord.

Vivian waits until my mother's walked out the door before she turns to me with a smile. "I'm sending you to Manhattan, Olivia."

"What?"

"This is a big meeting with our new account, and I can't make it. So you'll do it in my place. Sound good?"

"Do what in your place?" I say to her. "You're the president."

"And you're the deal closer," she counters me. "Perls is a huge client. You're awesome with new customers. This should be no different. And if it works out, there's a bonus attached, along with some great experience."

"Oh, gosh." I can feel the panic in my voice as I stare at her. "I don't know, Viv. The last time I was in Manhattan, things kind of went off a cliff."

Vivian nods sympathetically. "But this is just for one day. And it could be a great opportunity to maybe heal those memories, no?"

"Why Manhattan? Perls Retail is nearby here. Isn't that the only reason they're thinking of us?"

"The president of the regional offices is in New York," Vivian explains. "And he can't be bothered to come to little Liberty Falls. So if we want the contract, we need to go to him. I'll give you the notes I have, and you can do the rest of the research. If you're up for it, that is."

I take a deep breath. I'm not sure I'm up for anything that's happening in my life right now, but it doesn't really feel possible to turn back. And I doubt Vivian will ever have the same respect for me as her top employee if I turn this opportunity down.

"Sure," I say to her. "I'll do it."

Vivian gives me the thumbs-up. "The meeting's the Friday after the fair. If you want, stay for the weekend. Bring a hot date. The company will only pay for your plane ticket, but if you want to bring somebody, you can drive instead of fly. Doesn't matter to me as long as you're at that meeting at eleven a.m. sharp."

New York. Take two but without a cheating husband throwing off my game. Sounds like a plan.

————

Vivian lays a stack of folders on my desk after lunch with a, "this is just a fraction of what you'll need to know for your meeting in Manhattan."

I spend the afternoon poring over the documents, and by the time Mom picks me up outside the bank at six, I officially feel like I'm under water. Which turns out to be a perfect mood for tonight because Mom's surprise for tonight's Adult Education class is—water aerobics.

"I thought physical exercise might be better than another art class," Mom explains as I start to protest. "We'll pop by your house so you can grab your bathing suit."

"Mom, I don't even have a one-piece," I say. "I only have a bikini, and it's really skimpy. I'm not convinced it will stay on through a rigorous exercise class." I sigh as she ignores me and heads the truck in the direction of my house. "The other day, you said you signed us up for oil painting."

"Well, I did. But they called last night and said the class wasn't full, so it was going to be cancelled. The woman on the phone was very nice, and she said water aerobics still had room. I hear it's absolutely fabulous exercise," Mom says as we turn onto my street. "And so gentle on your joints. I'm hoping to get Bea into a regular class if tonight goes well for her. She's a little nervous about her suit as well," she explains as we pull into my driveway.

She turns off the truck and follows me up the front walk, despite me telling her I'll be right back. "But not for the same reasons you are. She's worried her suit looks too old-fashioned, but she needs the full coverage if you know what I mean."

I snap my head in her direction and give her a look, hoping to silence her.

But my mother has never been quick to quiet.

"She's always been hairy in the genital area," Mom explains as I block my ears. "What, Olivia—she has! It's been a source of great embarrassment for her. She hates to swim because of it."

"Mom, why doesn't she just shave then?" I head into my walk-in closet, turn on the light, and shut the door so I can change into my suit. "Or use a hair removal product, or go get a bikini wax or something?"

"She's thinking about it," Mom says. "Especially the home hair removal product. She won't do the wax because she's afraid of the pain. I told her I get my chin waxed, and it's not that bad, but I don't know how I'd feel about a bikini wax myself. Have you ever tried it?"

I've got my suit on now and I throw a tank top and jean shorts over it before stepping out of the closet.

"Yes, I've tried it," I say. "I don't particularly like it, though. I think Bea should stick with trying a product at home."

———

"I'm Angel." The instructor with bleached blond hair and a sunburned face appears in front of us as we all stand by the pool. Her bikini's more revealing than mine is, so I guess I needn't have worried. "Welcome to water aerobics. You're going to love it."

This time, other than Angel, I *am* the only person here under the age of fifty. Mom shushes me when I whisper that to her and tells me to count my blessings I'm still young and fit.

"Bless that body of yours, Olivia," Mom says as we step down into the pool together. "Don't be sorry you're here with us. Be happy your butt is so firm."

I playfully swat at Mom's arm with my hand. "Stop looking at my ass." I move further away from her and walk into the water up to my shoulders.

As soon as Angel begins the warm-ups, my cell phone starts to play U2.

Jenson.

I start moving past people and toward the stairs. Mom glares at me. "Is that your phone?" she says loudly.

"Be right back," I say as I apologize for nearly stepping on someone's foot. I reach the steps and dash up the stairs and across the tiled floor, being careful not to slip on the standing water.

The ringing has ceased by the time I get to my towel. As I pick up the phone to text him, he texts me.

Where r u?

I dry my hands on my towel and smile. *In Hell.*

Where's Hell?

Adult Ed. swimming pool with my mom & Bea. I'll be done in an hour.

I press send, turn off my phone, and hurry back to the pool.

————

Angel is in great shape. And it turns out water aerobics is quite the workout. By the time the hour is up, I'm more tired than after my walks with Mom. The thing about being submerged in water is that you don't know if you're sore or not until after you climb out. And I can tell I'm going to be sore.

Mom's exhausted, but Bea says she feels great and calls us both wimps.

"Love it," Bea gushes to me afterward in the locker room. "Could do it every day."

I smile at her. "Good for you, Bea. You've found your niche."

"Isn't that great?" Mom says as she pulls her shirt on over

her suit at a lightning-quick pace. "You don't mind if we skip the showering, do you girls?"

I shrug. "I can shower at home, sure." I pull my tank top over my bikini and reach for my shorts.

"Good," Mom says as she takes Bea's arm and urges her onward. "It's just so awkward in there," Mom whispers as we walk out of the locker room. "Some women parade around naked, talking to you all the while as if you're out to coffee together."

"But we're wet, Nora," Bea complains. "Wearing our suits underneath our dry clothes isn't very comfortable."

"I'm sorry, Bea," Mom says. "But your apartment's right next door. I'll walk you there myself."

We step out into the parking lot, and I swallow back a gasp.

Jenson's walking toward us.

His eyes catch mine, and I can read the promise in them from here. He glances at Mom and Bea and waves casually. He looks tanned, cool, and relaxed in shorts and a t-shirt.

"Whatever is Jenson doing here?" Mom says.

"He's here to see me, I think," I say, desperately trying to pull my soaking wet hair back into a ponytail.

"Oh, don't we all look a fright?" Mom says as she puts a hand to her own hair. "I guess we should have showered, after all."

Bea blanches. "I don't want to talk to any men right now. Let's send him away."

Too late for that.

Jenson grins at me as he reaches us. "Good time in the pool?" he says.

"Oh, Jenson, you turn right around now and take Olivia home," Mom says, turning him with her two hands and giving him a little shove. "Don't even look at us. Bea and I are a mess."

I hug Mom and Bea good-bye and start walking down the steps.

"Hi, Bea!" Jenson calls back over his shoulder as he follows me across the hot pavement.

"Nice to see you, dear," Bea says. "Olivia, remember to change before going out on the town. Your suit's making your ass look wet!"

"Jesus," I say under my breath as I keep walking.

Jenson laughs and leads me to his truck. "I'll get the door," he offers, opening the passenger side for me so I can climb in.

"I'm going to get your seat wet," I say to him.

"Doesn't worry me," he winks as he shuts the door behind me. "I find that sentence to be quite a turn-on, actually."

Once he's inside the driver's side, he turns to face me, his eyes bright. But I wave my hand at him.

"Step on it," I say. "If you don't, my mom's face may be peering into your window in a minute."

"Yes, ma'am." He pulls out of the parking spot and heads for the exit.

I smile. "Although her embarrassment would probably be enough to stop her. She and Bea didn't want to be seen after class."

"I was only looking at you, anyway," Jenson says as his gaze flicks over to me. "I couldn't take my eyes off you. Never could." He puts his hand on my bare thigh. "Still can't."

I feel water aerobics fading away. Bea and Mom drift out of my mind, and all I really want right now is this moment with Jenson.

"I'm envious you got to swim," he says as the light turns to green and he takes his foot off the brake. "It's hot as hell out tonight."

"You want to skinny dip? At the park?"

"How late is the gate open?" He's already yanking the wheel hard in the direction of the town lake.

———

Jenson parks in the dirt lot, and we walk together through the trees to the most remote area of the park. When we reach the water, Jenson pulls off his shirt and lets it fall to the ground. I've just taken off my t-shirt and shorts when I see him drop his shorts and boxers and dive into the water.

"Hey!" he says when I swim up next to him. "You said skinny dip!"

"I lied." I smile at him. "I wanted to see you skinny dip, but this bikini has to be good for something."

Jenson puts his arms around me, and I wrap my legs around his waist. "Will you come with me to Pittsburgh next weekend when I can close up everything?" he says, catching me completely off guard.

"Uh, no way." I wriggle out of his arms and swim away from him.

"Why not?" he says as he swims after me. "We'd get to leave Liberty Falls for a bit."

"And go to the place where you and Meghan lived together and had your twins." I stop to stand on the sandy bottom and look at him, hoping he'll see the pain in my eyes and drop it. "No thanks. I'll pass on that road trip down memory lane."

"Meghan and I never lived in this place together," Jenson says as he treads water. "She kept the house, remember? I've been in a townhouse ever since."

"I don't want to think about you two fucking on the streets of Pittsburgh." I avert my gaze.

"So don't think about it." Jenson stands up, too, and tips my chin up with his thumb, forcing me to make eye contact. "No fucking took place in public, believe me. What movie are you watching in your head?"

"The one that hurts," I say in a pinched tone. "The one that's always hurt."

Jenson puts his hands on my ass and pulls me in close to him. "That movie's over," he says. "The ending already happened. Didn't you see it? It wasn't happy. Ended in divorce."

"Oh, really?" I lean in closer to him. "How come?"

"Tragic," he says as he kisses my neck. "Turns out the guy's head over heels for somebody else. Some girl he's known his whole life. Seems like she stole his heart a long time ago. But circumstances kept them apart."

"What about his ex-wife?" I ask in a hoarse tone as Jenson reaches for the string on my bikini bottoms and unties it.

"She's otherwise involved," Jenson says as my bottoms slip off and hit the sandy bottom of the lake. "She's got a new boyfriend, and she's much happier. And the guy in this movie? He wants to show his kids how to follow your heart. Because if you cut that off, you really have nothing."

I put my mouth on his and close my eyes. When he pulls me closer, I take my hand and run it up and down his chest, causing him to let out a groan. Then I break out of his arms and duck into the water to retrieve my bikini bottoms. I glance around the lake and don't see a soul, so I carry the suit in my hand and walk half-naked to shore.

I wrap my towel around my waist and hide behind one of the large chestnut trees as I pull on my jean shorts. When Jenson meets me there, he's still naked. He's also soaking wet, and his hair's slicked back in that way I've always loved. I crave to touch him, to inhale him, but I don't. I stay where I am, a few feet away from him, and we eye each other cautiously.

"Glad you swam?" I ask him.

"Yeah." He stands across from me. "What's up?"

"Nothing." I dig my big toe into the dirt. "Why do you

ask?"

"Because you ran away just now. Do you think I'm going to hurt you?" He reaches for his towel on the ground and wraps it around his waist.

"No." I cross my arms over my bikini top and look past him at the cloud line. The moon's up, but it's not fully dark yet. You can still see the sun coming off the sky.

"What?" He frowns in confusion. "What's going on, Olive?"

I don't know why I'm pushing him away. Maybe because he asked me to go with him to Pittsburgh. I don't know. Part of me thinks I need to go there, to let go of all the ghosts I had in my head for years, and part of me is terrified.

"I have a big account Vivian put me in charge of at work, and it requires me to go to Manhattan the Friday after the fair," I say slowly. "Maybe we could do that and Pittsburgh in one trip."

"That works perfectly. Meghan takes the boys that weekend. We'll leave Friday night and be back by Sunday."

I take a breath and finally stop analyzing every single thing that's going on between us. As I stare into his green eyes that are so alive and lasered in on me, I relax.

The man I fell for is right here across from me. I'm pushing him away, and he's still here. That feels like a moment. That feels like something important.

Jenson comes closer to me and puts his lips to mine as the light fully disappears from the sky. He backs me up against the tree, his kiss growing harder. As our tongues find each other's, Jenson unbuttons my shorts. He puts his hand inside them, finding me slick and ready for him. Two fingers slide inside me and I moan. My head falls back against the bark and I writhe against Jenson's hand. He groans and kneels down in front of me.

"Let me worship you, Olivia." His voice comes out rough.

My shorts fall to my ankles, and Jenson's breath tickles my skin as his lips touch me between my legs for the first time. I squirm at the sensation, desperate to be as close to him as possible.

"Olive." His voice comes out uneven, barely audible. "You're gorgeous."

I rock into his touch, and he kisses me harder, using his mouth to give me what I need, what I've always needed from him but could never ask for. My hands go above my head, and I angle my hips closer to him, my body language begging him to keep going.

He licks and nibbles and sucks at my hot center, driving me into a frenzy of bucking hips and breathy moans.

"Oh, God." I claw at the bark over my head while Jenson absolutely rocks my world down below. "J. Oh, God."

My climax crashes over me like I'm sky diving through space, and I don't ever want to land. *So good.* Jenson holds me against his mouth, not letting up even as I come.

Eventually, I feel him shift. I open my eyes, and I'm staring directly into Jenson's green ones reflected in the moonlight. The depth of his emotions for me shines in his gaze. Out here by the lake, stripped raw of any covers, our feelings for each other are impossible to deny.

"Olive." His voice is barely a whisper.

I put my hand on his cheek. "I'm here. You're pretty good at that."

"You're pretty amazing." He wraps an arm around my waist and pulls me close. "I know you're scared. I know our pasts are painful and hard to let go of. And I know we're risking a lot, Olive, but I don't want to sit around for the rest of my life, thinking of you as the one that got away."

I swallow down the emotion clogging my throat. "I don't like to think of us that way. You've always been my best friend."

"Your best friend you've hardly been able to be around since you were seventeen because it hurts too much." He takes my face in his hands. "Remember my wedding?"

"I remember the first half of it," I say truthfully. "Then I kind of skipped out."

"So do you remember me walking down the aisle at the end?"

"No. Like I told you, I wasn't there."

"Exactly," he says. "Why not?"

I shift my gaze to the dropping sun. "I left and went out with some guy from school," I say, telling him the truth for the first time. "I tried to hook up with someone else to drown out the pain."

Jenson takes my hand in his and turns so he's looking out at the last remnants of the sun with me. "Did you get what you wanted?"

"Not any more than you did," I say. "I know you married Meghan out of obligation and guilt. You thought it was your fault she got pregnant even though you used protection. Things happen, Jenson. It's called life. Don't blame yourself for everything."

"I'm working on that," he says quietly. "Just like I want you to forgive yourself too."

"I'm trying."

"I have a lot of regrets, you know?"

"We were both young and scared. Maybe we still are." The warmth of his hand hits the small of my back. "I'm always scared. It's kind of a personality trait. I act fearless and independent, like I run the bank. Really, I'm just scared of losing the bank. Or breaking it, whichever way you want to put it."

Jenson laughs. "You'll never break the bank, Olive."

I lean my head on his shoulder, and we watch the sun disappear from the sky.

CHAPTER ELEVEN

The day of the fair comes quickly, and before I know it, I'm hustling along the sidewalk to make sure I get to the town square in time. Every year for the past five, Hayley and I have met at the liberty bell in the town square the day of the fair. She'll cheer loudly as my dad rings the bell, and then we'll take off and have fun, doing our best to ignore the cameramen who always try their best to get a few shots of "Mayor Graham's family."

But this morning, Hayley texted that she's running late, and Jenson mentioned offhandedly that Meghan's dropping off the kids today, so she may stop by the fair.

I like Meghan; she's a nice person and a great mom to Kyle and Connor. But she's always made me feel awkward, maybe because she's gorgeous and always perfectly put-together. I chide myself for feeling insecure as I make my way to the square.

I had wanted to wear an outfit that would activate my self-confidence, and I ended up pairing a fitted purple tank top and cut-off jean shorts with three-inch high wedge sandals, the sexiest and most uncomfortable shoes I own. I left my hair down the way I know Jenson likes, fixed myself up with a bit of lipstick and eye makeup, and I was ready to go.

As I walk through town, I take in the aromas of fried dough and hamburgers from a block away. I weave around the bouncy moonwalk and the portable bungee jump machine and head for the massive, bronze bell next to the gazebo.

My gaze lands on Jenson immediately. He's on a picnic blanket underneath a nearby tree, and Kyle and Connor are playing with some toys while Cindy and Dee sit with them. Meghan must have already come and gone as Jenson's in the middle of trying to break up a fight between his sons over a toy, and he doesn't see me yet. I smile and head toward him.

But then Matilda calls my name. She's with Auntie Sue, so I go over to them first and give Auntie Sue a kiss. I get choked up for a moment when she tries to smile, but her mouth freezes partway. I hate seeing her suffer.

"I'm going to tell you a secret later," I whisper in her ear. "I would tell you now, but your daughter's staring at me."

I glance up and smile casually at Matilda, who leans in like she wants to hear every word I'm saying to her mother.

I fall into Mom's habit of rambling about the beautiful day we're having until my father steps into our circle.

"Hi, sweetheart." Dad pulls me aside. "Listen, Olivia, I'm sorry about the other night..."

I put up a hand to stop him. "Dad, I know it was an accident."

He lowers his voice. "Your mother and I want to help. She has a surprise for you today..."

"What?!" I say in horror. "You don't mean..."

"Olivia!" Mom calls out from somewhere behind me.

I whip around and come face to face with my mother. She's wearing a bright orange sundress, and she gives me a huge smile. I freeze. Only one thing could possibly make my mother that happy, and it's got to be...

Mom takes my arm and turns me to face a man about my age.

"This is Will, Olivia. Will, meet my beautiful daughter."

Yep. It's got to be a man. Because only a man my mother is hoping will partner with me to give her more grandchildren could put that joyous look on her face.

Will gives me a crooked grin as we shake hands.

So this is the guy who's supposed to take my breath away. He's cute in an arrogant sort of way, and he kisses my cheek like we've met before, which immediately turns me off. As I make small talk with him, I glance in Jenson's direction. His eyes are on me, his expression unreadable. But I feel like I can see the smoke coming out of his ears from here.

"So you work at a bank?" Will says. "Union?"

I force my gaze back to him. "Yes, I have since college. I hear you just came from Manhattan."

"I did," he says. "Love the Big Apple. Hate this town. Too small."

I want to say that what I hate are shortened sentences that don't begin with a subject, but I keep smiling instead. "Why are you back then?"

"The offer coming out of Philly was just too sweet to pass up." Will throws his arms out wide. "The perks, the signing bonus, all of it. They wanted me bad." He winks at me then like that last sentence means something.

"That's exciting." I glance over at Jenson again. He's still watching me, but Kyle tugs on his arm and says something to him, and he gets distracted momentarily, just long enough for me to excuse myself from Will and head over to the man I actually want to talk to.

"Hi, J," I say as I reach the blanket.

Jenson looks up in surprise, and Kyle and Connor grab my

hand and ask me to sit with them. I take a seat on the blanket and say hello to Cindy and Dee. They greet me warmly, and Cindy asks me who the handsome man is I was just talking to. Before I have to answer her, Kyle spills Jenson's bottled water all over the blanket. I grab some paper towels to clean up the mess.

Cindy tells Dee he was supposed to watch Kyle better, and Dee tells her not to blame him for everything. Jenson intercedes and says it was his water, so neither of them should be blaming each other. But Dee keeps complaining about Cindy and her "attitude." I raise my eyebrows at Jenson, who shakes his head as he takes the paper towels out of my hand.

"Thanks for grabbing these," he says in my ear. "You're a lifesaver."

I pat his arm. "I'll help you clean up the spill."

"It's okay. I got it." He lowers his voice. "Super fun family picnic, huh? And who the hell is that guy hitting on you?"

"No one important," I murmur. "Just another of my mother's delusional ploys."

"I think my mom's got one of those ploys lined up too."

"Seriously?" I say.

"I'll explain later," he assures me.

"Dee, why can't you let it go?" Cindy says in a loud voice. "Goodness, I didn't mean to start anything. I just thought you could have been watching him better!"

Dee storms off to the drink table. Cindy exhales loudly as she mutters that apparently not everybody is in a sunny, picnicky mood today.

At that moment, Dad rings the liberty bell.

"Welcome to the Liberty Falls fair, everyone!" he calls out into the microphone. "As you all know, today is the birthday of our town, and we like to celebrate in style every year with our annual fair. The dog show is about to start!"

"Livia, are you coming on the carousel?" Connor asks me. "Daddy promised he'd take us now."

"Sure," I say, taking his hand. "Let's go."

After riding around on the carousel three times, Jenson convinces the boys he needs to stop spinning in a circle for a while.

I laugh. "Why don't we go see how Sheldon's doing with the dog show?"

The fair's crowded as usual, and it takes us a few minutes to weave our way through the throngs of people and variety of tents scattered across the lawn.

"This is my year, Olive," Sheldon says when we reach him at the dog park. "I can feel it." He rubs his hands together while Cara tries to corral Corkscrew, their hyper dachshund who's dressed up in a tuxedo-type coat.

I wave to Hayley as she heads toward us through the craziness of barking dogs, sniffing each other and romping through the man-made pond built just for them. This is the one park in town Mom and I avoid on our weekly walks— Mom says if you're not stepping in dog poop, you're trying to avoid a wet, furry animal running toward you at top speed. The leash law in Liberty Falls is not enforced here.

"So what prize are you aiming for?" Jenson asks.

"Whatever I can get," Sheldon says as he takes Corkscrew's leash from Cara. "They give out so many freaking awards. I'll take anything."

"I see you've gotten desperate enough to even try for best dressed, Sheldon," Hayley says as she reaches us.

I smile. "Cara, was the little outfit Sheldon's idea?"

"Of course it was," Cara says. "I don't give a crap about these contests, but Sheldon had me practicing bocce ball with him for weeks, along with searching for a tuxedo for Corkscrew. He's promised he won't enter any contest next year if he wins something today."

"I've got my fingers crossed for you then, Cara," Hayley says. She raises her eyebrows at me. "And you're looking hot today, Ms. Graham."

I cross my arms over my low-cut top, but not fast enough. Sheldon notices. "No, that's a good idea, Olive," he says. "The fair could be a great place to meet a nice guy. It's safe, unlike a bar, and it's family-friendly. Maybe you should hang out with me here at the dog park. I'll even let you hold Corkscrew's leash—some couples have been formed through their common love of dogs."

Jenson's hot hand on my back is the only sign of his reaction.

"Do you ever let up?" I say to Sheldon. "Mom is bad enough."

"I'm just saying," he says, "I know the single life is fun, but we can't do it forever, you know."

"What's that supposed to mean?" Cara snaps as she hits him in the arm. "I thought you wanted to get married!"

"I do!" Sheldon leans away from her. "I'm just saying there's a positive to being unattached, and maybe after her dumb-ass marriage, Olivia's enjoying the single life a bit too much. You know, nobody to answer to, no one to have to placate when they're pissed at you for this or that..."

Cara starts to yell at him, but Hayley quickly interrupts. "Look, the show is starting."

Jenson's breath brushes against my ear as he leans close to me and murmurs, "Your brother's driving me nuts. I'm this close to kissing you right now."

I step away from his close proximity and turn to face him. Fixing a smile on my face, I whisper, "Later. Don't let his baiting bother you."

For the next hour, my world is filled with dogs, barking, and slobbering. Kyle and Connor get bored, and Jenson leaves to get them ice cream.

"I thought Corkscrew did very well," I tell Sheldon as we wait for the results.

"Thanks, Olive." Sheldon clenches his jaw. He doesn't look sure of himself, a rarity, and my heart goes out to him.

"He really did do a good job," Hayley pipes in. "I mean come on. They've got to give him something."

The head judge walks to the center of the park and calls for attention over the microphone. Even the dogs go quiet as all of Liberty Falls Fair waits breathlessly for the panel's decision.

"The award to the winner of Best Dressed goes to..." The judge pauses. "Blossom the Chihuahua!"

I can practically see Sheldon deflate.

"It's okay." Cara pats his arm. "That's just one of the awards."

But by the time it's down to Best in Show and Best Bark, Sheldon's lost most of his confidence. "There's no way," he says. "I know he won't win Best in Show, and his bark even annoys me."

"But it's a distinct bark," Hayley says.

The judge calls for attention just as my cell phone rings. I answer it, but before I hear who's on the other end, the judge announces, "The winner of Best Bark is Corkscrew the Dachshund!"

We start screaming and shouting like lunatics, and Corkscrew barks and barks and runs as fast as his little legs will take him while Sheldon, leash still in hand, chases him toward the judge to accept his ribbon and get their picture taken for the Liberty Falls Gazette. Cara claps and stays where she is, saying this is Sheldon's moment.

"You just don't want your picture in the paper, do you?" Hayley says to her.

"Not even a little bit," Cara says as Sheldon holds up the ribbon in our direction, and we all clap and wave at him.

Shit. I forgot about my phone. "Hello?" I say, finally bringing it up to my ear.

"What the heck is going on?" Jenson says. "Did Sheldon win?"

"Corkscrew just got Best Bark. I got distracted with all the celebrating."

I start walking away from Hayley, who's watching me with a smile.

"Olive." Jenson's voice in my ear is somber, and I immediately tense.

"What's wrong?"

"I think I found my father."

"Oh God, J."

I start walking quickly, looking for somewhere I can be alone.

I always imagined Jenson might say those six words to me one day. But not like this. Not where I'm barely in the middle of a bunch of barking dogs and he's not here with me so I can read his expression and look into his eyes and be there for him...

"How did you find him?"

"I hired a P.I. last month. Kind of a last-ditch effort to track him down. Anyway, he just called me. Can we meet?"

"Of course. Where are you?"

"My mom's with the kids. I'm right outside the dog park."

I look around.

"Not there," he says. "Keep going, further to the left."

"Can you see me?" I say as I walk toward the gate entrance.

"Yep. You look gorgeous. Take about five more steps toward the fence. Now look right."

I turn, and then I see him. On his cell phone watching me just like I'm on my cell phone watching him.

I hang up and head over to him. When I'm close, he starts

walking, and I follow him. Past the gazebo and the large Welcome to Liberty Falls est. 1795 sign and behind the skateboarding park to a long line of thick trees standing between the park and the endless line of pastures. Nobody's skateboarding today because they're all at the fair. Jenson ducks behind the trees and pulls me in with him where he puts his mouth over mine immediately.

I melt into him and wrap my arms around his neck. His hands move to my ass as he kisses me more urgently.

Then, just as quickly as he'd started, he pulls back.

We stare at each other in silence.

I don't know why I'm shaking while Jenson flips through his phone. It's not my father we're about to identify. But it's such a huge missing piece of Jenson's life.

"Don't you be nervous." He smiles at me as we sit down on the ground and lean our backs against the enormous tree trunk. "I need you to be my rock right now."

I nod and search his face as we sit across from one another. The green of his eyes is bright, the way it is when he's curious and hopeful.

"Well, show me." I gesture to his phone. "Or tell me or something."

"The P.I. sent me this link. He's sure it's the right guy." Jenson sets the phone on his lap and points to a website of a real estate company called The Waverly Group.

I look up at him. "That's your father's company?"

He nods and clicks on the About Us page. Donald Waverly, President.

"There's only one other employee," Jenson says. "An assistant."

"Where is the company located?" I say, afraid he'll say California or Texas or somewhere else far away from here.

"Philadelphia," he says.

My mouth drops open.

"Philadelphia?" I say incredulously. "But we looked and looked for him!"

"We did. But that was a long time ago. This website was first put up two years ago. I don't think he had his own company before, so he must have been listed under somebody else's agency, and his name wasn't public."

I take another look at Donald Waverly.

He's distinguished-looking with gray hair and a dark suit. He has the same green eyes as Jenson, and when I keep looking at his face, I realize he's also got the same square, chiseled jaw. My eyes fill with tears.

"He looks like you," I say as I turn to Jenson.

Jenson closes the site and turns off his phone abruptly.

I touch his hand. "Are you going to contact him?"

"I don't know."

"It sounds like you came back to Liberty Falls to pursue what's in your heart," I say. "And I'm only part of the equation."

There's silence for a moment, and I don't think he's going to answer me. But then he says, "I've felt really lost, Olive. I love Dee as a father. I do. But the way my mom kept it all so underground, because of how things happened...it's like I've had this..."

"I get it. It's a hole you need to fill."

I reach over and put my arms around him.

His mouth tips up in a sexy grin. "I didn't get a chance to tell you earlier—you look super sexy today."

"Thanks," I say. "I dressed up for you."

He runs his fingers through my hair. "I want you. I've wanted to do this all damn day." His mouth covers mine again, and this time, we don't stop.

Jenson controls the angle of the kiss with his hand that's tangled in my hair.

"Harder," he mutters into my mouth. "Don't hold back, Olive. Give it to me."

Our tongues are wild as we kiss each other with abandon. It's urgent and out of control. Jenson's free hand goes to my waist where he slips his hand underneath my shirt and scrapes his rough palm over my burning-hot skin.

"Something's different," he murmurs. "We're different this time."

He's right. We've always been like this, passionate and electric together. But I feel something different too every time we touch, something more. I have since he's been back.

"Maybe because we're not holding back anymore," I say as he pulls me onto his lap. "Because we're both adults this time."

He sucks on my neck and moves his lips lower.

"I hated seeing that jerk flirt with you," he says as he trails kisses down my collarbone.

"It doesn't mean anything, and I didn't flirt back," I say on a moan.

"I know. But it doesn't mean I like it. And my mom—she tried to set me up with an old high school classmate before you got to the fair."

He moves his hand up my bare stomach and grazes the curve of my breast.

"Oh, God. J..." I barely remember what he was saying. Oh right, something about family wanting to set him up. Well, that's the story of my summer.

Jenson's fingers slip underneath my bra cup, and he tugs lightly at my nipple. I moan into his shoulder, trying to keep my voice down.

Our behavior is getting riskier. Even though we're hidden behind a stand of trees, we're in broad daylight. But the danger just makes it more exciting, more of a turn-on.

Movement behind a nearby tree catches my eye. But when I look more closely, I don't see anything.

Hmmm. Weird.

Before I can say anything to Jenson—

"Noooooo!"

We break apart and stand up. Jenson hurries to make sure my shirt is smoothed down, and then we run toward the sound of the high-pitched, agonized scream. When we emerge from the cover of the forest and I see what's going on, my heart comes up into my throat.

Auntie Sue is slowly rolling in her wheelchair down the grassy hill in the town square. Matilda's chasing after her, but before she can catch her, the wheelchair tips over and crashes on top of Auntie Sue. And then...silence.

"Oh, no." I bring my hand to my mouth.

"I'll call 911," Jenson says immediately.

CHAPTER TWELVE

When Jenson and I reach Auntie Sue, she's unconscious. My heart breaks for her, but for the first time in years, she looks at peace. It almost feels like a perverse sort of permission to take the leap into the unknown, to let go of the family ties that bind. Jenson locks eyes with me, and I nod at him even though he never asked me anything out loud.

———

Three hours later, we all stand around Auntie Sue's hospital bed and watch her sleep. As much as it seemed like God was trying to give her a leg up into the beyond, Auntie Sue is alive and sleeping like a baby with, miraculously, no broken bones and no head trauma. I'm more relieved than I want to admit, and I vow to spend more time visiting her this summer.

However, now isn't the time. Because while I love her, watching anyone sleep like this is its own little form of torture.

Unless we were excused, we're all here, and the hospital

room is hot and crowded. Kyle and Connor are too little to be expected to be here. And Cindy offered—more like absolutely *insisted*—to be the one to take Kyle and Connor home with her. Jenson tried to say he'd do it, but Cindy used the grandmother card, and now he's stuck here with the rest of us at the hospital.

My cousin Stacey whispers from my side. "Even if she had died, if she came back to life right now, she'd still be the same."

I shush her, but she won't stop.

"You know what I mean, Olive? People mourn the dead, but it's almost like they forget what they knew. Auntie Sue is awesome, but she was also bossy before she became incapable —remember that? She used to boss all of us around, and her sisters and kids, too. We loved her sassiness, but we used to get so mad at her too." Stacey shakes her head. "People don't want to admit the truth. I mean what's so freaking wrong with the damn truth?"

My gaze automatically shifts to Jenson standing across the bed from me as my mother keeps her arm around Cybil sitting at the foot of the bed. Cybil leans her head on Mom's shoulder.

"Such a beautiful paint job," Mom comments as she stares awkwardly at the wall behind Auntie Sue's head.

"Isn't it?" Cybil agrees. "Very tasteful."

Awkward silence follows until Cybil finally says what we're all thinking.

"My sister just won't let go," she says.

"It's like an iron grip," Matilda murmurs in a quiet voice.

"She'd feel so much better if she'd just give in and let God take her," Mom agrees. "Give in, Auntie Sue." My mother practically moans the words. "Let go."

Let go. Give in. Take me.

Oh, my God. I'm taking a conversation about death and turning it into sex in my head. I really have lost it. But I don't want to miss out on living when I'm so blessed to be young, healthy, and alive. Auntie Sue wouldn't want me to suffer like this. She wouldn't want me to hold back on love.

My eyes find Jenson's.

I want him so much that it aches. I tell Mom I have a message from work that can't wait, and I kiss Auntie Sue goodbye.

I'm walking through the parking lot when I hear him call to me.

I spin around with a smile. "You got out?"

"Of course." He steps closer until he's near enough to touch. "I've got some time before my coaches meeting."

Thank God. The ache between my legs is so intense I can barely stand it.

"Are you ready?" he asks me as he nods at his truck a few feet away.

Yes.

As soon as we get into the truck, I look at him. "Remember how I said I want everything with you?"

His eyes lock with mine. "Yeah?"

"I want it now," I say. "If you do. I don't want to wait anymore. I don't care about going slow and taking our time. What just happened with Auntie Sue—it made me realize even more how precious life is. It goes by so fast, you know? I don't want to waste any more time. She was always so good to me, and I feel like even now—she wants me to be happy."

Jenson grips the steering wheel tightly. "Olive. I don't want to wait either."

"So let's go to my house."

Jenson gives a quick nod and turns on the truck. He weaves his way through the parking lot and onto the street.

We don't speak during the fifteen-minute drive, but as we veer into my driveway, Jenson murmurs, "Thank God. I didn't think I'd make it here without pulling over and taking you in the backseat."

I think I say something in response, but I have no idea what. It's incoherent, much like my brain right now. All I know is how desperately I want him.

We barely make it inside and shut the door before he puts his mouth over mine.

"I've always wanted to know what it feels like to be inside you, Olivia," he says into my mouth. "I want to make love to you so much it hurts."

"I don't know why, but I've been nervous," I say as I slide my hands underneath his shirt.

He pulls off my top and unhooks my bra in record time. "Maybe because of how long we've wanted each other. What if I don't live up to your fantasy?"

His thumbs run over my hard nipples and I moan.

"What if I don't live up to yours?" I say.

"I went to Sequoia National Park once," he says in a rough tone as he reaches for the zipper on my cut-offs. "I was scared the trees wouldn't be as amazing in real life as they'd always looked in pictures. You know, awe-inspiring."

"And?"

"Awe-inspiring," he says.

————

Well, like Auntie Sue's day at the fair, not everything always turns out like it seems it will. Jenson and I will have to wait to find out if our lovemaking compares to the sequoia trees. As soon as he picks me up and carries me to bed, my house phone starts to ring. And ring. And ring.

Concerned something's wrong, I grab my phone off my nightstand, and we listen to the voicemail on speakerphone.

"Olivia, I assume you're on your way home now," Mom begins. "I'm driving myself. Oh, wasn't that so hard with Auntie Sue today? The poor thing..."

Jenson is still kissing my neck, but with a lot less enthusiasm. He finally stops altogether as Mom continues talking like she's right here in the house with us. "And I saw you talking with Will. He seems like a nice guy, doesn't he? So together and successful, too. Oh, but poor Auntie Sue—I just can't stop thinking about her..."

"Or talking about her, apparently," Jenson says.

I laugh as I reach over and run my fingers through his hair.

The voicemail finally cuts my mother off, and Jenson reaches for me again. He pulls me on top of him, and I catch my breath when I feel his hard length hitting me exactly where I need him most. Just as we start kissing, the doorbell rings.

"You've got to be freaking kidding me," Jenson says as I jump. "Who is that?"

I shrug. "Not a clue." I step out of bed and walk down the hallway so I can peek out the door peephole. *Crap.* It's a delivery. Must be that package of Todd's that Daphne had asked me to accept for them while they were away with his parents this weekend. I run back to the bedroom and throw on a t-shirt and shorts, then return to the door and open it. If this isn't proper foreplay, I don't know what is.

"Hi there." The delivery guy looks at me and gives me a creepy grin.

I give him a quick smile and sign the clipboard he holds out for me.

"Thanks," I say as I grab the package and shut the door.

I walk back into the bedroom, taking off my clothes as I walk. By the time I reach Jenson, I'm naked again.

"Delivery on behalf of Daphne," I say. "Let's not waste any more time—we may get interrupted again."

I reach down and carefully release Jenson from his boxers.

When his huge erection pops out, I immediately wrap my hand around it.

"Christ," he mutters. "Feels so good, Olive."

He guides me onto my back, and his hand slips in between us to the part of me that needs him so badly right now I'm shaking.

"Shit." Jenson's voice is raw. "You're so wet."

I reach for the condoms inside my bedside table and hand him one. "I need you inside me."

He's just rolled the condom on when his cell phone rings. He reaches over and hits ignore, but it rings again immediately.

"Just see who it is," I say.

He glances at the phone. "It's an 800 number. It's nothing."

He turns off his phone, and finally there's silence. It's just Jenson and me like I've fantasized about for so many years. He braces himself over me, and I wrap my arms around his back and look into his eyes.

But when he goes to push inside me, to take that final, irreversible step, something stops us. Me. My muscles tense and Jenson can't...get in, so to speak. I take a few deep breaths and tell him to try again.

Nothing.

Despite how intimate we've gotten this past week, intercourse seals the deal, and that seems to be the one thing I'm not able to do. We try everything, from different positions to taking a break to powering through. Nothing works. I'm just not having it today.

Mom's phone call certainly didn't help. But the truth is, I'm scared. The memory of my heart breaking when Jenson and I ended things all those years ago still haunts me. It's illogical, but the heart doesn't care about logic.

"It's okay." Jenson touches my cheek with his hand. "It's all right." He rolls off of me onto his back, puts his arms around me, and rests my head on his bare chest.

"Oh, Lord." I'm so embarrassed I don't think it's possible to feel more uncomfortable than I feel right now.

"So we practice," he says. "All good things take practice, right?"

I trace invisible circles over his chest with my finger. "I bet you and Meghan didn't need to practice."

"Hey." He takes my chin in his hand, forcing me to make eye contact with him. His are warm and tender. "I bet Meghan and I didn't have the history that you and I have. Nobody makes me feel the way you do, Olivia. Don't let this mess with your head."

I glance at the clock. "You have to go soon. You've got your coaches meeting." I hesitate, not sure I should say something, but I don't want him to think I've forgotten. "How are you doing? You know, about Donald?"

Jenson pats my leg. "Thanks for asking, but I'd rather not talk about it. I'm not sure what I'm going to do if anything. I just need some time on it."

"Okay." I put my hand on his. "I won't mention it until you do then. But I'm always here."

I walk with him to my front door.

"This is just the beginning for us," he says as he kisses me good-bye. "You and me—we're only getting started with how good this can be."

"Do you think in some parallel world we're married with two point five kids and a white picket fence?"

"It's what's kept me going," Jenson says, his hands in my

hair while he nibbles my lips. "The dream of getting to that universe someday."

I wave goodbye as he walks backwards out my front door. Once he disappears into his truck and turns out of my driveway, I reach for my phone to call Hayley.

I need a drink.

CHAPTER THIRTEEN

"How's your aunt doing?" Hayley asks me.

After I fill her in, I ask her about her editing project.

"My deadline's not until next week. You want to get drunk?"

After what happened with Jenson today, I can hardly wait.

"I'll meet you in ten minutes."

———

The Tap & Pitcher, the tiny bar on Main Street, is packed with people like us who left the fair early.

Hayley nods as the bartender delivers our drinks. "We have no cars parked out front, thanks to the taxi, so there's literally no incriminating evidence if we come staggering out at two a.m."

I laugh as we click shot glasses, and I swallow my whiskey and feel that comforting burn in my throat.

"So what's up?" Hayley asks me. "You look upset. You're dressed in your upset outfit."

I look down at the faded blue jeans and black top with the half-open back I only ever wear when I'm down.

"Things are going so well," I say to her. "But you know me —I'm a born pessimist."

"What worries you? That he'll leave again?"

I shrug. "Last time, he left for college, which was nothing unexpected. But then, he left forever to my teenage brain. I was just so young; it hit me harder than it probably would have as an adult. I didn't get over it easily. And it's like this reflex within me—I equate things going well between Jenson and me as the prelude to the end."

"I understand." Hayley pats my arm. "But you're grownups now. And he doesn't look like he's going anywhere. It will work out, Olive."

"We're too flawed people, Hayl."

"Everybody comes with something," Hayley says.

"It's not because he has kids," I say. "I love them. A lot. We just have this whole long screwed-up history together. Two divorces between us already, and we're not even thirty."

"Maybe you need to stop seeing Jenson as eighteen and see him for the man he is now," Hayley suggests. "You've known him at every age, but you're both grown up now. Maybe you wouldn't have been happy together before this and before all you both went through to get here."

I feel tears prick my eyes.

"I say this harshly only because I love you: stop avoiding your heart, Olivia. Tell Jenson how you feel, and don't hold back. Do you really want to give up what could be with him just because you both come with a past?"

Before I can answer her...

"Olivia," comes a flirty voice from behind me.

Hayley raises her eyebrows, and I whip around to see Will smirking at me.

"Will here, from the cook-out," he says to break the silence. "Remember me?"

I really wish I hadn't turned around. "Hi. Yes, of course."

"Right," he says confidently. "So, too bad about your relative there. Rolling down the hill and all."

"Yes. Rolling down the hill *was* too bad." My God, this guy is an idiot.

"How about we have a drink together?"

"No, thanks," I say immediately. "I'm here with my friend..." I turn and quickly introduce Hayley to Will. "If you'll excuse us."

"Your mom assured me you'd at least meet me for a drink," he says.

Oh, crap.

As if on cue, my cell phone buzzes with a text.

Olivia, please don't forget about poor Will in the middle of all this. Give him a chance, honey.

No one can lay on the guilt like a mother to her daughter.

I make eye contact with Hayley, who shrugs.

"I really am not good company tonight, Will."

He shifts closer to me. "That's okay. I'll hang out with you two anyway."

"Really, we're having a private chat," I say, but he's already turned to the bar to order us all drinks.

"Is this the guy you said your mom wanted you to go out with?" Hayley whispers in my ear. "She sure knows how to pick 'em, huh?"

I glance at Will's collared shirt with the sleeves rolled up. His dark hair's slicked back with gel, and he's wearing an expensive watch on his wrist. He may be handsome, but even if I were looking to meet someone, he'd be last on my list. He's clearly already buzzed with his glassy eyes and the way he's talking extra-loud.

"We don't need alcohol," I say, tapping him on the shoulder. "Just water would be fine."

"It's on the house," he says as he hands me some fruity-looking mixed drink. "Try it. Women love this shit."

I take it out of his hand and stare down at the red-colored beverage I'm holding. Looks like exactly what I would never order. Sweet and fruity. If I'm going to drink hard liquor, I'll take a whiskey over this any day.

Will downs another shot. He's starting to slur. Before I can protest, he grabs me around the waist and pulls me onto the dance floor.

I twist away, but Will keeps getting closer. His breath stinks of beer, and vodka, and then...he throws up on me.

"Oh, God." He tries to turn away, but it's far too late. "Shit!"

I think I'm going to puke now. I run to the restroom, where I clean off as best I can with paper towels and water from the sink.

When I open the restroom door, Will's leaning against the wall in the hallway. "Sorry about that."

"Let me call you a cab," I say to him as I reach for my phone.

Hayley's waiting for me when I make it back to the bar.

"What a nightmare. Are you okay?"

I roll my eyes. "I stink of puke. I just want to go home."

"No way." She points at my phone. "Call Jenson and invite him to join us. I want to get to know him better."

"Seriously, can we do this getting to know him better business when I don't have some other guy's vomit on me?"

"Ask him to bring a clean shirt you can borrow. You guys need a witness," she insists as I try to protest. "Like a pair of binoculars."

"Oh, God, you're getting buzzed." I laugh. "That just made no sense."

"No, it did." Hayley grabs my arm and leads me to an empty booth away from the crowd. "You and Jenson have always felt alone like nobody else has ever felt this same way. First of all, that's not true. There are forbidden affairs going on all over the place. Second of all, I think I can help. Let me try?"

I am really tired of carrying this secret all by myself. So I look down at the phone in my hand. He'll be done with practice and probably putting Kyle and Connor to bed. I start typing.

———

An hour later, Jenson slides into the booth next to me, takes my hand into his lap, and squeezes it. His green eyes lock onto my blue ones and hold me still. I'm mesmerized by his need for me, his unflinching, unwavering interest in me.

Whenever I would walk into a room, Jenson Beau would focus on me like I was the only person who existed. Nothing's changed except that maybe I have. Maybe it was my divorce. Or maybe it was the humiliation of the way that my marriage ended. But my guard is down, and that wall I used to have to raise between Jenson and me—it's quickly disappearing.

He hands me a t-shirt of his. "What happened that you need to change? I love your outfit."

I show him the vomit stains. "It's a long story. Be right back."

When I return from the bathroom a few minutes later, Hayley's deep into her interrogation.

"And your sons are so freaking cute," she says as I slide in next to him in the booth. "Oh! You never ordered a drink."

"I'll have a little of Olive's," he says as he takes a sip of my beer. "I think two drunk people at this table is enough."

"Where in Pittsburgh did you live?" she asks. "Are you

planning to buy a house in Liberty Falls eventually or just rent?"

After ten more minutes of Hayley grilling Jenson with question after question, all of which he responds to with clear amusement, I jump in.

"Max and Hayley are getting married soon," I say to him. "But Hayley doesn't like much about marriage."

"I like Max," Hayley says. "But I'm against a lot of marriage's traditions, and how it's legally binding."

"And that scares you," Jenson says calmly.

I look at Hayley in surprise. For some reason, I hadn't thought of that before. She turns red and picks up her beer instead of answering him.

"It *does* scare you," I say to her. "Doesn't it?"

Jenson runs his hand along my thigh underneath the table, and every part of me lights up.

"So what's your story?" Hayley says as she tries to turn the tables on Jenson. "What are you scared of with Olivia? Or is it just guilt?"

Jenson raises an eyebrow. "You're fairly blunt, aren't you?"

"And you're not?" she counters him.

I feel like I should intervene, but I want to hear Jenson's answer too much. So I sit quietly, drink my beer, and listen to them go at it, wondering who's going to break first.

"I'm not scared," he says firmly with a glance at me.

"But you feel guilty?" I say. "Because of our families?"

"Don't you?" His eyes dare me to be honest. "Your dad's a public figure. My mom works for him, and the whole thing will create a firestorm of gossip."

I swallow. "I'm aware of the repercussions. Obviously."

"What you two need to realize is that your feelings of guilt aren't helping anyone," Hayley says. "Not your family or yourselves. So you have to find a way to let all that go. It's just negativity you don't need."

"Are you a shrink as well?" Jenson asks her.

"Just a proofreader," Hayley says. "I told you I get paid to make things right. Nothing I get my hands on can be sent out into the world until it's been made perfect. I can do the same for you two."

Jenson grins. "You're quite the friend. I'll have to remember to call you up anytime I've got a problem."

"Absolutely," Hayley says. She leans back against the booth, suddenly looking exhausted. "No wonder you two are stressed out. I've only talked about it for fifteen minutes, and I'm tired."

Jenson's hand feels warm through my pants, and I take my left hand and put it over his.

———

Jenson drops Hayley off at her house, and when we pull up my driveway, he parks and walks me to the door. I invite him inside, and he asks me if I'm okay. I'm super buzzed from four hours of drinking with Hayley, and I elbow him in the side.

"You're teasing."

He chuckles. "I'm not. But you *are* drunk, babe."

He goes into the kitchen, and I take a seat on the couch in my living room. A couple of minutes later, Jenson hands me a glass of water and sits next to me on the couch.

I take it and nearly spill it all over him. He makes me take a few sips before putting it on the coffee table. I lean in to kiss him, and he puts his arms around me.

"I love kissing you," he murmurs as he takes my bottom lip between his teeth and tugs. "Could do it all day."

"That guy my mom wants me to date?" I mumble. "I ran into him at the bar tonight."

Jenson wrenches his mouth off of mine. "What the fuck was he doing there?"

I make a face. "Getting so drunk he puked on me. Freaking Patsy's dear friend Maureen has a son named Will. He worked in Manhattan as an investment banker, but he just took a job in Philly."

"An investment banker?" Jenson's tone is laced with irritation. "It sounds like you have a lot in common."

"Oh, please," I say to him. "You have literally nothing to be jealous about."

"I'll be jealous if I want to," he says. "Maybe it's time to tell them all the truth."

"I don't want their agendas pushing us into a decision," I say. "We promised we'd take things slow. Remember? I don't want to go too fast because of some silly fantasy of my mother's. There's nothing to worry about. You're a part of me, Jenson." I slip my hands underneath his shirt and feel his hot skin against my fingers. "You'll always be a part of me."

I don't want to stop this time. With the way I'm feeling right now, I don't know why we ever stopped.

"What was wrong with me earlier, anyway?" I say to him. I'm dizzy with alcohol and lust, and when I hear my own voice back in my ears, it sounds different, like I'm no longer guarding my heart. "Family? We're not blood related. The past? It's over and done with. Sex? I don't know why I was scared of that kind of commitment. Do you?"

Jenson pulls my hand away as I reach for his pants. "I'm not sure," he says. "But I'm not going to make love to you when you're drunk. We've waited long enough. Let's both be sober, Olive."

His green eyes are piercing as they fix on mine. But there's something else—

"You're afraid it's too soon," I say in surprise.

"Maybe so. But I know I'm not going to do this when

you've been drinking." He kisses my cheek. "I'll help you to bed, okay?"

I don't want him to leave. "Let's talk," I plead with him. "You tell me a secret, and I'll tell you one."

The corner of his mouth lifts in a grin. "Okay. I'll start."

"Okay." I curl up next to him on the couch, and he starts talking.

CHAPTER FOURTEEN

I wake up in the morning and roll over sleepily to glance at the clock. *Shit.* It's nearly eight o'clock. I never set my alarm, never need to. I usually wake up with a start every morning, so afraid I'll be late to work. I'm counted on to open the bank three days a week, but luckily today isn't one of them. Because it's Sunday.

And I am unbelievably hung-over.

Yesterday comes flooding back to me in snapshots.

Jenson.

And Hayley.

At the bar. So drunk.

And then Jenson at my house.

I can't seem to remember much of Jenson being here. Except I vividly remember I said I wanted to have sex, and he said I was too drunk. After that, it all goes blurry.

I get up gingerly. I have a massive headache to go along with my massive embarrassment for propositioning him when I was in that state of inebriation. Maybe I can avoid Jenson for at least twenty-four hours.

I'm showered and dressed and have just put on a pink

Randolph College raglan shirt and jeans when the doorbell rings.

When I open the door, Jenson is standing on my front step with his two sons and...a dog.

Looking incredibly handsome in athletic shorts, a fitted black t-shirt, and sexy day-old stubble, Jenson has Connor in his arms and Kyle's holding onto the dog leash.

"Hi." Jenson's sexy half-smile says much more than he can say in front of his kids. His gaze flicks to my lips, fresh with mauve lipstick, and then down to my outfit, fitted perfectly to my figure, and he winks. "How are you feeling this morning?"

"I'm fine." I lean in to give Connor a kiss and then bend down and put my lips to Kyle's sweet head. "Hi, boys. How are you?"

"Hi, Livia." Kyle hands me the leash, and I take it from him automatically, not understanding. "Surprise!"

"Did you get a new pet?" I ask him.

Kyle looks up at Jenson, who says, "I got you a dog."

"Why?" I stare down at the wriggly, floppy-eared creature with a giant tongue sitting at my feet.

"You said you wanted one," he says. "Remember last night?"

I stare at him. "No, not exactly. And how did you find a dog so quickly?"

"Funny story," he begins.

"Really," I say back as I give him a look.

His eyes fill with humor. "My mom volunteers at the Animal Shelter every week. A dog came in on Friday, and she never does this, but she took him home with her on a whim. She knew she couldn't keep him because Dee's not a dog person. But she was hoping somebody could because she said he's one of the cutest dogs she's ever seen in her life."

I look down at the dog in front of me. I don't think he's

especially cute. He's not ugly, but I wouldn't say he's super cute. There's something about him, though, that I'm falling for....

"And I take it this is him?"

"That's him. I figured you may not remember telling me you wanted a dog last night. It was one of your secrets," he adds.

One of my secrets? Oh, my God, what else did I tell him?

"It just gets more interesting," he says as his eyes lock with mine.

Shit. I had a feeling he was going to say that.

He grins. "Anyway, you can take some time to think about whether you want to adopt a new pet. I probably should have waited to confirm with you, but I thought you could use a dog in your life. You can take him on your walks with your Mom."

"I can't take care of a dog," I say to him.

"Daddy said you might say that," Kyle pipes in, his smile nearly as mischievous as his father's. "So he said you two could share him, and that way, Connor and I can play with the doggie, too."

I look up at Jenson, who swallows and waits for my reaction.

"Share him, huh?" I ruffle Kyle's hair. "Well, that's an interesting idea."

"Is that okay, Livia?" Kyle persists. "Can you and Daddy share the dog?"

"Please say yes!" Connor says, his green eyes pleading.

I smile at him. "Of course. You can play with the dog as much as you want to, honey. He'll be all of ours, okay?"

"He can stay at my mom's for now," Jenson says as he moves Connor to his other arm. "I'm taking the boys with me to practice this week, and Coach says the dog can come too.

By the way, my mom reminded me about Thursday's annual summer mayoral dinner."

Great. I completely forgot about the mayoral dinner on Thursday. That's the night before my meeting in Manhattan.

"Will that be okay for you?" he asks, his eyes reading the panic clearly crossing my face.

"Um, I guess it will have to be." I shrug.

Just one of those things I can't control. Kind of like whatever crazy things I told Jenson last night.

I hand Jenson back the leash as I stare down at this animal that's just entered my life. I reach out to pat him again, and he gets so excited he licks my hand with that giant tongue. Kyle giggles.

"He's a mixed breed, they think maybe part Rat Terrier, part Chihuahua," Jenson adds as they go to leave. "He's a boy, about a year old. He'll need some obedience training," he says as the dog starts to drag him down the driveway. "But we can talk about that later!"

I already know what I'm going to name him. Bernie, after the coffee house. Even as he's walking away from me, tail wagging, I'm already in love with him.

———

Jenson

"Daddy, Smith said Connor and I can play catch with him during his break. Okay?" Kyle pulls at my sleeve to get my attention.

I look up from where I'm sitting on the bench on the side of the field. I've got the dog leashed by my feet and my iPad next to me so I can keep working on the offensive scheme while I take in the practice going on in front of me. The dog ran around like crazy when we first got here until he exhausted himself and fell asleep on the grass.

"If Smith says it's okay and he has the time." I nod at Smith, who's making his way toward us. "How did those new plays feel out there?"

Smith gives me the thumbs-up. "Cool. Except for the one where I have to hand off to Dwyer. I should be throwing on that one."

I shake my head. "You can't throw on every down. Believe me, I fought my coaches for the same reason. But they were right. You'll have more success passing it off on that play."

"Hey, I looked you up," he says, a smirk crossing his face. "So you were pretty fucking"—he cuts off with a glance at Kyle and Connor, who are grinning up at him—"you were pretty darn good, Coach. State record for touchdown passes still stands, huh?"

"That's right," I say.

"Why didn't you pursue it? Coach said your knee, right?"

I point to the jagged scar that's still visible on my knee.

"Oh, wow. Sorry about that." Smith winces.

"The thing is, I feel like I was always meant to be a coach. So everything worked out the way it was supposed to."

"Hey, maybe one of your boys will pick up where you left off." Smith tosses the football lightly to Connor, who catches it in both hands. "Nice catch. You ready to play a little?"

"Ready!" Connor calls goodbye to me, and he and Kyle follow Smith onto the empty half-field behind where the second-team is practicing.

I watch them go, and the memory of yesterday when I located Donald Waverly for the first time hits me like a gut punch. Seeing his face, and myself in it, was so strange. I'm used to looking at my sons and seeing myself in them, but looking at a man who's a complete stranger to me in every way and seeing a physical resemblance—it was disconcerting.

And I don't know how to handle that.

I'm the only coach on this side of the field, and no player is within hearing shot of me. I reach for my phone and call Colton.

"Hey." Colton's greeting comes fast like he's hurrying somewhere.

"Colt. You busy?"

"On my way out of the locker room. We just finished in the field, and I'm headed to the film room. What's up?"

"It can wait if you're in a hurry."

I can practically feel him slow down his pace through the phone line.

"Now you've got me worried. What's up, J?"

I stare across the field. My gaze travels from the players and coaches gathered on the other side, and it's a moment before I can swallow through the tension in my throat enough to answer him.

"I found my biological father."

"Shit." Colton's tone drops. "That's huge."

"Yeah."

"How are you doing?"

"I'm..." I tell him the truth. "Freaked out. A lot more than I thought I would be."

"Have you reached out to him?"

"No." I briefly explain how I located him online. "Olivia thinks I should meet him. She would never say that to me directly because she wouldn't want me to feel pressured in any way, but I can tell she thinks it would help me."

"Maybe it would help both of you."

I let his words sink in. "How come?"

"Because she's kind of lived this alongside you your whole life, right? Maybe you need to find closure there of some kind —for you and for her."

Christ. He's right. "Thanks, Colt."

———

When practice ends, I call Olivia and invite her to pizza with the boys and me. Dogs are allowed at the local pizzeria, and ours is more than happy to tag along with us.

Olivia arrives looking put-together like always with her shiny black hair up in a high ponytail, her blue eyes bright and clear. She's dressed casually in a pink shirt that hugs her breasts, and black skinny jeans.

The dog nearly knocks her over the moment she arrives, and she immediately kneels down and pats him. Kyle and Connor rush to hug her, and then they grab "Doggie" by the leash and make a dash for an outdoor table. Olivia and I step into line to order.

"Is your hangover gone?" I ask her. "You look great."

"Right," she says. "I'm not convinced my hangover's even fully kicked in yet. I should never have done those shots."

I chuckle. "You guys wanted to do another round right before we left. I talked you out of it."

"Thank God."

"I didn't want to surprise you in a bad way," I say to her as we wait to pay.

"You mean by showing up outside my front door with a pet?" She breaks into a breathtaking smile. "And you brought along your two kids so I couldn't tell you no in front of them?"

"That part was unplanned. My mom was supposed to watch them, but she got tied up with Dee." I lock eyes with her. "So. Are we going to own a dog together?"

A long beat passes as we stare at each other.

"Yes," she says in a tone barely above a whisper. "I'd already made up my mind. I made it up within a minute of you blindsiding me at my front door this morning."

"This will be fun. I promise."

"How am I supposed to take care of Bernie?" she says. "I don't know what to do with a dog."

"Bernie." I smile. "After the coffeehouse?"

"Yeah. You like it?"

"It's perfect. I love it. And I'll help you. We'll take care of him together."

CHAPTER FIFTEEN

The next few days pass quickly, and somehow Olivia and I never get time alone to talk about the other night. Olivia's super busy preparing for her upcoming meeting in New York, and I'm up late every night after putting the boys to bed, trying to make sure I've got a great game plan in place for Randolph's first game of the season. It's the weekend after Colt and Dylan will be in town, so I want to make sure I'm prepared ahead of time.

Together with our families, we go visit with Auntie Sue, who's slowly improving, and Olivia and I spend time with Bernie and the boys. The four of us even take him to a dog training class together.

But on Thursday, Meghan and Andy are taking the boys to the shore for a few days, so after practice, I meet Meghan and hug my sons goodbye.

Saying goodbye to them like this never gets easier. It might get more comfortable, but I always feel that same ache in my chest.

"You'll be here when we get back from the beach, right

Daddy?" Connor asks me the same question he asks every time.

I rub his head. "I promise. I'm not going anywhere. I'll see you guys really soon."

I wave as they drive off, knowing they can't see me but wanting to make sure that if they do, they'll know I'm thinking of them.

I'm always thinking of them. But I also have something else I need to deal with. I pull into a parking space by the town square and text Olive.

Let's talk after the dinner tonight. Just you and me.

———

Olivia

I'm at work, in the middle of a hundred files in preparation for my meeting in New York, when my father pops in.

"Dad!" I say in surprise. "What are you doing here?"

My father's come by the bank a total of twice since I've been working here, and he's always called first.

"I'm sorry for the lack of advance notice," he apologizes as he stands awkwardly next to my desk. His gray wavy hair is in its usual haphazard state, and he's wearing what Daphne and I teasingly call his "mayor's outfit"—a blue tie with "Liberty Falls" written on it, and a navy suit. "I was supposed to visit Auntie Sue this afternoon, but with the dinner tonight, I just don't have the time. Any chance you could go in my place?"

"Of course, Dad. I always love to visit Auntie Sue."

He smiles at me. "You two always hit it off. Not everyone could handle Auntie Sue's personality, but you—you and she were kindred spirits."

"Still are. I'll go there after lunch."

"Speaking of, I thought you and I could grab a quick bite."

He holds up his cell phone. "Battery died, or I would have called."

"Um, I'm free for lunch, sure." I pick up my purse. "Where do you want to go?"

Dad suggests Burritoville down the road, so we walk there together and get into line to order. As usual, everyone in the place wants to talk to him, and it takes over twenty minutes for us to actually get our food.

As the mayor's daughter, I'm used to sharing my father with the town. But going out for a meal never really gives even a hint of privacy.

But Dad clearly came armed with a purpose other than requesting an Auntie Sue visit, and he leads us to a booth in the far back, away from the other customers.

Once we sit down, I get a hint of what this lunch is really about.

"So how are things?" He takes a chip and dips it in the salsa bowl sitting between our plates.

"Things are good." I look at him suspiciously and wonder for one brief moment if he's having some sort of father's intuition and knows I'm in a relationship.

But then he says, "Good. Olive, your mother told me about Will and how things didn't work out with him."

"Dad, he threw up on me," I say before biting into my burrito.

"Right," Dad says. "Not exactly impressive."

I shake my head and swallow my bite of food. "Not exactly."

Dad clears his throat, and I brace myself. I know what my father's throat-clearing means. It means he's about to launch into some sort of lecture meant to educate and guide me down the right path. Sheldon used to leave the room as soon as Dad cleared his throat; that way, he'd be long gone before Dad really got going.

I don't have anywhere to go other than back to the bank, and I have a nearly untouched burrito sitting in front of me, so I stay where I am but squirm uncomfortably.

"One's work is a wonderful thing," Dad begins. "Loving what you do and being inspired by it. Your mother and I are thrilled you love your job, honey."

I furrow my brow. "Thanks, Dad."

"Loving your home life is just as important," he continues.

Here it comes.

"Mom told me you may be feeling a little lonely since your divorce. And with Sheldon getting married..."

"Dad. I'm happy for Sheldon. Really I am. And..."

"I know you're happy for him," Dad says. "That's not what this is about."

"What is it about then?"

Dad puts up his hand. "I understand this is none of my business. But Mom said Will's a very nice man and very successful, and..."

"Dad, I'm not going out with Will, and that's final."

"That's fine. But maybe you and I can go over your options and plan this out. Two heads are sometimes better than one, you know."

"You want to sit down and plan out my love life?" I say to him. "Make a list of men, cross certain ones off, and move others to the top?"

"Now that's an interesting idea," Dad says.

Despite myself, I smile weakly at my father's well-meaning efforts. "Dad, no. That's a terrible idea. I was kidding!"

"Honey, I'm just worried about you." He drags a chip through the salsa bowl while he talks. "I want you to feel what true love is like. Obviously, your previous marriage isn't something to shoot for again. It takes longer for some people than others; I was older myself before I found real love with your mother."

I'm so tired of looking at his pitying eyes. "I do know what love is like. I've been in love. Deeply, crazily in love. Okay?"

Dad's bushy eyebrows shoot up to his hairline. "You have?"

I nod. "Yes. And that's all I'm going to say about it. But don't worry, please. I'll be okay."

Dad picks up his burrito. "It's a relief for me to hear you speak this way, Olivia," he admits. "I was worried you'd put so much of your attention on your work that you'd left your heart behind somewhere."

I force a smile at how accurate he really is. I did leave my heart behind somewhere, with a man I never forgot. I'm just lucky that we've got a second chance.

———

I walk through the nursing home and knock on Auntie Sue's open door before stepping inside her room.

She's napping, and the way the sun's rays are coming through her window and landing on her face—she looks like an angel lying there.

I take a seat in the empty chair next to her bed. First, I chat awkwardly about the weather. Then, I talk about the mayoral dinner tonight. But I feel like sharing my heart with someone in my family. And maybe telling somebody who can't say anything back, especially someone I've always looked up to, will help.

Holding her hand in mine, I start confessing.

I tell her about Jenson and me. Not every detail. Just enough that she gets the idea.

"He's the most important person in my life," I say. "And

you're the first person in my family that I'm telling. I guess I needed to get it off my chest."

Her eyes flicker open.

For a second, we stare at each other. And then, she squeezes my hand.

Emotion clogs my throat as I look into her wise eyes.

"Thank you, Auntie Sue."

———

Mom insists on picking me up for Dad's mayoral dinner, and I'm on my way out the door when my phone rings. I wave to Mom as I climb into the passenger seat. My long, black skirt gets caught up in my heeled shoe and I untangle it as I answer my phone.

"What's up, Sheldon?" I say. "I'm with Mom, and we're on our way."

Sheldon starts talking a mile a minute, but a car drives by and honks at the same time.

"I missed all of that. Can you start over?"

"Cara's driving me crazy. I try to help out as best I can, but it's never right, and she's at her mom's now in tears, and I don't even understand what I did wrong. I'm sure you can enlighten me."

"Let's talk when I get there," I say. "I'll meet you in ten minutes."

As soon as Mom and I arrive at the banquet hall, I rush the hors d'oeuvres station. I've just filled my plate with chicken satay strips and pastry puffs filled with spiced pota-toes when Sheldon rushes over to me. Between his stubble and the dark smudges underneath his eyes, he looks like he hasn't slept in days.

I gesture for him to join me at a table in the back of the hall. He and I are two of the first people here, and I'm enormously grateful for the lack of a crowd. The camera crew is still setting up by the stage, and a few reporters are milling around; I wave at Glenn, give a terse head nod to Calvin, and turn to Sheldon.

"Hate that damn reporter," Sheldon mutters as we take seats kitty-corner to each other.

"I know," I say. "He's the one who spread the lie about Dad having an affair with his assistant, remember? He doctored the photographs and changed the dates. Lindsay likes women, not men; I still don't know if Calvin's end game was to force her to out herself or to get Dad voted out as mayor."

"I say he wanted both things. Like I said, hate that guy." Sheldon grabs a puff off my plate and pops it into his mouth.

"You look awful. So what's the matter, big brother?"

"My wedding..." Sheldon pauses. "Olive, I'll be blunt with you because I can be: it's driving me fucking nuts. I'm not kidding here. I'm going crazy."

I look at his bloodshot eyes. "You do seem especially tense. What's the problem?"

I've managed to eat two puffs and start in on a chicken satay before Sheldon speaks again, which is fine with me because when I'm chewing, I can't answer him very well. I'm just in the middle of fantasizing that maybe I'll be able to finish my entire plate of hors d'oeuvres before I have to pay attention to anything other than the food in front of me when Sheldon starts talking.

"Cara's family is rude and demanding and can be quite crude..."

"I think I get the picture." I cut him off. "They're not helping things. But what's really going on?"

"Cara's miserable over it," he says. "I know our family's kind of overbearing and judgmental..."

I nod at him and purse my lips.

"But hers is just impossible," he says. "Everybody's divorced, and none of the exes can be in the same room with one another. Except they have to be for this one day, right? Which presents a problem. I mean what do they expect us to do—throw two weddings so half can attend one ceremony and the rest go to the other?"

"They're all divorced?"

"Some two and three times."

"Well, families are always hard. Especially around relationships." I think about Jenson and me. "You and Cara have to put yourselves first. You have to. Or else you'll drown underneath all these other people's agendas."

Sheldon picks up a chicken strip and points it at me. "*This* is why I called you. You're right. So what do I do?"

"Don't let them get in between you," I say. "Simple as that. No matter what you have to do, don't let that happen."

I take another bite of my chicken as Sheldon starts brainstorming about how to make sure he and Cara make it through their wedding intact. "You'd think your relationship would be the biggest hurdle," he says to me. "And it is. But it's the biggest hurdle because of all the other people in your life who are involved. You know?"

"Yes," I say slowly. "I think I do."

Sheldon looks at me more closely. "I ran into Hayley the other day. She said you two had yourselves some fun after the fair."

I rest my cheek on my hand. "We did. I should never be allowed to get drunk."

"God, I can't believe I missed that," Sheldon says. "You always tell secrets when you're drunk."

"How do you know that?" I ask him suspiciously. "I'm never drunk around you."

"Not in a long time, no. But remember my college graduation? You were underage, but we went to that party after—

you and that guy you were seeing, and me and Jeanne." He shudders. "God, they were both nightmares. Anyway," he continues, "you were plastered. And you took me aside near the end of the night—" He pauses. "Did I never tell you this?"

My tongue is in knots, and I can't answer him at all except to shake my head. I can't breathe for fear of what he's going to say next.

Sheldon grins. "First you started cursing that guy you were with. What was his name?"

"Ken." I pray he can't hear the way my voice is shaking.

"That's right!" Sheldon snaps his fingers. "Ken! God, I just kept drawing a blank. I wanted to say Ben, and then I thought Dale, for some crazy reason, and then..."

"Sheldon," I say tersely. "Finish the story?"

"Right," he says. "So you took me aside, talked about how much you couldn't stand to be with Ken another minute and said you were going to break up with him by morning. And then you said something else, something interesting." The curiosity in his face is clear. "You told me there was somebody else, a man you'd wanted for quite a while but that you'd been torn apart by circumstance, and the whole experience with him had made you lose all faith in relationships. But you never mentioned his name. No matter how much I tried to get you to tell me, you said that was a secret you could never share, especially with me."

Shit. I look away from Sheldon. The hall is starting to fill up now, and my father's up on the stage with Cindy, who's setting up his microphone.

"Olivia?" Sheldon's voice calls me back to the table.

I turn to face him and force my eyes to focus on his.

"Is it true?" Concern has replaced the curiosity. "Was there some guy who meant that much to you? And why couldn't you tell me who it was?"

Knowing I can't answer him without making it sound

even more mysterious, I simply shrug. Sheldon loves a mystery. He loves them so much I'm surprised he never cracked my secret when I gave him such an enormous clue all those years ago. But putting two and two together in this love story isn't something he would imagine: his sister and Jenson Beau, the little kid who came from nothing and was born into the Graham family? It wouldn't enter his mind.

"I'm sorry." I stand up. "I have to go see Dad for a minute."

"Olivia!" Sheldon calls after me, but I keep walking as fast as I can toward the stage. "Olivia, wait!"

CHAPTER SIXTEEN

I don't get more than twenty feet before a warm, familiar voice calls my name.

I turn to see Jenson standing by the long table of hors d'oeuvres.

He nods hello when I reach him, and his green eyes flash with mischief. His sexy scruff is still covering his square jaw, and his blond hair is combed back neatly. He's wearing dress pants and a collared shirt with the sleeves partially rolled up. Holy hell, he looks hot.

"Hey, J," I say softly.

"Olive." He takes a step like he's going to touch me, but then he doesn't.

We stand in silence for a moment as the tide of people grows around the table of food. Jenson tilts his head for me to follow him, and we walk toward the restroom hallway, stopping once we're alone.

There isn't a soul within ten feet of us, and all attention is focused on either the food or the stage where Dad is already standing at the podium and clearly close to speaking.

"I miss you," I say so softly I barely hear myself.

But Jenson's eyes fill with pain. "I know what you mean."

"Right this second," I say, my voice barely above a whisper. "I miss you. I didn't miss my ex-husband when I was away from him. I didn't ever miss anyone the way I miss you, J."

"You're killing me, Olive." He glances out toward the hall and then back to me.

I suck in a breath. "My brother was just reminding me of my penchant for spilling shit when I drink. Are you ever going to fill me in on whatever crap I told you the other night?"

"Let's wait till this dinner is over. It will be easier."

"Why? Was it that bad?"

He just starts walking back into the center of the hall. "You worry too much," he says over his shoulder.

I sigh and follow him.

We haven't made it five feet before Sheldon calls out to us. As we reach him, he hands me his phone, and I spend the next fifteen minutes chatting with Cara and trying to calm her down about seating for the reception.

As soon as I give the phone back to Sheldon, Mom waves from the front table where she, Cindy, and Dee are sitting together. The table is set up with benches for seating. Daphne rushes toward us, saying that Amy and Alec both got poison ivy and Todd's at home with them.

Before I can respond, Sheldon puts away his phone and picks me up.

"What the heck?" I say, mincing my language in front of Mom and Cindy. "Please put me down."

"Little sister." He hugs me tightly before letting me go. "Cara says you helped her so much with seating chart ideas. Saved my damn ass."

I nod. "Well, great. She had it pretty well covered already."

"She's so much calmer," Sheldon says. "I was pretty useless." He turns to Jenson. "Whenever Cara got upset, I told her not to invite so many people to the reception. That didn't go over well."

Daphne makes a face at Sheldon. "Of course that didn't go over well," she says. "A woman planning her wedding needs a solution that makes sense, not a cop-out plan."

Sheldon jumps to his own defense, and within five minutes he and Daphne are in a full-on argument.

Mom intercedes by reminding them the cameras are around. "My goodness, you two fight worse now than when you were kids," she says.

Sheldon turns to me. "See, Olive, this is why I like you. We don't fight as soon as you walk in the door."

I shake my head at him. "Don't put me in the middle, or I will start fighting with you."

Jenson claps Sheldon on the back. "Two sisters, man. You should know by now not to try to make them choose sides."

Sheldon puts his arm around me and pushes the two of us in next to Mom at the table, saying it's best for everyone if he and Daphne are separated. Jenson slides in on the side of Dee and his mother, and Daphne sits next to Jenson on the end.

"Olivia, how did you hit it off with Patsy's son, Will?" Mom asks immediately.

"Yeah, that's not going to work out, Mom," I say.

"Oh?" Mom says. "Did you give it an honest try, honey? Because sometimes these things take a while to sort themselves out."

"So true, Nora," Cindy says. "I introduced Jenson to this delightful woman at the fair, and he wouldn't have anything to do with her. He said something about no chemistry, and I tried to tell him chemistry is a tricky thing. Sometimes you don't feel it right away, or even all the time, but it doesn't mean you're not perfect for each other."

"Honey, let Jenson figure out his own love life," Dee says.

Jenson's focus doesn't leave my face as he says, "Mom, chemistry is important. And sometimes you do know right away."

Sheldon laughs. "So Olive, did you and this guy exchange bodily fluids?"

"Only if that includes his alcohol-induced vomit," I say.

Jenson breaks into a laugh as the waitress delivers our drinks.

"Ah, the old 'get so drunk you puke on your date' story," Daphne says. "We've all been there, Olive."

"Yeah, in high school," Sheldon says. "Seriously, how old is this guy?"

"He's twenty-eight in chronological years," Mom says. "Obviously that doesn't count for everything."

"Or anything," Daphne adds. "Sounds like you can do better than that, Olivia."

Mom starts tripping over herself in apology-mode, saying she feels like she pushed me into it.

"It's okay, Mom. And he wasn't my *date*. I ran into him at the bar. It was unplanned."

I'm still staring at Jenson. The green of his eyes dances flirtatiously as Dad's speech starts and goes on for so long that we're nearly through our meal by the time he's done.

As I reach for a roll, I accidentally bump Jenson's hand as he's reaching for the same piece.

"Here, you have it," we both say at the same time.

My body fires off on all cylinders, and I have to swallow hard. Jenson smiles softly at me and puts the roll onto my plate.

I want him so badly my chest aches. And I can't possibly sit in between Mom and Sheldon anymore. I excuse myself and hurry to the back hallway where I turn the corner and duck into the restroom.

Jenson

I watch Olivia walk away, clenching my jaw so hard I feel like I'm going to break a tooth. Being sandwiched in between our families is fitting for us, but I'm not a teenager anymore, and hiding the fact that the woman I want has been sitting across from me sucks.

"So who are you dating these days, Jenson?" Daphne asks me. "I never get to hear about your life."

I shrug. "Nothing to tell." Nothing that I can say out loud, that is.

"My son is so picky," Mom says. "Every time I fix him up with a new, wonderful woman, it's a bust."

"He and Olivia must be drinking from the same water cooler," Nora says. "I was so hopeful when she got married, and then bam—she divorced him! I know he brought that on himself, but..."

I blow out a deep breath.

"Olivia's ex-husband was an ass," Sheldon says. "She never should have married him."

I want to fist bump Sheldon for defending Olivia.

"I only met him once, but I didn't like him, either," I say, unable to keep my mouth shut. "He was completely wrong for her."

Sheldon nods at me. "We're guys, Mom. We can read the asshole vibe from a mile away. You're too busy trying to see the good in all these jerks you're setting Olive up with that you're missing the fact none of them have been right for her."

"Well, what can we do about it?" Nora asks, furrowing her brow. "Olivia doesn't seem too adept at finding 'the one.' And she deserves that in her life."

I open my mouth and nearly say something I can't take back.

I have to tell you something.

I blink. Apparently I say that out loud without realizing it because the entire booth is staring at me like I'm about to announce something life-changing.

"What did you say, honey?" Nora asks me. "You have to tell us something?"

"What is it?" Sheldon asks.

I let out a deep breath and try to sound casual. "I just mean that Olive will be okay. She's going to be so happy in love one day soon that you'll forget you were ever worried about her."

Nora beams at me. "Thank you for that, Jenson. You know Olivia better than anyone, and I really hope you're right."

"Excuse me for a moment." I stand up and walk down the hall toward the restrooms.

———

Olivia

It's a one-person bathroom, and I turn the lock in relief before rinsing my face at the sink.

I turn off the faucet and look at myself in the mirror. My face is wet with water, and my eyes are sparkling blue. I look better than I feel, a feat women have perfected over the years. How can make-up and putting on a brave front help to hide the pain so well?

A knock on the door startles me, and I don't answer. But it comes again louder.

"Just a minute!" I call out.

"Olive." It's Jenson. "Can you open the door?"

With my face still damp, I unlock the door and pull on the knob. Jenson's standing right outside. His eyes are blazing with heat, and I stare up at him as he steps into the bathroom and closes and locks the door behind him. Before I can say anything, he backs me up against the wall and puts his mouth over mine.

I kiss him back like I'll never get enough. His tongue sweeps across my lips and inside my mouth, and I clutch at his back. Then, I come to enough to remember where we are, and I pull back.

"My face is wet," I mutter to him.

"I know. You want to dry it?" He puts his hands on my ass and lifts me off the ground and tighter against him.

"I can't," I say. "There are no paper towels in here."

Jenson tears his gaze off of me to glance around. "It's just that dryer thing?"

"Hot air's more economical than paper. Not to mention more green."

Jenson lets me down to the ground so he can untuck his t-shirt and hold it out. "Dry your face on me."

"It will show," I say. "Our mothers have eagle eyes."

"Use the bottom, and I'll tuck it back in. Come on."

I smile at him as I dry my face on his shirt. It smells like his cologne; it smells like him. I lift it up to kiss his stomach, and then his chest. Jenson sucks in his breath.

I raise my head to make eye contact with him. "I'm sorry my mom keeps bringing up Will. I never want to hurt you."

He kisses the top of my head. "I don't care about him. I only care about you. We have enough demons. Let's not worry about someone our mothers are talking about."

I tug on his shirt, pulling him closer. "I agree."

He braces his hand on the door by my head, his face inches from mine. "You're irresistible," he says against my lips. "I can't wait to touch you, Olive."

He reaches for the hem of my skirt.

I gasp. "J, what..."

"Shh." He slowly lifts my skirt up over my thigh until it reaches my hip. "This will be quick."

When his hand sneaks underneath the band of my underwear, I clutch at his arm. "Hurry," I beg him. "I've been dying for you the entire dinner."

Two fingers enter me, and I sink my teeth into Jenson's shoulder to muffle my cries. His thumb circles me while he moves his fingers in and out in an erotic motion that makes my legs shake.

"I'm going to...I can't..." *Hold myself up anymore.*

Jenson shifts so he can wrap his arm around my waist, holding me close as he continues to pump his fingers into me.

I come so fast I can't contain my moans, and I chant his name into his shirt as I climax.

"You're going to get us in trouble," I whisper after I finally regain the ability to stand without my knees buckling.

Jenson helps me fix my skirt. "I'm getting tired of hiding," he says. "I nearly lost it out there. I really almost told them."

I widen my eyes. "Just now?"

He nods. "I wouldn't do that without talking to you first, of course. And I know it's not quite the right time, and I don't want to get suckered into it just because their cluelessness is driving me mad. But listening to them drone on about potential dates for us..."

"It's maddening," I agree.

"So," he says, looking at me closely. "Sorry we still haven't gotten a chance to talk. But of course things didn't work out the way we hoped on Saturday. I got those calls, your mom called and left that super long message, the delivery guy dropped off a package..."

Silence fills the tiny bathroom.

I put my hand in his. "I hope we aren't going to put a lot of focus on what happened—or rather, what *didn't* happen—

between us. Because that's going to make things really awkward..."

"Not going to be awkward. But I have an idea. The boys are with Meghan, and my mom's thrilled to take Bernie for a few days. So tonight—you, me, your house? With a quick stop at my new place first."

"You already got the house?"

He pulls a key out of his pocket. "Just signed the lease before coming here. It has no furniture yet or I'd say let's stay there tonight."

"That's amazing, J."

"That's where my mom thinks I'm sleeping by the way, so she won't worry when I don't come home. And this weekend, they all think I'm in Pittsburgh and you're in New York."

"It's like a regular undercover story. So tonight. Déjà vu?"

"Not exactly. We'll draw the blinds, turn out the lights, turn off our cells and unplug the landline, open a bottle of wine..." He brushes my cheek lightly with his hand. "We'll shut out Liberty Falls for twelve hours. And when we go to Manhattan tomorrow?" His question is laced with promise. "How about we think of this weekend away as a mini-vacation? Just us."

That does sound romantic. "I can definitely do that. You think it'll do the trick?" I'm already imagining having Jenson with me, all to myself, for an entire night and day.

"Yeah. I think we can pretty much bank on it." He grins. "No pun intended, Ms. Deal Closer."

"Baby, I'll be home in about an hour."

We both jump at the sound of Sheldon's voice. Jenson wraps his arms around me and holds me close.

"No worries," Sheldon's saying. "Love you."

"He must be on the phone with Cara," I whisper into Jenson's ear.

He kisses my neck. "He'll go back to the table in a minute."

"So should we," I say as I step back from him and begin straightening my hair. "Or we'll be noticed. Right now is definitely not the right time or place to tell them about us."

"I know. We'll wait for the right moment."

———

After Jenson leaves the bathroom, I wait a few minutes before opening the door and stepping out. As I hurry through the hallway, I bump into Calvin rounding the corner.

"Ms. Graham," he says, his face masked by the shadowy light of the dimly-lit hall.

"Calvin, hello." I instinctively cross my arms over my chest. "How are you?"

"I think I should be asking you that question," he says, his tone laced with sarcasm.

"I'm great. If you'll excuse me..." I go to walk around him.

"Ms. Graham." Calvin matches me step for step as I hurry toward my table. "I'd like to ask you a few questions."

I spin on him. "Are these questions about my father's campaign?"

He stumbles backward. "Um, in a manner of speaking."

"I don't have time to play your games tonight, Calvin. I remember the things you've done in the past, the rumors you spread, and the lies you told. I would suggest you keep your distance from me right now if you want to continue to be invited to these mayoral events."

"You can't stop me from attending," he spits out.

"Try me." I turn away and head for my table.

Jenson's seated and chatting with his mom as if he never left. I push in next to Sheldon, who takes one look at me and asks what's going on. I take a big sip of my soda rather than answering him.

"You're all flushed and bright-eyed," he presses. "Did you get a phone call from somebody? You were gone a little while."

I know he's just curious and probably half-joking, but his aim is far too close to home. I deflect by telling him he's got too vivid of an imagination.

The rest of the meal goes smoothly, but leaving with Jenson proves tricky. I tell Mom I don't need a ride and that I may go to Bernie's first. Sheldon overhears and says he'll go grab Cara, and they'll meet me there.

"Um..." I stall.

"I'll go with you to Bernie's, Olive," Daphne says.

Sheldon and I stare at her.

"You're going to Bernie's?" Sheldon says. "You're going to sit around and be idle, and waste time doing nothing productive?"

Daphne gives him the finger. "Fuck you, Sheldon. Fine, I won't go then."

"No!" I say, grabbing her arm. "Of course you should go. Don't let our irritating brother stop you, for God's sake."

Sheldon nods. "I want you to go, Daph. It'll be like old times." He turns to Jenson. "You want to join us, J?"

"Yeah, that sounds good," Jenson says. "Does anybody need a ride?" He looks at me when he says it.

I want to say yes, but I know Daphne may chicken out and not go. "I'll ride with Daphne," I say. "We'll see you there?"

He grins at me. "See you there."

CHAPTER SEVENTEEN

Daphne's barely turned on her car before she says, "Sheldon's always so mean to me now. Don't you think? He doesn't get me anymore at all."

I look over at her frowning profile as she backs the car out of the parking spot.

"You know Sheldon," I say. "He looks for openings. He wants to push everyone's buttons. If he could irritate every human being on the planet, he would do it."

"But he likes you still," Daphne says, and it's not until she says it like that, that I realize how much it hurts her. "Ever since I had kids, he thinks I'm no fun anymore."

"You're just really busy. You have a lot of responsibility, and that can make it hard to find a balance. I mean, I don't know—I'm not a mother."

"Not yet," Daphne corrects me. "You will be, Olive. I know you may lose hope sometimes, but I just know that you're meant to be a mother."

I put my hand on her arm. "And I know you're meant to be happy. You should hang out with us sometimes. Hire a sitter or have Todd watch Alec and Amy for a couple of hours. You need it, Daph. You need time for you."

She sighs as we pull onto the street. "I know. Todd and I just don't seem to enjoy being together anymore. We don't enjoy much of anything these days." She laughs a little, and I look at her in surprise. It's been a long time since Daphne's laughed at herself. "I can't believe what a whiner I sound like! Jesus, how do you stand me, Olivia?"

I reach over and take her hand in mine. "You'll be okay, Daph."

———

We all hang out at Bernie's until Daphne eventually starts yawning. I text Jenson that I'll meet him at the bookstore, and I leave the coffee house.

I head across the street to the bookstore where I go over to the erotica section. I open the first book on the shelf and have made it to page ten when Jenson puts his arm around me.

"Maybe this will help us," I joke as I show him the book.

He flips the novel to about halfway through and reads aloud, "As he grabs her by the small of her back and presses his cock between her legs, she moans and..."

I take the book out of his hands and slam it shut. "I don't need a live read in public."

His breath brushes my ear as he chuckles. "We'll have more fun in private, believe me. My truck's out front. It's live parked."

"Great. A quick getaway, just what I need."

Once we're inside the safety of the truck and Jenson's pulled away from the curb, he reaches inside the console and flips a set of keys onto my lap.

I look down at them and then over at him.

"For my house," he says as he stops at the light. "You ready to see it?"

"I'm ready. Let's go."

———

As soon as he pulls into the driveway, I jump out of the truck and have the door shut before Jenson's barely opened his door.

"Hey, slow down," he says as he hops out and shuts the door. He meets me in the driveway and kisses my head. "You nervous?"

"No!" I say too loudly.

His mouth tilts up. "You're nervous." He takes my hand and leads me up the front walk and toward the door.

Just a bit. Okay, fine—I'm freaking out. But I have no idea why. It's not like this is our home. But it does mark the first time Jenson and I have lived in the same town since I was sixteen. And that's significant.

His house is a one-story ranch painted pale green. Jenson insists that I open the door, but I toss him the keys.

"All you."

"Should I carry you over the threshold?" he jokes as he opens the door.

"It's not our house. It's yours."

"What about if it was our house?" he asks me as we step into the foyer. "Would you let me carry you then?"

"Probably," I admit. "But that's another parallel universe dream."

I follow him into the empty living room and look around as Jenson turns on the lights.

"It's really nice," I say to him. "I love it, J."

Jenson leads me down the hallway to the master suite. The bedroom is large with a nice bathroom that has a separate garden tub and stand-alone shower as well as double sinks. He puts out his hand to me, and as we slow dance around his empty bedroom, I say to him, "This is one of those moments we're supposed to remember, isn't it? Like a measuring stick in time or something."

"Yes." His arm around my waist tightens, and he lifts me up so we're at eye level. When his mouth touches mine, goosebumps cover my arms. "I want to be with you, Olive."

He kisses me sweetly and lets me down to the ground. "I want to make love to you. Let's go to your house."

———

When we reach my house, I put out my hand and Jenson comes inside with me, shutting the door behind us. He goes over to my phone and unplugs it and shows me his cell phone is on silent. I do the same with mine. Then, he holds up a bag from Bernie's.

"Two pastries," he says.

"Blueberry turnovers?"

"Of course—they're your favorite."

"They smell so good," I say as I open the bag and lead him into the kitchen.

He opens my cabinet and pulls out two plates. I grab the wine, pour us each a glass, and we sit down at the table.

The dessert is delicious, and the company is the best.

But I eat my pastry nervously, wondering whether Jenson will finally share the secret I told him or whether I should ask him about it again. Before I have to decide, he taps my arm and I look at him.

"My secret that I shared with you?" he says. "It was sexual in nature."

I bite my lip, pastry forgotten as I stare at him.

His lips quirk up. "A fantasy I've always had—of you and me."

"Wha—" I clear my throat. "What's the fantasy?"

"I told you that I dreamed of slowly taking off your clothes, piece by piece, until I'd stripped you bare." He reaches out and gently traces my lips with his index finger, and I shiver. "Then, I'd put my mouth on you, starting with your mouth, and then moving down to your breasts, and last, between your legs."

I grip my wine glass so hard I'm afraid it will break.

"Once you're done screaming my name, I'd slide inside you, driving into you over and over until you come again. And again." He leans forward and brushes his lips against my cheek. "I'd take you there as many times as you want, as many times as you need."

"Wow." I blow out the air I'd been holding in. "Maybe we should go to the bedroom now."

"Hold up." Jenson catches my wrist before I can stand. "Don't you want to hear what your secret was?"

After the way his confession turned me on, I nearly forgot. "I suppose I need to know. What secret did I tell you?"

"First you said you'd always wanted a dog," he says.

"And now I have one. It's like instantaneous gratification week." My stomach twists with nerves. "What else did I say?"

He hesitates and looks at my face before grinning. "You told me one of your sexual fantasies as well."

If I'd been given a million guesses, I wouldn't have expected that to come out of his mouth.

"Really?"

"Really. You want to know what it was?"

I look back at him, my defenses completely down. "I already know what it is."

His lips part. "I need to hear you say it, Olive."

I flush with heat. "Well, while I don't remember saying it the other night...my fantasy has always been for us to have sex...in the shower. Me in your arms, my back against the tile wall."

"And?" His green eyes are smoldering.

"And you drive into me slowly until..."

"Until..."

"We both come so hard we're screaming each other's names." My face is so hot it must be flaming red.

Jenson kisses my cheek. "Do you remember our first kiss?"

"Did you honestly think I would forget?"

I was fifteen and Jenson was seventeen and a half. We were at a party Cindy was holding for Dee's birthday, and we were the only two who stayed outside when the rains started. No thunder or lightning, so the adults couldn't force us inside, and Jenson led me over to the side of the house with no windows. Best of all, there were no reporters—the paper was on strike that week.

"No one could see us when I gave you a hug," he says. "You were wearing a pink tank top that fell off your left shoulder, and jean shorts. Your gorgeous jet-black hair was in a high ponytail."

I sit up and stare at him. "You remember what I was wearing?"

"Every detail from that day is permanently inked into my memory." The green of his eyes darkens with heat. "You were so beautiful and so innocent. You kissed me first. Remember?"

"Yes." I had never felt emotions as big as what I felt that day with Jenson. I didn't know where to put my feelings, so I did the only thing that felt right. I put my mouth over his.

By the end of a half hour, I was lying on top of him with my tongue in his mouth, and he had his hands underneath my top. The next day, I woke up and was sure I was going to hell. Not for going to second base. Mom and Dad had never made a big deal about sex. I just knew that Jenson and I weren't supposed to like each other that way.

But later that afternoon, Jenson showed up in my driveway on his bike. We rode down to the apple orchard, and we talked. He told me that we weren't doing anything wrong, and we couldn't help what was in our hearts. He said he couldn't imagine being with anyone other than me, but he thought we should wait until I was older to do anything like that again.

So we did.

"We didn't kiss again until my sixteenth birthday," I say now. "You were leaving for school, but you surprised me with the best present—a dinner date and then a walk by the river."

"I gave you my heart that night," he says. "I'd given it to you already, but that night I did it consciously. I knew I would never care for anyone the way I cared for you, Olive. That certainty has never changed. Even when I thought our time was over forever, I never let go of you."

———

When we finish dessert, Jenson washes the few dishes and I dry, and then we make our way to my bedroom.

As soon as I get within sight of my bed, panic sets in.

My palms start sweating, and my pulse is racing. It's from this place of anxiety that I rush to my dresser, grab some clothing, and excuse myself for the bathroom.

I change into a pair of red lace underwear and bra and then put on a simple black t-shirt and pajama bottoms.

When I return to the room, Jenson's lying on his side on my bed. I take a seat next to him and he sits up and puts his arms around me.

"J?"

His mouth goes to my neck and he rubs his hand in slow circles on my back. "Mmm?"

"How about we wait to have sex until we get to Manhattan?"

He jerks his head back to meet my gaze full-on. "What? Why would we do that?"

"Because we'll be staying in a hotel." I start to fidget but keep rambling. "I mean, that seems more romantic. But I do have some sex toys here. I can show them to you later—well, I can show you right now if you'd like..." I break away from him and head for my dresser across the room.

I pull out a vibrator, dildo, and a tin of body butter, and then I grab a lighter, flick it on, and start lighting candles before Jenson can utter a word. "I'm not sure body butter qualifies as a sex toy, but I'm counting it. And I'm wearing sexy underwear to celebrate the occasion, this red set I bought with Hayley a while ago. I've never actually worn it for anyone before because normally I think it's making too much of a statement. I also have these essential oils, which smell really nice. I'm not sure I'm an oil kind of girl, but maybe you're into that kind of thing. I don't know. I guess there's a lot I don't know about you, J, at least in the bedroom."

"Hey." Jenson takes my wrist. "Can we sit down?"

I take a seat next to him reluctantly on the bed and open my mouth to speak again, but Jenson starts talking quickly. "I really appreciate all of this," he says, gesturing toward the dresser. "Although I don't need anything but you. And I understand your idea of waiting until tomorrow night. It's only one more night, right? And we've been waiting for years for this moment."

I nod.

"So we could wait patiently until tomorrow," he continues

as he takes my hands in his. "But the thing is, I don't need a special place for this night to be amazing and unforgettable. You're all that matters. Olivia Graham, I love you."

My breath catches in my throat. Tears fill my eyes, and I have to look away from him and out my window where I can't see a damn thing because it's pitch dark outside. Hearing Jenson say those three words out loud to me—it means so much. It feels like a fantasy, and yet he's real. And he's here. Jenson puts his hand underneath my chin and turns me to face him again.

"I've wanted to tell you that every day since I was old enough to know what love meant, Olive," he says in a hoarse tone. "I fell in love with you a long time ago, and my feelings never changed. No matter what was going on or how far away we were from each other. I love you. And I really want to take off your clothes right now, including the sexy underwear you told me about, and make love to you right here. No pulling back the covers, no worrying about the candles. Let's just blow them out and love each other all night long."

I close my eyes and brush a tear away. Jenson puts his arms around me and says in my ear, "What do you think?"

I take a deep breath and keep my eyes locked with his. "I love you. I really do love you, Jenson Beau. I always have, and I know I always will."

His green eyes glimmer with emotion. "Olive. I..."

But I put up my hand to stop him. "That's why I'm so scared. Having you here with me feels so surreal, and I'm still adjusting to the reality. I love the reality, but my brain is still getting on board with my heart. I felt bad after things had to end between us. Sometimes, even though it was silly, I hated myself." It's an uncensored remark, one I would take back if I could, but it's the truth, and I let it stand.

Jenson tucks a stray hair back behind my ear. "Please don't

ever hate yourself, Olive. We'll get this right. Practice makes perfect."

I respond by reaching for the buttons on his shirt. And this time, it's like Jenson, and love, slip right into my heart.

He leaves a trail of kisses down my neck and down to each breast. "This is sexy," he says as he takes off my top and his gaze lands on my red bra. He reaches a hand behind my back and easily unhooks it. "But you know what's even sexier?"

"What?" I say hoarsely.

"How beautiful you are bare." He slides the bra straps off my shoulders and down my arms until the bra's left my body and I'm half-naked. "And you look so damn hot in these paja-mas, babe. But you know what turns me on so much I can't stand it?"

I shake my head, too aroused to answer him verbally.

"Peeling them right off of you." He slips his fingers in the waistband of my pajama bottoms and does just what he said he was going to do. And he doesn't stop there. My little red panties come off next. "This scrap of lace isn't nearly as sexy as what's underneath it, Olive." His fingers graze that spot between my legs that sets me off like a lightboard when he touches me.

I let out a long moan, and Jenson nibbles my neck. Then his mouth goes south, and he closes his lips over one nipple. I arch my back, and he keeps moving, across my stomach, until he's planting kisses on my inner thighs.

"I want to taste you again, Olive. Can I?" His voice is rough and needy.

I nod as I thread my fingers through his hair and guide him between my legs. And...oh, God. Jenson's kisses start out gentle, and then he licks and sucks the most sensitive parts of me until I'm writhing on the bed and he has to hold onto my hips to keep me still. He brings me over the edge so quickly and so intensely that when I come to, both my hands are clutching the sheets in a death grip.

"Now, J. I'm sure." I reach for a condom and hand it to him as I cup my hand over his hardness straining through his pants.

He lets out a low growl and puts his hand over mine. "Never felt like this with anyone else." His lips brush my ear. "Ever. Only you, Olive. It will always be only you."

He sheds his pants, and I reach over to pull off his knit boxers. His hard length juts out to greet me, and I wrap my hands around him while he groans. I lean down and press a kiss to the tip of him, and then I lick him.

"Christ. Olivia."

I lick him again, this time letting my tongue trail all the way down his erection. He threads his fingers through my hair and urges my mouth off of him.

"I want inside you, babe," he says to me. "And I won't last long enough with you sucking me off like that."

He tears open the foil packet and rolls on a condom. And this time, I'm more than ready.

At the first sensation of just the tip of him inside me, we both let out a moan. He pushes inside me slowly, inch by precious inch. Beads of sweat line his brow as he braces himself over me with his arms on either side of my head.

"We'll never have another first time," he whispers into my lips. "I'm going to go as slow as I possibly can. Because I don't think I'll last very long once I'm all the way there."

I'm already at the edge of bliss. The way Jenson feels inside me—there are no words. And now he's moving. *Oh, God.* With one thrust I can feel him so deep inside me that I climax.

He immediately follows me, murmuring my name and then collapsing on top of me.

All I hear is his breath in my ear, and I hold him as tightly as I can.

"Too fast?" he says, and I can hear the smile in his voice.

"Not for me," I say. "That was the most amazing orgasm I've ever had."

"Me, too. But I promise you next time, I'll take you there more than once." He rolls to the side so he's not crushing me and then buries his face in my neck. "I love you, Olive. That was so damn perfect."

I pull him closer to me. "I love you, Jenson."

CHAPTER EIGHTEEN

Jenson

Olivia and I are in our own little world all night long. We fall asleep with me spooning her, but I wake up a couple hours later, and I'm harder than I've ever been in my life. I crave to be inside her again, almost more intensely than I ever have. Now that I know just how incredible it feels to make love to her, I don't ever want to stop.

I lift her silky black hair off her bare shoulder and kiss the skin softly. She lets out a sleepy sigh. I shift my hand down her bare stomach, and keep going until I'm touching the soft insides of her thighs. She moans and opens for me so I have better access.

I run my fingers between her legs until I find the place I love to have my tongue. She grinds her perfect ass against my erection as I work her until she's climaxing all over my hand.

Then I grab a condom off her nightstand. Once it's on, I lift her leg so I can slide into her from behind.

Holy fuck.

The way she feels the second time is even better than the first, something I didn't think possible.

"Olive. Baby..." I murmur into her ear.

"Oh, God. Jenson. Shit." She reaches for my hand on her hip and clutches it. "This is so...good."

I thrust into her faster, and when I know she's on the edge, I move my hand over the inside of her leg and to the apex of her thighs.

She bucks against me hard, and we both lose it at the same time.

I bury my face in her neck, nipping at her skin harder than I meant to. I kiss the same spot, murmuring an apology as I come down from my orgasm.

"I loved every single thing that you did," she says. "Don't be sorry for any of it."

I pull out of her slowly, and she turns to face me. "You know exactly what I like, and I never even told you."

"I love you," I say as I plant kisses along her jaw. "And if there are things you like that I'm not doing, please fill me in. I'm happy to please."

———

We fall back to sleep until just before dawn. I glance over at the clock. Five thirty-three. It's still dark out.

I lean my chin on Olivia's shoulder and ask her what time we need to leave for New York.

"Let's get going now," she says. "That way I won't be stressing the entire way about being late for the meeting. I have everything laid out in my closet—I'll just jump in the shower and we can go."

Jump in the shower. Exactly the words I was hoping for.

"I'll jump in with you."

She looks over her shoulder at me. "What are you going to do in there?"

I grab a condom from the bedside drawer and edge her

toward the bathroom. "Lots of very bad things that will make you feel really good."

I turn on the water in the shower and make sure it's a good temperature before I invite Olivia in.

"Jenson, seriously, I have to get ready." She's already ducking under the stream of water and wetting her hair.

"And I am seriously here to help you."

I uncap her shampoo bottle, pour some into my hand, and angle her head back toward me. As I massage the shampoo into her scalp, she sighs.

"I've never had someone else wash my hair for me before."

I guide her underneath the water so I can rinse out the suds. "I've never shampooed anyone else's hair before."

I soap her body next. She starts laughing when I move the soap between her legs.

"Let me shampoo your hair," she says. "Or we'll get distracted."

I'm fine with getting distracted, but I let her put shampoo on my head and stretch her arms up to try to work it into my hair. I bend down as much as I can, but we end up laughing too much for her to finish on her own. So I rinse off, and then she soaps me up—everywhere.

By the time she's finished, I'm ready to get dirty again.

And when Olivia's eyes go soft and wide, and she steps closer to me, I know we're on the same page.

"Remember your fantasy?" I whisper in her ear.

"Yes," she says, her cheeks flushing the perfect shade of pink.

"Let's do something about that."

I slip my hand between her legs. Finding her wet and ready, I pick her up in my arms, and back her up against the tiled wall. I keep one arm under her ass for support, and she wraps her legs around my waist. Grabbing the foil packet off the side of the tub, I tear it open.

Olivia inhales. "You certainly came to the shower prepared." She helps me roll the condom on, and then I'm inside her.

"You're beautiful, Olive." I tip my forehead to hers.

When we make love this time, it's slow and deliberate. My thrusts are steadfast, and I draw out each one, trying to make the moment last.

We come together in an intense, prolonged climax. When we finish, instead of pulling out, I lean in to kiss her.

Our kiss becomes as intense as our lovemaking just was. This one, incredible, long kiss that feels like it has no beginning and no end—and I'm so far in love with Olivia Graham I can't imagine living another day apart from her. Ever.

"Wow." Her voice is breathy when we finally break apart.

"I know." I slip out of her and make sure her feet are solidly on the tub floor before I reach over to turn off the water.

"That was..."

I bring her close to me in a hug. "Yeah. It was."

———

Olivia

Yeah, so Jenson and I definitely got a little carried away in the shower, and by the time we step out, I'm not feeling as anxious about my meeting. In fact, I'm probably not anxious enough. I love Jenson so much, and I'm slightly head over heels obsessed with that fact. So, the idea of heading to Manhattan for business? Not so scary right now.

"I'll drive," Jenson offers. "And you can go over your notes."

———

When we reach New York City, I kiss Jenson good-bye outside one of the endlessly tall buildings on Lexington Avenue.

"New York is like a different world," I say to him as I open the truck door. "As you know, the last time I tried to work here, things kind of imploded. I don't know if I can handle this."

"You can handle it better than anyone I know." He leans across the console and kisses my cheek, and my nose, and my lips, one last time. "You'll do an amazing job."

I grab my notebook and folder. "I'll call or text you. Find a nice hotel but not too nice! They're all going to be overpriced as it is. Try to stay around two hundred dollars if that's even possible here. I can treat us, or we can split it."

"I'm treating," Jenson says. "You brought us here; I've got the hotel." He pulls away before I can protest.

I walk through the building and head for the elevator bank. When I reach the top floor, I take a moment to glance out the floor to ceiling windows to the left of the elevators. Manhattan's skyline is beautiful. And I feel like I'm in over my head. I see Perls in big black letters outside the door, and I open it cautiously, knowing I'm a few minutes early.

The receptionist is on the phone when I step inside, and she gestures for me to have a seat. I sit down in one of the chairs and leaf through the magazines stacked on the table next to me. I tap my foot on the ground and take the moment to silence my cell phone. As soon as I do, the receptionist hangs up the phone and offers to help me.

I tell her why I'm here, and she says she'll let Harry and Estelle know.

———

Harry, Estelle, and I meet in a windowless room. They both

sit silently for the first forty-five minutes while I give what I had hoped would be an interactive presentation. Instead, I make jokes only I laugh at and ask questions into the air that nobody answers.

When I finish, I take a seat more out of exhaustion than any sort of optimism that I'll be asked to stay. I compile my folders and start to put them into my bag, half-expecting that when I do look up, Harry and Estelle will have disappeared from the room and I'll be left here alone.

"Olivia, that was an interesting presentation," Estelle says.

I look at her smiling face and want to ask her where that smile was for the last forty-five minutes. Instead, I smile back and tell her I'm glad.

Harry buzzes the receptionist for lunch and invites me to eat with them.

As I take a bite of my chicken sandwich, Harry asks me to tell him about Liberty Falls.

"It's just a small town," I say. "I love it, but I've lived there my whole life."

"Is that right? Sounds interesting." His eyes lose some of their dullness. "I grew up here."

"In Manhattan? Wow."

"Yep." He gestures around the room. "Took over this business from my dad, who took it from his dad. It's been a work in progress for years. We finally got our heads above water about ten years ago, and we've been flying ever since. Things are looking up, I tell you."

"That's great," I say. "Union Bank has been growing steadily for the past few years as well. It's exciting to be a part of something positive."

"It is," Estelle agrees. "And I was intrigued that your president is a woman."

"Yes," I say. "She's done a really amazing job."

Harry grins suddenly. It's the first time he's smiled since I walked into the room, and the sight of his teeth almost scares me because I wasn't expecting to ever see them. I smile back, hoping against hope he'll give me good news and I can finally breathe.

"You know what?" he says. "I'm impressed. I'm going to give you a shot. You and Union Bank."

I stare at him, wanting to make absolutely certain I understand what he's saying. "Are you saying..."

"I'm saying we're going to give you the contract," he says. He then stops smiling and takes a big bite of his sandwich.

I thank him profusely, but the conversation peters out after that. By the time we've finished eating, I'm ready to run out of the building. There's only so much awkward small talk I can take.

After we say good-bye, I take the elevator down to the lobby. I blink when the bright sun hits my eyes as I step outdoors.

Before I can text Jenson, I hear, "Olivia Graham? What the hell are you doing here?"

I whip around.

Nate. My ex-husband. My *cheating* ex-husband, is standing three feet away from me.

His gray suit looks tailor-made and expensive. His brown hair is slicked back, and his dark eyes still narrow when he's confused.

And I feel...nothing.

I can barely even summon up righteous anger.

Because the truth is, he did me a huge favor. Not the way he did it, of course, but forcing an end to our marriage, a marriage that held little love and even less passion, was the best thing that could have happened to me.

"What are you doing in New York?" he asks.

He gives me a quick peck on the cheek, and I hug him quickly and without any affection.

"Closing a deal." I gesture to his suit. "You look very dapper."

He tugs at his suit jacket and grins sheepishly. "Playing the role, I guess."

"It suits you." I roll my eyes at myself. "No pun intended."

He laughs. "You look good, Olivia. Happy."

"I am. You?"

He shrugs. "I don't know if happy's my thing. Driven? Sure. Busy? Absolutely. But happy? I think that's a longer road for me."

At the sound of honking directly behind me, I turn around.

Jenson's live parked on the curb, and he waves at me from his truck.

"Is that Jenson?" Nate says as he stares into the truck window.

I turn back to face him. "Yep. He drove me here for my work meeting."

"Does he still live in Pittsburgh?"

"Actually, he's moving back to Liberty Falls. He got a coaching position with Randolph."

"Nice." Nate gives me a second look. "Must be good to have him back in town."

I fidget with the strap of my bag. "Sure."

"Olivia." He glances around and then lowers his voice. "I saw the way you looked at him whenever he came home."

I nearly drop my bag. Instead, I clutch it more tightly to my side. "What do you mean?"

"Come on." He locks eyes with me. "I was your husband. A shitty one but still your husband. And I knew when another man had your attention. In a way I never did."

Shit.

I blow out a breath. For the first time in my life, I drop

my defenses around the topic of Jenson, and I speak the truth.

"I'm truly sorry for that, Nate. I had no idea I was so transparent."

"You weren't," he assures me. "Only to me. Your families —I could tell they didn't have a clue. Mainly because they didn't want to."

"Right."

"And he looked at you the same way, in case you didn't know."

I bite my lip.

"So are you two..."

I take a deep breath as I look at him. "That's...complicated."

He nods. "Piece of advice? You and I wasted way too much fucking time worrying about what other people would think," he says. "If I'd been honest with you about...well, anything over the last couple of years, I wouldn't have had to cheat my way out of our marriage. I would have been a man and talked to you about why I thought us separating was the best thing for both of us."

"Nate, thank you, but..."

"Olivia." His dark eyes grow even more serious. "Nothing's more important than love. Right now, all I've got is love for my job. But you? You were never like me. And it's obvious that you two—" He tilts his head in the direction of Jenson's truck. "—have years of love between you. Looks like a lifetime from where I'm sitting. So do yourself a favor, and realize you deserve love."

I reach over and give him a real hug this time, and then I turn away and head for Jenson.

As soon as I get into his truck, he pulls out from the curb. Jenson keeps his eyes on the road as he maneuvers through traffic. "So. Odds of running into your ex-husband in the middle of Manhattan—pretty fucking high apparently, huh?"

I shake my head. "I couldn't believe it. He was right on the sidewalk when I stepped out."

"You two seemed to be getting along." Jenson's profile is neutral. "Everything okay?"

"He knew about us. I was so shocked; I didn't deny it either."

"That's one point in his favor. Didn't know he was that perceptive when it came to you."

"Me neither. Did Meghan ever think anything?"

"No. I thought maybe she would, but she was always so focused on the boys. Our marriage was all about them from the start."

I lean my head back against the seat, but I can feel Jenson shift to look at me.

"So did you get it?"

"Get what?" I say.

"The contract. How'd the meeting go?"

"It went awesomely. I closed the deal, baby."

"So you're now the number one deal closer in the Northeast?"

I laugh. "Right. I'm still working on that title. But I will get a good bonus from this."

He leans over to kiss me at the next stoplight. "Congratulations, Olive. I'm proud of you. You worked really hard for this."

"Yeah, I guess. I know Liberty Falls is a joke to people here."

"Liberty Falls isn't a joke," Jenson says. "You want balance in your life. There's nothing wrong with that."

"I know." I never actually wanted to move to New York City. I didn't want the long hours or the intense pressure, as much as I tried to convince myself I needed it. And if I were living here now, I would have missed Jenson's homecoming, which means I may not have gotten a chance to heal the hole in my heart that I've had for as long as I can remember.

"Did you get us a room?" I ask him.

"Yes, sugar, I got us a room," he says in a teasing tone.

I laugh. "How is it?"

"It's nice. I'm not big on fancy hotels, but it's got a great bed and a good view of the city."

"I think that's all we'll need."

CHAPTER NINETEEN

As soon as Jenson and I step out of the truck and hand the keys to the hotel bellhop, I drop my purse. It flies open and the condoms I brought sail out. But they don't just drop out of my purse—no, they literally fly out and disappear down the gutter, which happens to be right next to my feet.

"Oh. No." I kneel down and desperately look down into the gutter, even sticking my fingers into the spaces. Maybe I can still reach them; after all, it isn't every day I get to have sex with the love of my life as often as I want to.

Jenson touches my arm. "Just let them go, Olive. It'll be all right."

I know he has no condoms with him because I showed him the box of specialty ones on my dresser and told him I'd pack plenty for our trip.

I stand up reluctantly and take his hand as we walk into the hotel lobby, which looks all gold and glittery and pretty.

"We'll buy some later. There are drugstores in the city. I know yours were special," he adds at the look on my face. "But we got to use those last night, right? I guess we're due for some good old-fashioned rubbers."

I hit his arm as he laughs. "I hate that word. It's so unromantic."

"Because condom sounds so sexy?" Jenson says as we enter the elevator. The couple already inside the car stares at us, and Jenson grins at them until they turn away.

When we get to our floor, Jenson leads me to the left and down the hall before stopping outside our room. I kiss his neck as he puts the keycard in the lock, and as soon as we step inside the door and close it behind us, he backs me up against the wall.

"I love your work clothes," Jenson whispers to me as he takes off my jacket. "But I love taking them off you more."

He shifts me toward the bed, unbuttoning my blouse at the same time. I fall back onto the mattress, and Jenson joins me. He stretches out onto his back and lifts me on top of him.

"I missed you the whole meeting," I say to him as I pull off his shirt. I start kissing his chest and then move my lips down to his stomach. "I'm glad you came with me."

"Honey, I don't want to be anywhere else." Jenson fumbles with the zipper on my skirt and then slips his hands up the insides of my thighs.

I let out a moan and reach for the belt on his jeans. "I want you so much, J."

His hands are all over me, dragging my skirt down my legs. But then he freezes.

"We don't have a condom, Olive."

Every part of my body and heart is screaming: *That's fine!* I always knew that if I were ever going to have kids, they would have to be Jenson's. My brain warns me to be careful.

But I've been holding back with Jenson for years. I'm sick and tired of listening to the jury panel in my head as they sit back and deliver their verdicts over and over again.

I grab at his boxers. "That's okay." I flip onto my back and pull him on top of me. "I don't think I'm ovulating. We'll be okay."

"All we need is us." He nibbles my neck. "Love is all that matters. And I'm okay with whatever happens as long as I'm with you, Olive. I want everything with you."

After that speech, he rolls off of me and starts putting on his pants.

"What the hell are you doing?" I prop myself up on my elbows and watch him get dressed. "I just worked to get you out of those clothes."

He chuckles. "And I look forward to you doing that again in a few minutes. I'm just going to go grab us some protection."

"You're leaving? To get condoms? I thought you just said love is all that matters and you want everything with me."

He bends down to kiss me gently on the lips. "I do want that. And I really am excited to have a baby with you as soon as possible. But I don't want it to happen by default. We waited too long to do everything right, so why would we get careless now?"

Good point. "I'm not sure..."

Another tender kiss. "Olive. You deserve to have a baby on your own terms, when you're ready. And I'll be right by your side. Okay? I'll be back. Keep the bed warm for me."

———

Later that evening, I'm lying across Jenson's chest, enjoying that the only sounds I can hear are his heartbeat and his breathing and, of course, the constant background buzz of city traffic down below.

Then my cell phone rings.

I jump and glance at the clock, certain it must be the middle of the night.

"It's only nine?" I say to Jenson as I grab my phone.

"Hi, Mom," I say into the receiver.

"Hi, honey," she says. "How are you doing in New York?"

"I'm great. How are you?"

"Everything's fine here. Auntie Sue's doing as well as can be expected. I just hope she can make it to Sheldon and Cara's wedding."

"I hope so too."

"I figured you were done with dinner, and I thought maybe you were lonely in the city all by yourself."

"Oh." I pull the sheet up over me and lean back against the pillows. I feel like she can see my naked body through the phone. "No, I'm okay, Mom. Not lonely." I look over at Jenson, who smiles and starts pulling the sheet back down so he can kiss my stomach.

I push him away as Mom keeps talking. "And with the whole Nate business that took place there..."

"It's okay, Mom."

"I know. But the city can be very lonesome. So many people but no connections, you know? No green grass to lie down in, no trees to stand by you as you take walks..."

I have no clue what she's even talking about. "Mom, the trees don't stand by you as you walk. They stand still, and you walk by them."

Jenson starts laughing. I push his head to get him to stay quiet and press the phone closer to my ear.

"But nature is so comforting," Mom waxes. "I remember the year Dad and I lived in Philly while he was an adjunct at the university. It was terrifying."

"There's nothing to be scared of around here, Mom," I assure her.

Jenson leans closer to the phone and whispers, "What the hell is she talking about?"

I put my hand over his mouth as I say into the phone,

"I'm safe and secure in my hotel in a very safe part of the city. Don't worry, but I've got to go, okay? I'll call you when I get back. Love you."

Jenson's kissing the hand I'm pressing over his mouth, and he keeps kissing it until I hang up the phone. I turn it off and throw it across the room to the couch, and then I scoot back down under the sheet and climb on top of him.

"That was not fun." I kiss his neck and run my hands through his hair. "You made that very distracting."

"I'm sorry." He puts his arms around me and reaches for my mouth with his. "But you're irresistible."

And then everything grows fuzzy, and love feels easy. Jenson and I waited so long to get to this point, and all of a sudden, in a different state and a different place, it all feels so easy.

———

A while later, I stand in Jenson's t-shirt in the dark room and open the curtains to look out at the city lights of New York below me.

"It's weird being this high up," I say as Jenson leans his head on my shoulder and puts his arms around me from behind.

"I called Donald Waverly today," he says abruptly.

The mood in the room changes in an instant.

I whip my head around so I can face him. "What? When?"

"While you were in your meeting." He sits down on the edge of the bed, wearing nothing but his black boxer briefs. "I guess being in Manhattan felt far enough away...like I could be anonymous."

Kind of like how we feel right now because no one in our families is here to see us together.

"What was he like?" I say as I take a seat next to him.

"He was very businesslike," Jenson says. "I told him I was interested in condos or possibly houses in the Philly area. He talked to me for about ten minutes about the different options and neighborhoods. Then I said I had to go, but he asked me to call him next week to set up coffee and then some viewings. He told me he'd take me around personally. I said I'd get back to him when I was ready."

"Wow. Does he typically offer to meet people himself?"

"I'm sure." Jenson clasps and unclasps his hands on his lap. "It's just him and one assistant. The assistant was out to lunch so I lucked out. Or else I may have had the wrong person talking to me about real estate I'm never going to buy."

I put my hand over his. "I'm proud of you. At least you got to hear his voice. It's a good start."

"He lives in a high-rise, and he's one hundred percent single and living the good life. He sounds like he's got his whole life in place," Jenson says. "Who am I to go and screw that up?"

"He may want to know that he's your father. He may not. I don't know what I'd do."

Jenson turns and puts his arms around me, and I hold him close to me. "He doesn't know I exist. Imagine if I didn't know about Kyle and Connor? I have to tell him. I'm just not sure what to say yet."

"Keeping secrets is exhausting," I say, picking at the comforter on the bed.

"Why do I get the feeling we're not just talking about my situation?" Jenson asks.

I raise my eyes to look at him. "Part of me wants to tell our families soon. But we'll have to wait until after Sheldon and Cara's wedding; I couldn't live with myself if I ruined their wedding because things got awkward."

His expression relaxes into relief. "I've been feeling the same way. The thing is, when I decide to tell my mom about you and me, I'm not going to stop there. I'm also going to tell her I found Donald, and I don't know if I can keep that secret from Dee."

I look at him in surprise. "You're thinking of telling Dee about Donald?"

"I wouldn't ever do that without my mom's permission," he says, but his voice is strained with pain. "You remember how, the day I found the birth certificate, my mom asked me not to tell anyone who my biological father is? And I get it—she wanted to protect her marriage. But keeping the truth from Dee has made things incredibly awkward. He's raised me the same as if I were his biological son, and I love him. But to pretend that Donald doesn't exist is hard; I'm uncomfortable not telling my sons the truth, and the older they get, the more uncomfortable I feel."

"I understand."

His eyes look greener than ever and more intensely bright when he says, "Once we tell them about us, Olive, it's not going to be easy at first. Your family's amazing and welcoming, but some of them, not to mention the people in Liberty Falls, truly believe I'm related to you by blood. They're going to feel like we've betrayed them, and we're going to need to be strong no matter how hard they come at us."

———

We check out of the hotel early the next morning to make sure we get to Jenson's townhouse in Pittsburgh before the moving company does.

We run into traffic leaving Manhattan, but by the time we hit Pennsylvania, the roads are clear. Jenson tells me he's mapped out the back roads to Pittsburgh.

"Cool." I look over at him. "Who's on the back roads?"

"Hopefully just you and me." He winks. "I'm hoping that somewhere along the way, we can pull over and have a little fun. You want to?"

"How soon can you find a place?"

———

About an hour later, we pull onto a dirt road that leads us past pastures of cows and horses to fields of wheat and corn. Jenson pulls the truck off the road so we're nearly hidden from view by the cornfields growing over the fence. Not a soul is around, and he looks over at me and grins.

Jenson moves over to the passenger seat, and I climb on top of him and look into his green eyes. He's got my skirt hiked up and has unhooked my bra before I hardly know what's happened. Then his hands are underneath my skirt, and I start working his pants down past his hips. He puts on a condom and then pulls my underwear to the side just before I sink down on him abruptly, bringing him all the way inside me immediately.

He jerks in surprise, and grips my hips as I start riding him.

"Olive." His voice is heavy with lust. "Come for me. I want to feel you come for me."

My orgasm hits me so fast I clutch Jenson's biceps to keep from sliding off him. He thrusts up into me hard a few more times and then follows me over the edge.

"It will always be you and me, Olivia," he murmurs as I lean my cheek on his. "Forever."

———

After our private rendezvous, we're forty minutes late to Pittsburgh. The good news is, so are the movers.

"I'm impressed by how organized everything is," I say to Jenson as I help him take a few of the boxes out of his town-house and into his truck. "You've labeled the stuff you want to take back so you're not fishing around for it all afternoon like I would be."

"The moving company said they'd get the furniture to my house next week. But Kyle and Connor had a few things they don't want to wait for." He gives me a kiss. "The landlord's on his way now so I can hand over the keys. We'll sit tight until he shows, and then we can get food downtown if you want. There's a good pizza and ice-cream place. It's called Pitts Stop."

"That sounds perfect. So, how far away from here does Meghan live? You know, your old house?" I ask him. Mentioning the elephant in the room doesn't feel great, but I'm curious where they lived together.

"She and Andy are away with the kids," Jenson reminds me. "We won't run into them."

"I know," I say. "That's not why I asked."

"Oh. Why did you ask?"

I put my hand on one of the belt loops on his jeans and slip my fingers inside it. "I think I want to see where you lived when you were out here and I was in Liberty Falls."

He doesn't ask me why I need to see it, and I love him for that. He puts his hand around mine, which is still clinging tightly to his belt loop. "We can drive there before we get food. It's about ten minutes away."

———

"That's it." Jenson slows the truck and points across the street.

I look past him at the bluish grey two-story house he and Meghan lived in for their brief marriage. It looks surprisingly normal in a normal suburban neighborhood. Doesn't look like a place where divorces happen.

I nod at him and don't say anything. Jenson pulls away from the curb and drives off. Neither of us speaks until he parks outside Pitts Stop.

"I was living my life wrong," Jenson says to me as we sit in the truck outside the ice-cream parlor. "I remember sitting in Pitts Stop with Kyle and Connor after Meghan and I agreed to try again after our separation. They couldn't even talk yet, but I was sitting there trying to explain to my two babies how Mommy and Daddy were going to live together again. And I'm ashamed to admit it, but part of me wanted to jump in the truck and run like hell." He looks at me. "Things were never good between Meghan and me, and all it took was a few months of living in the same house again for us both to fully accept that we were never supposed to be together. We went forward with the divorce, and that was it."

I exhale, feeling past pain that I've been holding onto finally disappear. "Thanks for showing me the house, and I truly appreciate your honesty. But I don't need to talk about it anymore. I'm just so grateful we have a second chance, Jenson."

He brings me into his chest. "Me too."

CHAPTER TWENTY

Now that Jenson has his own place, it's easier for us to spend time together. It's also easier for us to sleep together, which we do quite often over the next few weeks.

When his sons are with him, we all go to the park with Bernie, we go out for pizza, or we cook at home. We put the boys to bed after reading them a story, and then Jenson and I stay on his couch and make out like high schoolers until I leave for my own house.

Jenson's busy game planning for Randolph's first game of the season, but he takes time out to arrange to meet Donald Waverly at a coffee shop in Philadelphia.

"I told him I decided I was interested in buying a house. For me and my fiancée."

"Oh, no." I put my hands on my hips. "Why did you bring me into it?"

"Because I want you there, too." He gives me a shy smile. "Can you make it to Philly tomorrow morning at eight-thirty? I'll drop you off at work as soon as we're finished."

I put my hand on his cheek, enjoying the feel of his sexy

stubble. "Of course. So you didn't tell him who you are yet, right?"

"No." He kisses me. "I'll see what I think of him first."

———

On the way to meet Donald Waverly, Jenson misses the exit three times. Three times we get off the highway an exit late, turn around, and get back on, only to drive right past the exit again.

"Freaking hell," Jenson says as we careen off onto the ramp.

"Why don't I drive the rest of the way?" I suggest.

I don't know that I've ever seen Jenson this frazzled. He's always so in control of his emotions, but going to meet Donald has him understandably thrown off.

Jenson pulls into a fast food parking lot, and we switch seats. As I put his truck into drive and we start back onto the highway, I say, "It will be okay, J."

———

Thirty minutes later, I sit next to Jenson in a booth at the Freedom Coffee House with Donald Waverly across from us. He's got a full head of gray hair, thick eyebrows, and Jenson's green eyes. He's outgoing and friendly and intent on enticing Jenson and me into buying a home in Philadelphia.

"So how long have you two been engaged?" he asks as he pours three creamers in a row into his coffee.

I can't stop staring at the cream disappearing into the black steaming coffee in his cup. And I can't believe the three of us ordered hot coffees in this heat. I really should have asked for iced.

"Just a month," Jenson says. "But we've always known we'd get married someday."

"Well, congratulations." Donald opens four sugars at once and pours them into his cup of coffee.

"Thank you." Jenson keeps his hands around his cup of coffee but doesn't come close to taking a sip.

"There are so many great options in Philly these days," Donald says. "Me, being a single guy with no kids, I live in an awesome condo with panoramic views. There are clubs right down the block and plenty of places to eat. Now, for you two, being on the verge of marriage, partying and nightlife may not be what you're looking for."

I clear my throat. "Right. Probably not."

———

After we say goodbye to Donald, Jenson and I return to his truck, and he pulls out of the parking lot.

"He's a grown man, and he talks like he's still afraid that a wife and kids will tie him down," he says as we hit the highway.

"Jenson..."

His jaw clenches. "He's rich and single and does whatever the hell he wants. He's kind of a mess, Olive."

His profile is still filled with tension, and I don't know how to help him.

"Maybe you could use some time alone," I suggest as we enter Liberty Falls. "You can call me later."

But he insists on coming into the house with me to pick up Bernie for the day. We spend the first ten minutes being slobbered on by Bernie, who acts like we've been gone for a month rather than two hours.

"I'll take you to work, babe," he says.

"Do you want to talk about it? I can take the rest of the morning off."

"I'm okay."

"I get it, J, more than you know. You're tired of living with this secret buried inside of you. I've had a secret, too, one that I'm sick and tired of hiding from the world, which is not being able to shout, 'I love Jenson Beau,' from the rooftops of every building."

Jenson takes my hands in his.

I hold his gaze. "Meeting your biological father was kind of like meeting the man behind the dark curtain at a puppet show. He's holding the strings because he's the point where all the different threads connect for you. If he hadn't disappeared, my father wouldn't have made you an unofficial Graham. A secret father is a hard thing to carry, and other than you, I know that better than anyone."

I want to be the strong one who stays calm and lets Jenson have his space because this is his story. But my story became inextricably linked to his a long time ago, and my emotions are all over the place.

Jenson pulls me into his chest and holds me close. "You're right. About everything. Let's go inside."

We settle Bernie in the living room with a toy and then go to my bedroom. Jenson pulls back the covers, lifts me up, and lays me down on the bed. He takes off everything but his boxers and climbs in next to me. "I'm going to love you," he says as he pulls the sheets over us, and I rest my head on his chest, "forever." He lightly traces my lips with his finger. "My whole life flashes before my eyes, Olivia, when you touch me. And I want that always. I love you."

I start trembling. "J..."

"I love you," he repeats firmly. "I don't know why this is how it happened, why this is our love story..." He draws in a shaky breath. "But it is. It's our story. Everybody has a story to tell. And this is ours."

———

Jenson

I go for a long run after I leave Olivia's house, and then I bring Bernie, Kyle, and Connor to the park. We spend over an hour tossing Bernie a ball until all three little guys are exhausted.

Kyle sacks out on my chest, and I sit down with my back against a tree, cuddling Connor next to me. Bernie happily flops down in front of us and goes to sleep.

"I love you, Daddy," Connor says sleepily.

I kiss his head. "Love you too, Con."

"What about me?" Kyle says, too tired to even keep his eyes open. "Do you love me, too, Daddy?"

I chuckle. "Remember what I tell you every night when I tuck you into bed, or when I call before you go to sleep at Mommy's?"

"You say you love us, no matter how near or far, and you always will."

I hug him close to me. "That's right. And I always mean it."

Within seconds, both boys are sound asleep. I doze off for a minute or two myself, enjoying the peace and quiet. Nobody else is at the park, and the sun is shining.

Only one person is missing. Olivia. My heart.

As soon as Kyle and Connor wake up, I urge them up.

"Come on, boys." I take them each by the hand and let Kyle hold Bernie's leash. "We're going on an errand."

"Where?"

"To the jewelry store."

"Why?" Kyle demands.

"To get something I should have gotten a long time ago."

By the time we reach the store, Kyle's in my arms, and Connor insists he wants to sit on the bench outside.

"You sit right here by the window where I can see you," I instruct him. "And keep Bernie with you, okay?"

I walk into the store with Kyle, knowing exactly what I want.

"Daddy!" Kyle squirms in my arms as I carry him through the building. "Why are we here?"

"I'm buying someone a present," I say. "We'll just be a minute, buddy."

I put Kyle down as I stop at the counter and nod hello at the saleswoman.

"Do you know what you want?" she asks me.

"Yes," I say. "I know exactly what I want. It has to be custom-made, though."

"Not a problem, sir. We have a jeweler on site, and he can get started right away."

"What's cupsom?" Kyle asks as he tugs at my shirt.

"It means there's only one like it," I say. *Just like her.*

Olivia

A couple days after meeting Donald, Jenson invites me over for dinner. As soon as we've put Kyle and Connor to bed, we snuggle on his couch, and he pulls a jewelry box out of his pocket and puts it on my lap.

I look up at him and joke, "You're proposing? Don't you think we should deal with some other things first?"

His green eyes sparkle. "It's not an official engagement ring. Not yet. But you can think of it like that."

I put my hand on his cheek before carefully opening the box on my lap.

I gasp at the beautiful ring inside. It's got tiny diamonds around the top half and is a pretty white gold.

"This is beautiful." I lift it out of the box. "You know exactly what I love, J."

"You showed me before," he reminds me, his eyes intense on mine.

My heart comes up into my throat. "But that was a long time ago. We were still in high school."

"But I never forgot." He leans forward until our foreheads touch. "I never forgot a single thing you told me, Olive."

"It's so perfect for me." I turn away from him in an effort to rein in my emotions, which are getting the best of me. Tears are threatening behind my eyes, and I try to force them back. "I keep thinking I'm going to wake up, and you'll be back in Pittsburgh, and I'll be here."

"Olive." Jenson takes my chin in his hand firmly. "Listen to me. Everything we're doing is for real. Just because we've decided not to let people in on our reality yet doesn't make it any less true."

I hold out my hand, and he slips the ring on my finger. It fits perfectly.

I lean in and give Jenson a long kiss. "I love it. I love you."

———

Later that week, the Wilds and their significant others fly into town. The Cougars play a preseason game against Philadelphia, and Dylan and Colton were nice enough to give Jenson a block of tickets. Because it's preseason, the players have a little more leeway than they normally do during the regular season, so Jenson's organized for everyone to come to his house the night before the game for a cook-out.

The Wilds mean so much to Jenson, and they always will.

And they're all really good guys—I just want things to feel natural between us.

"Did you tell Ayden and Cam about us?" I ask Jenson in a low voice as we stand by the grill and wait for everyone to arrive.

Connor and Kyle are bouncing around the backyard, throwing a football and then practicing how to spike it. They'll stay for a couple of hours, and then Cindy's going to come by and take them to her house for the night.

"No, and I'm not going to say anything with the boys here." Jenson runs his hand down my back. "Don't worry. All the Wilds remember you fondly."

The back door flings open, and Colton's blinding smile is all I can see.

"J, nice place!" He jogs down the few steps to the yard and flings an arm around Jenson.

He brings him in close for a hug, and I step back to give them space. But Colton turns and wraps me up in a hug as well.

"So good to see you again," he says, his blue eyes bright with an emotion I can't decipher.

"Thanks, Colt." I swallow as I remember the last time I saw him in the hospital nursery. I don't know if he ever told Jenson we chatted then, and I never brought it up. "It's been a long time."

"It has." He leans in close to me. "And I still remember exactly what I said to you the last time we saw each other. Do you?"

His eyes study me as he waits to see how I respond.

I break into a soft laugh. "Yes, I do. You were quite the optimist as always."

"Hey, looks like I was right."

He glances back at Jenson, who's raising an eyebrow at him.

"So Olivia," Colt adds as he waves his hand to someone, "You haven't met Skylar yet."

A beautiful redhead with creamy white skin and a friendly face approaches us. Her pink and yellow sundress hugs her curves, and she walks slowly toward us as she eyes me curiously.

When she reaches us, Colton kisses her temple and puts his arm around her. "This is my wife, Sky. This is Olivia, Jenson's best friend since they were babies."

Sky shakes my hand warmly. "Yay! More women to help balance out all this testosterone."

Before I can answer her, what sounds like a stampede of elephants storms Jenson's backyard. Ayden walks toward us holding hands with a pretty blond woman, Brayden and Cameron follow close behind, and Dylan is last. All the guys are wearing jeans and t-shirts that stretch across their broad chests. They saunter through the yard casually, confidently, like they're used to being stared at. They make quite a pack, and even though he's bringing up the rear, Dylan is clearly the leader.

He's carrying two six-packs of beer in one hand, and his free arm is around a tall woman with long legs that never end. She could easily pass for a model.

"That's Jasalie, Dylan's wife," Sky says to me. "Isn't she intimidating?"

"She really is," I say.

"She's so freaking nice, though," Sky gushes. "And she knows self-defense. She could literally take out an attacker if she had to. Dylan's head over heels for her."

That's obvious. He and Jasalie seem perfectly matched and not just because she's the only woman here who's nearly on his height level. She's wearing black skinny jeans, matching black heels, and a hot pink spaghetti-strap top. Like her husband, she really is flawless looking like she just wakes up beautiful. Dylan gently brushes his lips to her blond hair as she laughs.

He gives me a kiss on the cheek and introduces me to Jasalie.

She shakes my hand and glances from me to Jenson. "You two are..."

"Old friends," Dylan says quickly, and I send him a grateful glance. "We all met Olivia years ago as kids."

"That's so cool," Jasalie says, her guarded expression dropping some. "It's nice to meet you."

"Hey!" Cam and Ayden greet Jenson, who brings me close. "You remember Olivia, right?" he says.

Ayden's blue eyes flash with recognition. "Of course. You were one of the best parts of coming to visit Liberty Falls. You were always fun to hang out with." He introduces me to Bella, his girlfriend, who smiles shyly. Bella's dressed casually like me, in blue cut-offs and a simple tank. I like her immediately.

Cam surprises me by picking me up in a tight hug. "It's been years, hasn't it?" he says.

"It has." I marvel at how grown up Cam is. His dark hair and eyes, plus that mouth that constantly looks like it's trying not to laugh, make a lethal combination. "I think the last time I saw you, you were fourteen or fifteen and already in a serious relationship."

Cam chuckles and waves a hand in the air. "Done. All done."

"Really?"

"High school love. Didn't last." He grabs a chip out of the bowl by the grill and pops it into his mouth.

"I'm sorry."

"Don't be." His eyes flash with mischief. "I'm done with anything serious. For a long, long time. Trust me."

The guys all want a tour of Jenson's house, and Kyle and

Connor insist they do too. Cam lifts Kyle onto his shoulders, Brayden does the same with Connor, and all six men disappear into the house.

I don't know what to do with myself once they're gone. I busy myself at the grill, which I told Jenson I'd keep an eye on until he returned.

When I look up from the steaks, Bella, Jasalie, and Sky are all watching me from the opposite side of the grill.

"Um, hi," I say awkwardly. I gesture to the bowl of chips. "Please help yourselves. There's salsa and cheese over there."

"Yum." Sky grabs a chip as she says casually, "We didn't mean to make you uncomfortable, Olivia."

"Oh, you didn't," I lie.

Three beautiful, curious faces stare back at me.

"So." Jasalie speaks first. "You and Jenson."

My mouth drops open at her bluntness.

Sky breaks into a fit of giggles, and she gives Jasalie a little shove. "You're making her blush!"

Jasalie's expression softens. "I'm so sorry," she says to me. "I didn't mean to pry."

"I just haven't heard of Jenson dating anyone serious since his divorce," Bella explains.

I nod, not knowing what to say to that.

"Are you and Jenson..." Bella pauses, her voice hitching as she hesitates. "Together?"

I let out a deep breath. "You all seem really nice," I say. "So I don't mean to be evasive. But things are more complicated than just giving you a simple answer to that question."

Sky's eyes widen. "Holy crap. We're making you really uncomfortable with all these questions, aren't we?"

I crack a smile. "You could say that."

"My boyfriend and I just moved across the country, and we've only been dating for a few weeks," Bella offers up. "Can't get much more 'surprise!' than that."

"How do you like L.A. so far?" I ask her, loving her for changing the topic away from me.

"I love it in its own quirky, unique way. I lived there once before, but for Ayden, this is all brand-new. He's still adjusting."

"So you all live in L.A."

All three women smile and nod.

"It's awesome having girlfriends around," Sky says. "You should definitely come out and visit us sometime, Olivia. I'm from Connecticut, and the west coast is a breath of fresh air from the long, cold winters of the northeast."

"That would be really nice, thank you," I say.

———

Jenson

After Mom picks up Kyle and Connor, the get-together becomes a little more adult-friendly. Cam and Ayden get involved in a drinking contest with the beers Dylan brought but can't drink because he has a game tomorrow, and Sky decides to try to outdrink them.

Olivia's laughing, but she's standing back, almost on the periphery of the group.

I put my arm around her and say quietly, "This is supposed to be fun."

"I know." An emotion passes through her eyes. She masks it quickly but not fast enough.

"You're sad." I run my thumb over her hip.

"It's stupid."

"It's not stupid. Tell me."

"I wish I could have known them better." She gestures toward the group, but I already knew where she was going. "They're all so nice, and kind, and funny. And they love you so much, J. It makes me realize how much time we lost."

I pull her into my arms. "We're not going to lose anymore. You'll have years and years to hang out with these crazy guys and their partners; so much that you'll get sick of them."

She leans in close to me, and I kiss her head.

When I hear the sudden silence, I shift slightly so that I'm facing everyone.

Yep. Just as I thought.

Every last one of them is staring at us. Cam and Ayden most of all. Only Colton seems at ease; he leans against the nearby tree and crosses his legs at the ankles. His expression's calm like none of this is a big deal.

And the thing is, it isn't. The big deal is the woman to my right.

I gesture toward Olivia. "Olivia's not really my cousin as you know. And the truth is, I'm in love with her. I have been forever."

Cam points from me to her. "I knew something was going on...you two always had that damn chemistry. I couldn't just come out and ask you, though..."

"You knew?" Dylan asks him. "How did you know?"

Cam shrugs. "I was with someone young, so I guess I got young love. Jenson and Olivia always looked like a couple to me. Or two people who should be a couple."

Ayden jerks his chin toward me. "You two okay? Because you seem stressed."

Keeping my arm around Olivia, I say, "Our families don't know. We don't expect them to be super supportive. Olivia's father is the mayor of this town. He's running for re-election this fall, and the residents look at me as her cousin. They don't take to change very well."

"We're your family too," Sky says. "And we're a hundred percent supportive."

Everyone nods.

"That is so sweet," Olivia says softly.

Cam raises his beer and points it at us. "To you two," he says. "The newest couple in our group. Bray, you and I are going to be partying alone soon. All these losers getting hitched and growing up and shit. When did that happen?"

Brayden grabs a fresh beer and clicks it to Cam's. "To staying single," he says solemnly.

"One of you will have a date to Dylan and Jasalie's wedding renewal," Sky says confidently. "I have a strong hunch. You could call me psychic."

Cam shakes his head emphatically. "No way. Won't be me."

"Me neither." Brayden backs away from Sky like he's allergic to her prophesy, and we all laugh.

CHAPTER TWENTY-ONE

Olivia

The rest of the week passes in a blur of football, more football, and wedding stuff.

Going to the Cougars game in Philly is fun. Colton gets us seats behind the team bench, so instead of being in a box, we're super close to all the action. Hearing Kyle and Connor scream out, "Uncle Dylan" and "Uncle Colton" whenever either of them touches the football makes the experience worth it on its own. The Cougars win the preseason game by a touchdown, and Dylan delivers two game footballs—both signed by a bunch of the players—to Kyle and Connor before he and Colton have to leave for the team plane.

Three days later and the night before Sheldon and Cara's wedding, I walk down the stairs of Randolph's football stadium with Hayley and Max.

Our seats are on the sideline, and Hayley clutches my hand in excitement.

"We're so close!" she squeals. "I don't know a thing about football, but I'm stoked."

So am I. Randolph's first game of the season and my first

time in a while seeing Jenson coach. I went to a few games with my family when he coached in Pittsburgh and his team came to Philly, but obviously he and I weren't together then. So when I saw him afterward, it was always awkward and painful.

This is a whole new game. My smile's so big as we head for our seats I'm sure the entire stadium can tell how happy I am.

We take seats at the end of the row, right next to Kyle and Connor, who are with Cindy and Dee. My parents are on their other side, along with Sheldon and Cara, and Daphne and her family.

"Livia!" Connor grabs my hand. "Daddy's out on the field. Do you see him?"

I do. My pulse picks up as I watch Jenson striding through the field as he chats with players as they warm up. He's wearing a gold and maroon Randolph sweatshirt and black pants. His shaggy blond hair is blowing in the wind. He takes the football from one of the guys and steps back to deliver a laser to another player about forty yards away. The ball spirals through the air perfectly before landing in the player's outstretched hands.

"Shit, he's still got it," Max says admiringly from the other side of Hayley.

He sure does.

"He's gorgeous," Hayley whispers in my ear.

Jenson turns and looks up over at our section. He and I lock eyes, and he grins as he puts his hand to his ear.

I know what that signal means. So while he's waving at Kyle and Connor, who are bouncing up and down and calling out to him, I check my phone.

A single text.

Love you. See you after.

Five words that mean everything. Because every other

game I've been to, we couldn't see each other after. Our feelings for each other were lost in the sea of family and
obligation.

But this time, tonight, we're changing all of that. Even if
we're keeping it private, we're together, and that means
everything.

———

As soon as the game starts, the butterflies in my stomach are
huge, and they just get worse as the game proceeds.

Randolph gets on the board first, but the Saints score on
the kickoff return, and the coaching staff for Randolph is
screaming on the sideline.

"What are they so angry about?" Hayley asks me.

"The refs missed a holding call on the return team," I
explain. "And now the game's tied because of it."

"You know this stuff?" She looks at me like I'm a
complete stranger to her. "I didn't know you understood
football."

I laugh. "I grew up with Jenson. He made sure I understood football, believe me."

Like he hears me, Jenson glances up from the bench. He
gives me the thumbs-up, and my irritation over the missed
call disappears.

"The Hawks are going to be okay," I say to Hayley. "Jenson
has a great game plan."

Sure enough, the Hawks score on their next possession.
They march right down the field with a variety of pass and
run plays.

But they can't stop the Saints from scoring, and by the
end of the first half, the game is tied 21-21. Jenson jogs off the
field with the rest of the team, but he makes sure to wave up
at us before disappearing into the tunnel.

He smiles, but his jaw is tight. I know how much this game means to him; to get win one under his belt with a new team, and to do it in the backyard of where he grew up, is an important homecoming for him.

"Football games are so stressful!" Hayley says. "I'm going to get something to eat. You want anything?"

"I'm good," I tell her.

I turn to Kyle and Connor. "Your dad's doing a great job with the offense. Smith looks fantastic."

"But the game's tied," Kyle says with a frown. "We want to win."

"It's a long way from over, boys," I say. "I have a feeling your dad's got a few tricks up his sleeve. And hopefully, Randolph can stop the Saints from scoring, huh?"

The second half goes quickly, and with two minutes left in regulation, the score is tied yet again at 42 all.

"Randolph has the ball, so they've got a great chance to win," I say to Kyle and Connor.

"This is going to be awesome!" Kyle says enthusiastically as he stands up and starts shouting "Go Hawks!"

Randolph makes it to the fifty-yard line, but then forward progress stalls. Before I can blink, it's fourth down with only twelve seconds left in the game.

"Last chance," I murmur to no one in particular. "Come on."

I clench my hands together on my lap as I watch Jenson call the next play into his headset. Smith takes the snap, drops back, and rolls to the right. Jenson's shouting from the sideline now, and Smith shifts left and throws without hesitation.

Emery, the wide receiver, breaks off a crossing route, sheds his defender, and bolts downfield. I can hear the rush of energy from the crowd as the ball arcs through the air, angling down toward a wide-open Emery.

Hayley shouts next to me about how fast he is, but my attention is back on Jenson as he runs up the sideline next to Emery. Jenson keeps pace as Emery catches the ball and heads for the end zone.

The crowd erupts when he crosses the goal line.

He spikes the ball, and Jenson pumps a fist in the air. Time runs out on the clock as Randolph wins 48-42.

Smith runs off the field and leaps into Jenson's arms.

"Hot," Hayley says next to me. "That was an awesome ending."

"Can we go see Daddy now?" Kyle tugs on my shirt sleeve.

I look at the field filled with media, coaches, and players.

"Let's wait a little bit," I say. "It's really crowded out there. We'll see him really soon."

———

Jenson

I move through the locker room, congratulating our players on the hard-fought win. I take questions from the media, and Dee brings Kyle and Connor in so they can share in the moment.

My boys have just left when Calvin, the annoying-ass reporter, steps out from the corner and beckons to me.

"Olivia's outside waiting for you." His tone is neutral, but the gleam in his eyes isn't.

Making sure to keep my expression blank, I give him a quick nod and turn to leave.

"Jenson." He steps uncomfortably close to me. "I'd be careful if I were you. Randolph's board members are as conservative as our town's residents."

Hoping he's just fishing to see if he hits a target, I say coolly, "And your point is?"

"I think you know what my point is." Calvin rubs his

thumb over his lip. "I wouldn't kiss and tell if I were you. For example, if you're in the trees by the skateboarding park, say during the annual fair? I'd maybe be a little more careful about who I bring into the woods with me. Because not everyone's going to be as understanding..."

My jaw's turned to steel, and it's all I can do not to punch this guy out. "Calvin, you have no idea what you're dealing with here."

"I think I actually have a pretty damn good idea." He smirks. "And you could lose everything if you keep acting on your impulses. I'm a reporter, not a confidante. And there's only so long I'll keep quiet for."

"What do you want?" I ask him. "Because if you didn't want something, you wouldn't give a shit about threatening me."

"I want the one thing I've never gotten with this paper—a front-page story." He shrugs callously. "And I don't personally care who I have to take down to get it."

I lean in close to him, my hand on his shoulder like I'm casually telling him something. But my intent is clear, and Calvin's eyes widen the closer I get.

"You want some advice?" I say in a deadly-calm voice. "Stay the fuck out of my private life. Because if you cross that line, I swear to God, you'll regret it for the rest of your life. Your career as a reporter will be over."

I leave the locker room, determined to talk to Olivia.

But before I can even look for her—

"Jenson!" Sheldon calls out from behind the metal gate where he's standing with Max and Todd. "My bachelor party starts now! Let's go!"

———

Olivia

Cindy and Dee take Kyle and Connor home with them for the night so Jenson can hang out with Sheldon and his wedding party. Max goes with them, and Hayley and I take Bernie with us to the coffee shop and proceed to drink far too much caffeine.

"I don't want to keep things quiet about Jenson and me anymore," I confess. "I want to go public. No matter what happens or how much it upsets the apple cart of Liberty Falls and our families, I want to take that risk. I need to."

"Any other day, I would say 'yay!' But Sheldon and Cara are getting married tomorrow night," Hayley points out. "Just because Cara hates bachelorette parties and isn't having a pre-wedding soiree doesn't make her wedding any less real. And assuming your families will need a little time to adjust to the news? It could ruin the night."

"God, you're right. I can't run the risk of wrecking Sheldon's night. It'll be okay. We can wait a little longer."

Hayley laughs. "Speaking of...look who just walked in."

I turn on the couch and lock eyes with Jenson walking toward us.

Hayley gives me a hug. "I'm going home. See you tomorrow at the wedding."

I wave goodbye to her and invite Jenson to join me on the couch. He pats Bernie, who whines happily.

"I thought you'd be out with my brother," I say.

"Sheldon's friends are cool, but they plan on going all night at the bar." He stretches out his jeans-clad legs on the coffee table. "I'd rather hang out with you."

I smile at him. "And I'd rather hang out with you. Let's go to my house."

We don't say much as we walk slowly through town, but as soon as we're inside my house, Jenson says abruptly, "Calvin confronted me after the game. He knows."

My skin goes cold. "What do you mean?"

"About us, Olive. He made some insinuation about kissing someone in the woods during the fair."

"I saw him!" I say, remembering the movement I'd noticed. "Right before Auntie Sue's accident. I was going to mention it to you, but I forgot about it."

He puts his arm around me, and we sit on the couch in my living room. Bernie settles at our feet.

"I wonder how close he was to us that day."

"Why?"

"Because that was the same time I told you about Donald."

"Oh my God. You think he overheard that as well?"

Jenson shrugs. "Calvin's an ass. He just wants a story to bolster his career. But I've decided I'm going to tell my mom I met Donald. And when you're okay with it, I'm going to tell her about us."

"Are you sure?"

"Yes. Hopefully she'll be able to handle it. I won't share her secret with anyone because that's her story to tell. But I can damn sure tell my story to her." He pauses and tips my chin so we're staring into each other's eyes. His expression looks exactly like I feel: excited and hopeful. "Are you ready to tell your parents?" he asks me softly.

I nod. "Something changed when we met Donald. Something important. I'm ready."

He puts his mouth over mine.

"What do you think they'll all say?" I whisper into his lips.

Jenson's hand is rubbing my back in small circles. "It'll be town gossip until the next big secret comes out. It'll blow over. These things always do." His mouth brushes mine again. "We're not doing anything wrong, Olive. We've never done anything wrong. So let's tell this freaking world of Liberty Falls what we've been so afraid of and let them stare at us. I don't give a shit about any of it. All I want is you."

My phone lights up with a text. I glance down at the screen. "Daphne says she needs to talk to me tomorrow at the wedding. I wonder what that's about."

Jenson shakes his head. "Sheldon said something about her needing to rekindle the magic she and Todd once had." He furrows his brow. "I don't remember that magic, do you?"

I wave my hand in the air. "You know the two of them used to do it in the town park at night when no one was around. On the slide or something."

"Weren't they in high school then?"

"Yes, but my sister said she sometimes still wants to be eighteen. I get it. She and Todd are having some issues right now."

"I'm sorry to hear that."

"Do you want to get married again?" I say softly.

"I want to get married again if you'll be the woman standing across from me at the altar," he says, and my heart melts. "Or the courthouse, or the beach. Wherever we do it. As long as I'm with you, Olivia, I'm exactly where I want to be."

CHAPTER TWENTY-TWO

Jenson and I finally go to bed, but I sleep fitfully. I'm worried about Calvin telling my family before I have the chance to. When I wake up for the third time, I get out of bed quietly and grab my cell phone. I take it to the bathroom, sit on the floor with my back against the tub, and call Sheldon.

He answers on the fourth ring. "What's up, little sister?" I can hear music in the background.

"Not much. Just wanted to see how the boys' night out is going. I thought the bars closed by now."

"Yeah, they do." Sheldon's voice comes through the phone so loudly I'm afraid Jenson will hear it. "But McArthur's says they'll stay open as late as we want. Isn't that great?"

"Great," I say unenthusiastically. "And you'll be hung-over and nauseous for your wedding tomorrow."

"Oh, Olive, don't be such a downer," Sheldon says. "I can sleep till noon. That's the great thing about a night wedding."

I don't say anything. My throat tightens as I feel how real it all is, my brother's wedding, and I feel like a rebellious teenager hiding a boy her parents would disapprove of. I suddenly feel like I might scream and cry at the same time.

"Hey, what are you doing now?" Sheldon asks me.

"Just can't sleep, I guess."

"Why don't you come meet us for a drink?" Sheldon suggests. "You're like one of the guys, right?"

I sigh. "Sure. I suppose."

"See you in fifteen minutes." Sheldon's hung up before I can answer him.

I leave a note on the bed so Jenson won't worry if he wakes up and finds me gone, then I go get dressed.

————

When I arrive at the bar, I take a moment before walking through the doors to fix the bun I hastily fastened my hair into. My hair's a mess, really—I've been in bed for hours, tossing and turning. I take a breath and walk into the bar, not really sure of what I'm going to find. I've never been to a bachelor party before.

Sheldon and his group of seven are the only people here. The bartender looks up in surprise as I come through the door, but Sheldon calls out, "Hey, Olive! Come on, and get a beer!"

His face is flushed from the alcohol, but his blue eyes are mirthful. He gives me a drunken hug as soon as I reach him and makes sure I know everybody. Darryl, Finn, and Boo, his three best friends from high school; Cara's brother, Seth; and Daphne's husband, Todd, who can barely stand up straight. Darryl, who I've known since the third grade, immediately brings me into a conversation they're all having on politics.

"Oh, God," I say. "Politics and drinking are not a good mix."

But I get drawn in for over a half hour while I nurse a beer Sheldon throws into my hand. I come to my senses when I see Todd beginning a game of quarters.

I try to get Todd to quit drinking, but he won't hear of it. Then Sheldon calls me over to a table. "I'm getting hitched in less than twenty-four hours," he says to me, clinking his beer to mine. "Awesome, isn't it?"

I smile at him. "It is awesome. I'm happy for you."

I take a big sip of my beer and look out again at Todd and Seth playing quarters. I think of Jenson and of the conversation I had with him earlier that's caused me such a sleepless night. "So, you haven't run into any reporters tonight, have you?"

Sheldon clinks his beer to mine again. "Nope. I think they're all sleeping so they're well-rested for my wedding tomorrow. Not because of me but because the mayor's only son is getting married."

"Maybe you're right," I say slowly, hoping he's onto something and the media will be more focused on Sheldon than any sort of potential scandal.

"Of course I'm right. I'm brilliant when I'm drunk," he says.

I roll my eyes. "On that note, I think I'm going to go home."

"I'll come with you to your house!" Sheldon says.

I hear the panic in my voice even as I try to sound calm. "I'll drop you at your place, sure."

"No, let me stay on your couch."

"Won't Cara worry?"

"She's not home. She's at her mom's. Wedding tradition to sleep apart on the night before the big event."

"God, wedding traditions make no sense," I say. "You guys have lived together for two years, and now she pretends she's a virgin so you can 'deflower' her tomorrow night?"

"You're so cynical, Olive." Sheldon pulls playfully at the messy bun in my hair. "Let me come over. Like old times. We can sober up with black coffee on your front porch."

I don't have the heart to tell him I don't need sobering up. I'm plenty sober and have been all evening.

But as long as I can keep him on the porch or in the living room, and out of my bedroom, this should be okay. I agree because I can't think of a good reason to say no, and I know Cara will be relieved to hear Sheldon left with me rather than stayed out drinking until dawn.

———

I text Jenson as we're walking out of the bar, hoping against hope his phone will wake him and he'll read my warning to stay in the bedroom.

The television's on when we walk in the door, but Jenson's nowhere in sight. Panicked, I grab the dog leash and tell Sheldon to take a barking Bernie out to the porch.

"You left the TV on?" Sheldon says to me. "You're usually so anal."

Yes, I am usually. I look at him and shrug. "You caught me." I shove him and Bernie outside and tell him I'll be out with coffee.

Sheldon pokes his head back in the door. "Hey, I forgot you got a dog."

"Yep," I say, trying to sound casual. "His name is Bernie, after the coffee house."

"Cool," he says, but I know he won't stop there, and he doesn't. "You know, this is a very good sign, Olive."

I try to cut him off. "Uh-huh. Sure."

But Sheldon can't be stopped. "Usually when you get a dog, a partner isn't far behind. A dog can help you pick up a good guy this time, Olive."

"Great." I go to shut the door on him again, but he stops it with his foot.

"A lot of people get dogs to own with their partner," he continues. "But I guess you're one step ahead of the game, huh? You got the dog in place early."

"That I did." I push his foot out of the way. "Be out in five minutes."

I shut the door and then grab the spare set of sheets out of the linen closet and start to make up the large couch before I go find Jenson.

Looking back, I don't know why I made the decision I did. Obviously I should have found out where Jenson was first, and perhaps all that happened could have been avoided. But I was intent on making up the couch, and it ends up taking me a few minutes longer than I planned.

When I hear Sheldon call out, "Jenson Beau! What the hell are you doing peeing in my sister's toilet?" I cringe.

I hear the toilet flush. I don't want to walk around the corner to the guest bathroom. But I do it. Jenson's in his boxers, thank God, but nothing else.

Shit.

"Jenson!" Sheldon's so drunk he doesn't seem phased by Jenson's underwear-only attire. "What are you doing here?"

Jenson's eyes flash with panic, and he turns to me.

"Jenson's drunk, too. Wasted," I say quickly, the lie coming off my tongue a little too easily. "He locked himself out of his house and can't find his keys. So I told him to take a cab over here."

Sheldon looks from Jenson to me and back to Jenson. For one horrifying second, I'm certain he's going to guess the truth. And if I'm truly honest with myself, a tiny piece of me is relieved that the secret will finally be out.

But Sheldon breaks into a laugh. "I was wondering why you left my party early. Did those rum shots go straight to your head?"

"Straight to it," Jenson gets out. "Great party, though, Sheldon."

Sheldon grins. Then he says, "But where were you sleeping?"

"In my bed," I say quickly. "He was sick. I was on the couch."

I point to the bed I just made on the couch, hoping Sheldon won't remember it wasn't there five minutes ago.

He doesn't, and the secret continues.

"See, you're the cousin, so you get special treatment," Sheldon teases Jenson. "I'm just the brother, and I always get the couch."

"Ha, ha," I say. "I'll make up the smaller couch for you, Sheldon. Go use the bathroom."

I drag Jenson into the bedroom. While he throws on his jeans and t-shirt, I whisper into his ear, "Didn't you get my note and text?"

"I got your note," he whispers back as he kisses my neck. "But no text."

We walk quietly out to the porch to check on Bernie, who's sleeping through this whole charade. I close the door behind us so Jenson and I can talk privately.

"I woke up, got your note, and decided to wait up for you in the living room," Jenson explains in a low voice. "That's why the TV was on, and I was using the main bathroom."

"Didn't you hear Sheldon when we walked inside?"

"No," he says. "I must have been in the bedroom at that point. I went in there to grab my shirt. Which I obviously didn't quite get on," he adds as I throw up my hands.

Sheldon opens the door and nearly dances out to us. "This is so cool! I get to spend the wee hours before my wedding with my favorite sister and cousin. And you're 'friend-dating' to my wedding! You guys make the perfect pair."

I know my face must be bright red, so I turn for the door, saying I'll be out with coffee.

———

The three of us go to sleep eventually with my brother and me on the living room couches and Jenson in my bed. I don't want to even try dissecting that little fucked-up triangle, and I fall into a fitful sleep.

The next morning, Jenson leaves early to go see Kyle and Connor. I wake up Sheldon a couple hours later and send him home to shower and eat so he'll be ready for tonight.

I get dressed in a cream strapless slinky dress that I pair with a matching silk scarf. I hadn't planned to wear the scarf, but Jenson and I got a little carried away last night, and he gave me quite a love bite on my neck. Since my family thinks I'm as single as I've ever been, I don't think advertising a hickey at Sheldon's wedding is the way to tell them about my love life. So, scarf it is. I pin my hair up into a twisted bun and wear pearl-drop earrings to match my dress color.

And then before I know it, Jenson and I are at my brother's wedding. I watch Sheldon and Cara exchange rings at the altar, and I put my arm around Mom when she cries. Daphne cries too, on my other side, and whispers to me, "Our only brother's all grown up now."

I smile at her and nod, but I don't get it. It's just a legal exchange, for goodness sake. Sheldon's been "grown up" for a while now.

Jenson and I follow the group of guests down Main Street to the reception. We take the elevator to the rooftop of The Lounge and clap when Sheldon and Cara are introduced as husband and wife for their first dance.

I spend some time chatting to Auntie Sue, who looks

paler than usual. When I ask Matilda about it, she says the doctors cleared her mother to come tonight and that she wouldn't have missed it for the world.

Auntie Sue turns to look at me, and for a moment, I swear she sees into my heart. She knows who I want to marry and what my wedding would look like if I could have one right now. And she nearly smiles.

I give her a big hug before Dad beckons me onto the dance floor.

I dance with Dad and then Sheldon, and finally Jenson pulls me over for a dance.

"You look fucking gorgeous," he says into my hair.

"Thank you." I tilt my head at his black tie. "So do you."

We talk and laugh while we're on the dance floor, but I feel a million miles away from him. I feel the hundreds of pairs of eyes around me even though nobody's paying a bit of attention to us. Jenson squeezes my hand to get me to look at him, and I force a smile. But he keeps grinning at me until I laugh, and the tension breaks.

And keeping the secret ends up being fun, in a way. It feels illicit and daring to make out behind the tree in the pavilion and then walk back into the hall like nothing's happened.

Sheldon and Cara are hanging out at an empty table, and he calls us over.

"Hey, you two," he says as we sit down. "How's the friend-date working out?"

"Fine," I say with a casual shrug. "With two divorces between us, we couldn't be expected to find decent dates last minute."

When I realize that Sheldon's mind is currently nowhere near me and my dating issues, I relax. My brother is one hundred percent distracted by his other sister's love life.

"Have you seen Daphne and Todd? They were fighting on the dance floor in front of all the cameras."

Jenson tries to urge him to lower his voice, but Sheldon can't be contained.

"I feel bad," he says. "It's like Daphne went to a wedding and got lonely."

I stop fiddling with my hair to stare at him. He's right. I turn to scour the crowd for Daphne. I don't see her anywhere. Sheldon's still rambling on about weddings, about how much pain they can cover up and that, if you're not careful, you'll soon find yourself lost in the middle of a reality you didn't want to be lost in. I excuse myself and walk toward the dance floor, hoping to catch a better view of the crowd.

I finally spot Daphne. She's off in the corner, talking to Mom. I head over and insert myself into their conversation.

Mom's talking about the weather, never a good sign. "... slight potential of thunderstorms next week. It would mean loads of lightning and tons of water. There could be flooding off Main Street if Mother Nature plays it just right."

I nod politely as Mom turns to me. "Olivia, you need to keep your eyes open for that rain," she says soberly. "Your house is off Main, after all."

"It is off Main," I agree as I glance at Daphne. Her mouth is set in a thin line, and her hands are clenched at her sides; one more weather comment from Mom, and Daphne may very well slug her. "Mom, I think Dad's calling for you."

"Oh..." Mom turns to where I'm pointing and sees my father. He doesn't exactly look like he's calling for her, but when he turns to see us all staring at him, he waves and smiles. Mom gasps. "Thank you, Olivia," she says. "I don't know where my hearing's gone lately." She walks away, and I turn back to Daphne.

"Thanks for the save, Olive." She releases her fisted hands and exhales. "Mom was making me lose it."

"The ceremony was very nice. How are you doing?" I say to her.

"Great." She bites her lip so hard it bleeds. "Couldn't be better."

I take her arm. "Let's get some air. You know how I hate crowds."

When we reach the edge of the rooftop, in the back where there are no people, I reach over and hug my sister. "You look beautiful, Daph."

She makes a face as I step back and lean my elbow on the guardrail. "No, I don't," she says. "And you know it. You must have seen Todd and me fighting. I'm so embarrassed to do that to Dad during his campaign year."

"It's okay. Honestly, I didn't notice. I'm telling you the truth."

"What has you so preoccupied?"

I fidget with the scarf around my neck, accidentally pulling it down just enough that Daphne gasps.

"Where'd you get that love bite?" she says suddenly, pointing at my neck.

I immediately cover it up again with my scarf. "Nowhere."

"Nowhere? What's that supposed to mean?"

I sigh. "It means it's private. For now. No offense."

Like Sheldon earlier, Daphne's too caught up in her own issues to push me about mine.

"You and your new lover, whoever he is, have these romantic secrets, and my husband doesn't even want to be with me. He sleeps in the guest room all the time now."

I stare at her. "The guest room? Why?"

She frowns. "It started when Amy was born. She needed to be fed all the time, of course, and so she stayed in our room at first. Todd was tired, and he had to be up early for work, so he started sleeping in the spare room to get his rest. But after Amy left our bedroom, he never came back to me."

She reaches into her purse and pulls out a cigarette. I haven't seen her smoke since she and Todd got married.

"You're smoking again?"

She lights up and blows smoke over the railing before speaking. "I hate to smoke. But I miss having something to do with my mouth. I miss having someone to kiss, to talk to, to fight with even. I miss being in a relationship."

My eyes fill with tears. At a loss for what to say, I look across the rooftop and see Jenson at the other end. He's at the bar, ordering a beer. He turns in that moment and spots me. He smiles that smile I adore and holds up his beer to me. I wave and turn back to Daphne as I feel the words come.

"It's too much pressure," I say to her. "Your whole life is too much pressure, Daph."

Her eyes water, and she takes the tissue I offer her.

"You've always felt like you had to be perfect, you know?" I say. "The happiest girl in high school, the top cheerleader with the best boyfriend, but also the girl who had the most fun and who loved to be a rebel. You can't be happy when you're trying too hard to be happy. It just doesn't work."

She dabs at her eyes, and dark mascara comes off onto the white tissue. I hand her another tissue. "You and Todd are both stressed out," I say. "He was slamming shots at Sheldon's bachelor party like he was still eighteen."

"You were there?"

I don't want her to get jealous that Sheldon didn't invite her. "Accidentally. And for about five minutes. Just long enough to drag Sheldon out of there."

"Can you drag me out of here?" Daphne says with a half-smile.

"Do you want to be dragged out?" I ask her seriously. "Because yes, I will help you leave discreetly if that's what you need."

She takes another puff of her cigarette and stares out over

the deck. "I don't know. I'm just upset tonight. It reminded me of my wedding. Todd and I met too young. We never learned how to be adults together. We just had kids and thought that would be enough to teach us how to grow up. And the thing is, they're two separate subjects—there's being husband and wife, and there's being parents."

As she's talking, Todd rounds the corner.

"Everything okay?" He looks first at my face and then at Daphne's.

I nod encouragingly at Daphne, who hesitates before saying, "No, not really."

Todd's eyes flash with concern, and he puts his hand on Daphne's arm. I excuse myself just as Todd says, "Can we talk about it, Daph?"

I walk over to the bar and order a beer. While I'm standing there, Sheldon comes up to me.

"Awesome. Two full beers!" He holds up his bottle.

I follow suit, and as I do, the scarf I was using to hide my neck slides off me and down to the ground.

And that's when Sheldon notices my hickey.

"Who's the guy?"

I flush so hot that even Sheldon can't miss it. His eyes bug out of his head, and he leans in close to my ear. "Why didn't you bring him tonight?"

Tears sting my eyes, and I surprise both of us when I reach out and put my arms around him.

"Hey." He holds me close. "Are you okay?"

I can't answer him because I truly don't know. I've risked more in the last month than I ever have in my life, and I'm not sure how my heart is holding up. Keeping Jenson a secret from my family has never proved harder than right now. I excuse myself from Sheldon and tell him we'll talk later.

On my way to find Jenson, I get waylaid by Mom and Veronica, Todd's mother.

"Olivia, don't you look lovely tonight," Veronica says as she gives me a hug.

"Thank you, so do you," I say. "If you'll excuse me..."

"And where's your date for the evening?" Veronica glances around the room.

Mom gasps. "That's right! I never asked if you brought someone." She looks at me expectantly. "Is it someone we know?"

"Well," I pause. "I...I brought Jenson. He and I are both currently unattached. It just made sense. He's my friend-date."

"So Jenson helped you out," Mom says with a knowing smile. "What a gentleman to do his cousin a favor when she's lonely. Isn't he so sweet?"

"Oh, isn't he good?" Veronica agrees. "I've only met him a handful of times before, but he stuck out in my mind. So handsome and so kind."

I nod and quickly excuse myself for the restroom.

I take my time and when I exit the bathroom, I hear low voices coming from the dark part of the hallway behind the stairwell.

"...I took care of Calvin."

I can't see who's talking, and I shift forward until I recognize Glenn's large form and white head of hair. His back is to me, and he's blocking his companion, who says—

"How?"

Jenson. Glenn's talking to Jenson about Calvin?

"Let's just say I've been at the paper a long time. And everyone's got some skeletons in their closet. I just happen to know what Calvin's are. And I told him if he breathes—or Christ, if he *writes*—so much as a word about you and Olivia, he'll wish he hadn't. Because if what I have on him gets out, he'd be fired faster than he could refute it."

"I appreciate you protecting Olivia like that, Glenn. We're not planning to keep quiet forever."

"You sure about this?" Glenn's tone turns to genuine concern. "Because I wasn't just protecting Olivia. I was looking out for you too. I hope you realize that if this comes out, your situation will be more precarious than hers."

Jenson doesn't say anything in response, but Glenn continues, "Randolph is a tight-knit school, and they pride themselves on a family-oriented community. I don't know how they'll react to this. And your mom...she was the outcast in town until the Grahams took her in. I'm worried how people will treat her."

"I am too," Jenson admits, and I flinch. "But Olivia's not my cousin, and you know it."

"I do, but this town's got a short memory and is big on gossip." Glenn puts his hand on Jenson's arm. "Olivia comes from the golden family. She'd come out of this okay in the long run. Her father may be pushed out as mayor, which I know they'd all take hard, but she shouldn't be too scathed on a personal level. But you...just think about it. Take your time before you act."

When he leaves, I step out from the stairwell and head for Jenson.

"J."

His green eyes widen. "Olive. Did you hear any of that?"

"Most of it."

"It's good news about Calvin." His expression is warm and calm.

"But not about you." My voice sounds cold to my own ears.

Jenson cocks his head. "What are you saying?"

"I'm saying what Glenn just said—you have far more to lose than I do."

"Your father could lose the election—you don't think

that's a lot to lose? Glenn's making no sense. We're in this together, Olivia, no matter what happens."

"But..."

"And no matter what happens," he repeats, "I'm never letting you go again."

CHAPTER TWENTY-THREE

"Jenson..." I flush with emotion. "I don't like the idea of you losing anything because of me."

He takes hold of my arms. "Do you really think a damn job is more important to me than you? I can do something else if I have to. As long as I can take care of my sons, I'm happy."

"You love football. It's in your blood. And I know how hard it is to get a coaching position. Openings don't just pop up every day. Maybe we should wait until the season ends..."

"Olive..."

We stop speaking as my mother hustles toward us from the other side of the rooftop.

"Oh, Olivia. Jenson." Mom's tone is clearly agitated, and we turn toward her immediately.

"Mom, are you okay?"

"Honey, Auntie Sue just went home to God. God rest her soul."

My breath catches in my throat. "Where is she?"

"She was sitting at the table with Matilda when she slumped over. Cara's uncle is a doctor, and he performed CPR right away. The paramedics have been called, but it's already too late. She's gone."

I feel hot tears burn my eyes.

Mom leaves us when Dad calls for her, and Jenson and I are alone.

"Auntie Sue must finally be feeling better than she's felt for a while now," Jenson says quietly as he kisses my cheek. "And we'll see her on the other side someday, you know?"

I nod at him through my tears.

This wedding quickly goes from a celebration to a mourning. Auntie Sue was my constant in the Graham family. She was everyone's constant. The matriarch who never flinched no matter what life threw at her. She was always there. Until now.

And what I overheard between Jenson and Glenn? That weighs on my already-heavy heart when the evening finally ends hours later and I drift off to sleep.

———

The next few days are filled with making arrangements for Auntie Sue's wake and funeral. Meghan takes the boys, but Jenson and I are never alone, and when he tries to make plans with me, I come up with excuses.

"Olive." His voice is terse as we separate from the rest of the family at the wake. "You're avoiding me."

"I'm sorry," I say. "I just...Glenn's warning threw me for a loop. I don't want you making a rash decision based on your feelings for me." The words catch in my throat. "I want you to take the time to think about what he said."

Before Jenson can respond, Sheldon walks in the door. He comes over and gives me a hug, and I know he won't be able to resist. Sure enough, his voice goes low as he mutters, "Olive, I didn't even know you were dating anybody. Or screwing anybody, for that matter. Whichever it is, you've really kept it quiet."

"Yeah." I pause. "It's been that way lately." I lift my left hand to brush my hair out of my eyes and tuck it behind my ear.

"Do you think you'll reveal the mystery guy someday?" Sheldon asks me as his gaze lights on my ring. "Looks more serious than just screwing, by the way."

He turns to fist bump Jenson. "So do you know anything about my little sister's love life?"

Jenson coughs and takes a sip of his tea before saying, "I don't think I'm the right person to be answering that question tonight, Sheldon."

Mom dances toward us. "Oh, Olivia! I almost forgot to tell you Will may stop by in a bit."

Sheldon's eyes get so big I think they may pop out of his head. He starts pointing at me. "Is it Will? Is that the guy?"

"No," I say firmly. "It is not. And Mom," I say to her. "You know I don't like Will. I told you what happened the one night I agreed to meet him."

Sheldon snaps his gaze from Mom to me. The confusion is written all over his face. He doesn't understand why I'm keeping a secret at my own expense. He knows I could shut Mom up quickly if I just told her I had a boyfriend, if I just showed her the ring I'm wearing. If he only knew.

I excuse myself and go kneel at Auntie Sue's casket alone.

Auntie Sue looks serene, much more at peace than the last hundred times I've seen her. She doesn't look like she's fighting so hard anymore to just...breathe.

Good-bye Auntie Sue. God bless you.

I look at the beautiful photograph Matilda placed on top of the casket. It's a picture of Auntie Sue when she was nineteen years old. The photo is a bit blurry and torn around the edges, but it's been perfectly framed, and Auntie Sue's face shines through the glass. Her eyes look so full of promise, so filled with hope and optimism.

I bow my head and thank her for holding up our family for all of these years.

"It can't have been easy," I say under my breath. "This is your time now."

———

Vivian comes to the wake to "pay her respects to the matriarch of your family." She runs into Dad's second cousin, Ed, whom she worked with years ago, and they end up sitting with me on the couch.

Jenson stops by, but a second later, Dad comes over and asks if we're doing okay.

"Fine, Dad," I say to him. "How are you?"

He kneels down next to Jenson. "These things are always difficult, aren't they?" he says as he pulls at his tie. "I can't imagine working in a funeral home."

"I'm with you on that," Jenson says.

A noise at the door gets our attention, and we all turn our heads to witness Daphne and Todd making their grand entrance. I say grand because they practically skip into the funeral parlor. They look like they barely had time to clean up after their latest roll in the hay, and I'm not exaggerating.

Dad gets called away by Cybil, and Jenson stands up to say hi to Daphne, who gives him a big hug before going to wait in line to see Auntie Sue.

"Not to be crude, but Daphne literally looks like she has semen in her hair," Jenson whispers as he squats down next to me.

I refuse to look in Daphne's direction. "Do not say that sentence aloud again," I say to him. "I forbid you."

Not more than a minute later, Sheldon kneels down next to Jenson and says the same thing.

"God, you boys have such dirty minds," I say just as Cara joins us.

"Did he just run right over here and tell you?" Cara says. "Don't even answer that. I don't need to ask."

"Like Cara, I would rather not talk about it, or think about it, for that matter," I say.

"No offense, Olivia," Sheldon says. "But there's not much else going on in the funeral parlor. Daphne's given everyone the story of the evening."

In fact, Sheldon and Jenson aren't the only ones noticing Daphne and Todd. Half the guests are staring at them or whispering when they pass by.

I excuse myself and hurry over to my sister.

"Hey!" Daphne says.

"How are things with Todd?" I ask her.

"Okay," she says. "We talked."

"That's good."

"We had sex," she continues.

"You don't say."

"We spent the whole night in the same bed," she adds.

"That's awesome! You're on your way back."

"Yeah, I don't know. I hope so. We decided to go to couples therapy, too. So time will tell."

I beckon her out of earshot of anyone else before I say in a whisper, "I'm happy things are going better with Todd, but your hair has a residue in it."

Daphne puts her hand to her head and smiles.

"Right," I say. "And it's obvious. You must respect the dead in a funeral home. That's the only reason a funeral home exists."

"Oh, Olive. You're so uptight."

Daphne always was the rebellious one out of the three of

us. It's funny to think of now because she's been locked up in her house, playing mother and housewife for so long, but she was the one who snuck Dad's beer out of the cellar and got wasted on our roof. She was the one who got high on weekends freshman year and tried to cheat on a geometry test. She was the one who was sleeping with her boyfriend and got caught by his parents in their bed in the middle of the school day. She was smart and demanded a lot of herself academically, but she also loved to be a wild child.

I look at her with fresh eyes. "I think you've let the rebel go too much," I say suddenly.

Her pretty blue eyes widen. "What?"

"You're the rebel in our family, Daph. You always were. I think you put that part of yourself away when you got married and had kids, and now she's locked up somewhere in the closet of your mind. You miss her, don't you?"

Daphne's mouth drops open. "Jesus. You're right."

"I think you should bring her out again. Not by drinking or getting high. But somehow, you need to reconnect with her. You're dying inside without that part of you. Let your kids see who you are, Daphne. Don't just show them a 1950s housewife. That's not you."

Daphne pulls me in for a hug. "You are so freaking smart, you know that? No wonder you make so much money."

"I don't make so much money. I make money. Will, on the other hand," I say as I see him stride through the door, wearing a designer suit and sunglasses, "makes soooo much money. Look at what he's wearing."

"Did you have sex with him?" she asks as he waves at me and heads in our direction.

"You sound like Mom. And the answer is no. Not on your life."

"Olivia." Will leans down and kisses my cheek. "So sorry to meet you again under these circumstances." He looks at

Daphne through his shades. "I'm sorry, I don't believe we were formally introduced. I'm Will."

"This is my sister, Daphne," I say. "Now if you'll excuse me..."

"I want to take you out," Will says loudly as I try to walk away.

Daphne's eyes flash to mine.

"No, thank you. I'm busy."

"I didn't mean tonight necessarily," he says.

"I'm busy every night," I say as Jenson approaches us.

He gives Will a hard look, and Will acts like Jenson doesn't even exist.

"You can't be busy every night," Will says. "Your mom says you're single and divorced."

As if on cue, Mom comes over to our group. "Oh, hello Will," she says pleasantly. "I see you and Olivia have found one another."

I breathe out heavily. Jenson's clenching his jaw, and his eyes have turned cold.

"Mom," I say. "Please stay out of this. I told Will I'm busy."

Sheldon, never one to miss anything interesting, strolls by with Cara. He stops on a dime as soon as he hears what I say to Mom, and then he shifts his gaze over to Will. When he sees Will wearing shades, even though we're inside and it's nighttime, Sheldon starts to laugh.

"What's so funny?" I say to him.

He leans in and whispers to me, "I just know this guy's not your type. I may not know much, but I know that. So I believe you when you said it's not him."

I turn to Will. "Excuse me. We're leaving for the burial soon," I say before walking away.

———

We pile into our cars and follow the funeral procession through town from one end to the other until we arrive at the cemetery.

I sing along with everyone else to Come Labor On while Dad and the other pallbearers lower Auntie Sue's casket into the ground.

Afterward, we drive to Cybil's house where she has a three-course meal spread out in her dining room. Miraculously, Will has disappeared, but before I know it, Cindy's next to me asking if I can help her find Jenson a good woman.

Jenson's across the table with my mother, who's rambling on to him about Will and what a shame it is that I won't give him a second chance.

"I think Jenson can work out his own love life," I say to Cindy, trying to be as polite as I can.

Vivian's next to me on my other side and she laughs. "God, if only my mother had learned that rule."

I want to ask Vivian why she's here, but when I see Ed putting a piece of meat on her plate, the light dawns. Apparently wakes are a good place to meet someone.

"I'm just worried," Cindy says as Sheldon shakes his head and shoots Jenson a sympathetic look. "He's already been divorced once. And you too Olivia. I want to see you both settled and happy."

Not one minute later, my phone buzzes with a text.

You and me. I'm taking you home after. I know you've been avoiding me, but don't even try to argue me.

I look over at Jenson, and his hot green eyes lock onto mine.

I give him a nod, and he walks away from Mom at the same time that I get up from the table and stand by the bay window. Jenson joins me as I stare out at the rain, which provides a welcome relief from Cindy, who's behind me again and talking in a loud whisper.

"Missy called last night to pay her respects to Auntie Sue," Cindy says. "I had forgotten about her."

I raise my eyebrows questioningly at Jenson.

"Missy from my senior prom," he explains. "She met Auntie Sue one time. Prom night when we took pictures. Missy and I were always just friends."

"She read about the death in the obituary," Cindy says. "And she was just so sweet and kind and single..."

Of course Missy's still single. Why else would she scour the obituaries and find a way to try to worm her way back into the life of some guy she had a crush on in high school?

Meanwhile, Mom is STILL talking about Will, this time to Sheldon, who doesn't want to hear it.

"Mom, the guy's a tool," Sheldon says. "Let's call a spade a spade here."

"Sheldon, don't be rude," Mom admonishes him. "If not Will, then maybe that sweet boy you mentioned the other day to me, Cindy. What was his name again—Howard?"

"Howard!" Cindy says. "Olivia, I think you'd love him. He's corporate like you are, and..."

And then it happens. Jenson loses it. But not in a way that would look reasonable and acceptable. No, he loses it in a way only he can.

He bends down to put his plate on the ground.

Then he stands up straight, and out of absolutely nowhere, he puts his hand on the back of my neck, pulls me flush to him, and kisses me.

Right on the mouth.

I hear the loud gasps as I put my arms around his waist and kiss him back.

We don't kiss for long, just long enough to make our intentions clear.

When we pull away after several seconds, the room has fallen into a hush.

I look around at the sea of confusion blanketing everyone's faces: Mom, Cindy, Sheldon, Daphne, and Dad. They're so confused that they try to make it right, try to pretend it's okay at first. Mom smiles, Cindy smiles, and Sheldon...well, Sheldon doesn't know what to do, I think, because he's slowly putting two and two together. I actually see the realization flash across his face the moment his mind registers the truth behind my secret boyfriend. His mouth contorts into knowing, and he just...stares at Jenson and me in shock.

Daphne cheers, but then her eyes grow big like she doesn't know what to do next. Dad shifts awkwardly in his chair and looks around like he's making sure there are no reporters around. And Vivian...she turns toward Ed and kisses him. His eyes widen, and he kisses her back with enthusiasm.

Then Cybil starts to cry.

At the sound of her shrill, insistent wails, everybody freaks out. I mean *freaks* out.

Mom starts screaming at no one in particular, wondering how she didn't uncover this love affair herself and then asking me why I couldn't find someone outside of the family to date.

Cindy begins to berate Jenson, asking him what he thinks he's doing by betraying the Grahams' trust this way.

Cybil cries louder.

Matilda worries out loud that our kids will be like the royals, "who we all know are inbred."

Dee catches wind of what Matilda says and tries to tell her that Jenson and I aren't blood related, but then he turns on Jenson as well, telling him I'm family regardless.

Cindy quiets down first, and I can see the blood absolutely drain from her face as she realizes that her secret would be treated with just as much judgment and horror as ours is. And Jenson could reveal his father's identity right now, right this minute in order to save himself and turn the attention onto his mother. All he'd have to do is tell the truth about his birth, and in about two seconds flat, the whole room would turn on Cindy. And Dee would turn on Cindy. Her world would come crashing down around her feet, and she knows it.

But of course, Jenson keeps his mouth closed. So does Cindy. And the rest of the room keeps shouting. And criticizing. It's painful, but I realize that I'm strong enough to take it now.

"Hey!" Jenson whistles, and the room goes eerily quiet.

All eyes shift to us as we stand with our backs to the window. I have half a mind to turn and use the window as my escape from the unwanted attention, but Jenson puts his arm around me firmly.

"Are you okay?" he asks me softly.

His green eyes shower me with love. His flushed cheeks tell me all I need to know: he's going to fight for us. Even though he doesn't need to because we've already made our decision, Jenson's going to speak his mind, anyway.

I nod. "I'm good."

He presses a kiss to my temple before turning to face our irate audience.

"I'm in love with Olivia Graham." Jenson's admission is met with gasps, but his expression is calm and resolved. "I've loved her for as long as I can remember."

"Shit." Sheldon's stunned reaction breaks the tension in the room, and I nearly smile.

"Olivia's in love with me, too. We're together, and we're not blood related."

"But you're family!" Matilda cries out.

"There are a lot of different ways to define family," Jenson says. "My mom and I were incredibly lucky to be invited into yours. But my feelings for Olivia were always different and ran deeper than what you all thought and understood us to be. We aren't actually cousins, and we aren't going to deny our own happiness by pretending to be something we're not. I love her more than life, and to be without her anymore—it's just not an option. I hope you all have a good meal."

Jenson nods his head, signaling that the "conversation," if you can call it that, has come to an end.

I don't add anything to what Jenson already said so perfectly. But as I stand in front of my family, it's absolutely liberating to finally face what I've always feared. I thought my family's negative reaction would literally crush the life out of me. But I'm okay. I'm more than okay. And that is so freeing.

Jenson doesn't say anything else. He just reaches over, takes my hand in his, and we turn and walk out of Cybil's house. We get into his truck and drive away.

CHAPTER TWENTY-FOUR

We drive out of town and keep going for over an hour until we're at the Delaware border. Jenson pulls off at a gas station and shifts to face me. His eyes shine with emotion, and his mouth turns up in a lopsided grin.

"That didn't happen the way we'd planned it," he says.

"Not exactly." I unbuckle my seat belt, and he pulls me onto his lap. "Okay, not at all. But I don't care."

"Are you sure?" His hand rubs my back gently. "I know we said we were going to wait. But our moms were driving me so damn crazy with their set-up plans. I finally lost it. And God, it felt good to just be open and honest about our relationship."

I lean my head on his shoulder. "For me too. When you kissed me, it was like we were the only two people in the room for that moment."

"I felt that too," he says. "I care so much more about you than their verdict, Olivia. I'm sorry we didn't figure that out when we were younger. But maybe we just weren't ready."

I bite my lip. "I don't think we were. I look at Daphne and how she and Todd were so young when they got together, and they didn't have to go through the outside pressures like we have. And it's still hard for them. For me, having gone through all the stuff I did on my own first, it makes being with you now even better. We're stronger together."

"Nothing can come between us now," he says to me. "Nothing."

"Are you okay keeping the story of your father a secret still?" I study his expression as it turns from calm to stormy.

Jenson clears his throat. "It's my mother's story, Olive. But mine is in there, too. My birth father lives twenty minutes away in a high-rise in Philly, and the man who raised me is on Elm Street in Liberty Falls. And they used to be friends, but Dee has no idea about my mom's night with Donald. What if I want my sons to meet Donald? Am I going to keep the truth from them forever? Or from Dee?"

I shake my head. "I don't know."

He takes my face in his hands and kisses me hard and urgently. "But you and me—this—is ours. No one can touch it, okay?"

I nod and rest my forehead against his. "We did it."

Jenson slips his hand underneath my shirt and I shiver. "We did. And we're going to celebrate all night long. Sound good?"

Sounds perfect.

———

We go to my house and make love all night long. And it's... intense. Some of it's a reaction to death, I think, to try to feel as alive as we can for as long as we can. I hold him in my arms and tell him how much I love him, and he kisses my face as he drives into me over and over again.

I moan at the intensity of him inside me as his thrusts touch me deeper than I've ever been touched before.

We come together, something we've been making into an art lately. And it's bliss.

His sexy sounds drive me wild, and I come one more time as he finishes moving.

"J. I love you."

———

When I arrive at Union Bank the next morning, Vivian immediately calls me into her office.

I walk in, trying hard to act casual, but inside, my heart is pounding.

But she surprises me when she immediately says, "I'm so happy you're happy."

I exhale in relief. "Well, you're in the minority. My mother's left me three voicemails explaining that it's urgent I get back to her so she can talk to me about 'the kiss' she witnessed and can't get out of her head."

"Even when love should be easy," Vivian says, "we make it hard. Or the people around us do."

———

Mom shows up at the bank at lunchtime, and I can no longer avoid her. But I still try. I run behind the teller cages, but Mom calls out, "Olivia, I saw you run back there. Come out because your mother needs to talk to you now!"

I stand up straight and lift my head as high as I can before stepping out from behind the teller cages and looking right into the eyes of my mother. Her gaze is bright but guarded, and I know what she's feeling. She's happy I'm in love but hurt I never told her.

I take her arm and lead her outside the bank and down to the patch of grass by the gazebo. We take seats on the bench before I turn to her. "I'm sorry you had to find out this way. I wanted to tell you a thousand times, and I chickened out. But this isn't some little fling, Mom. Jenson and I are in love with each other and have been for years."

"That's what's so astounding about all of this..." she begins. "For—years?"

"Yes, years," I repeat firmly.

"But your marriage..."

"Was forced," I say. "I wanted Nate to be right, but he wasn't. You all wanted Jenson and me to be cousins so much, with the best intentions, of course. But we always had that spark between us. As a teenager, I was too young, and when Meghan got pregnant...the timing was just never right. And I never wanted him to lose the Grahams as family."

Mom leans her head against the bench. She looks spent. "Of course he won't lose us. Don't worry about that. So you and Jenson have always had a thing for one another?"

"I can't remember a day when I didn't love him." I'm surprised how raw my voice sounds and how laced with emotion.

"Was it the same for him?"

"Yes. We were each other's everything. We always will be."

"Olivia." Mom's voice is hushed. "This is...big. Big love."

"Yes."

Silence.

"Mom," I finally say. "How are you feeling?"

Mom starts. "Oh, pardon me, Olivia. Of course I'm happy you're in love. I adore Jenson. And you two have always been so attached to one another even though I missed the fact that it was romantic attachment. You know we always wanted him to feel like a member of the family. So the circumstances..."

"I've let circumstances hold me back for years," I say. "I'll hurt too many feelings; I'm too young; he's too old; it's not the right time; I need to wait a while; I need to wait forever; I need to marry the wrong man and stay far away from the right one..." I brush the tears off my cheeks as Mom reaches hastily into her purse for a tissue. I didn't even realize I was crying until I feel the wetness on my face.

"Oh, sweetheart." Mom reaches over to hug me. "Dad told me you two talked about love and life the other day. I didn't realize what you were hinting at. I mean, your words were clearly a cry for help." She gasps.

"Mom, you weren't even there."

"Oh, honey, I'm always there," she says knowingly. "Dad and I are like one soul, honey. He spoke to you, felt your issues peeking out from the surface, and he came to me. He said he thought you might be on the edge."

"The edge of what?" I say to her. "He did not say that, Mom! You're speaking reflectively now that you know about Jenson."

"Well." Mom doesn't know how to argue her way out of that comment, so she hands me another tissue and begins to talk about her undying love for Dad.

"That's great, Mom," I finally get out. "I'm glad you and Dad still stoke the fires as you say."

She fixes her attention on me. "I'm happy for you, Olivia. And your father and I both support this union. We may have been taken off-guard, and some members of the family may not be as comfortable with your relationship as they could be..."

"I know that Cybil and Matilda and others may always judge us. They literally seem to think Jenson is blood-related. Not to mention the town."

"All you can do is be happy. Don't pay the haters any mind, okay? Listen, Bea is excited to talk to you about Jenson. She's on my side of the family, and we've always been more open-minded. You two can chat tonight. She found the perfect Adult Ed. class."

"Mom, I'm not sure..."

"It's some extreme form of yoga, supposedly to open up your sex chakra. They say everybody stays clothed, but it may entail a little disrobing of outerwear..."

Oh, sweet Lord. "I can't possibly do that right now. Sex yoga is not the right match for my mood today."

Mom nods solemnly and then gasps so loudly that I jump.

"What?" I ask.

"I have an even better idea," she says so enthusiastically I think she's going to suggest she, Bea, and I climb into our own spacecraft and orbit the moon. "I saw this class at the center, and I didn't say anything to you or Bea because I thought it might be too extreme."

"Oh, no. More extreme than sex yoga?"

Mom nods and looks like she may burst with excitement. "It's called HypnoFantasy."

"That sounds frightening," I say.

"It's a class where each student undergoes a short period of hypnosis in order to unlock her deepest sexual fantasies."

"No," I say immediately.

But Mom thinks I'm saying it in enthusiastic disbelief.

"Yes," Mom says. "I didn't believe you could find a class like that in Liberty Falls, either. Although this town has always been a bit quirky. Which may be a good thing for you and Jenson," she adds with a knowing look.

"Mom, please."

"I'm just saying. This class sounds fascinating, don't you think? I confess to having lots of fantasies lurking inside me, as must you, Olivia. And we could do it together."

My mother has hit a whole new level of liberation. I take a deep breath. "Mom, I really don't think I can handle something so..." I search for a word. "Intense right now. I fully support you and Bea attending, though. It sounds like it could be very therapeutic."

"That's exactly what I thought!" Mom says. "See, it's like one mind, honey."

———

I walk home from work slowly. I've just rounded the corner into my driveway when I notice somebody on my front step. I can't make out who it is because the big bush in front of my walkway blocks the view quite well. As I get closer, Sheldon's profile comes into focus. He's fidgeting with his hands and pacing back and forth in front of my front door.

"Hey," I call out.

Sheldon waves and waits for me to reach him. I invite him inside, and he follows me. Bernie's barking like crazy, so I take him out and then get his dinner ready for him while Sheldon takes a seat on my couch. Once Bernie starts to eat, I sit down on the other end of the couch from Sheldon and wait for him to speak.

"I just want you to know that when the assholes come shouting, because you know they will, Olivia, I am here for you. And for Jenson."

I let out a long breath. "I appreciate that more than you can ever know."

"So you guys can be together now. You are together now." Sheldon watches my eyes. "What do you think of that?"

"I've been in love with him since I was a kid, and nothing has changed that. No matter how hard I've tried, no matter how many other men I've hoped to love, nothing's worked."

His eyes go wide. "At Cybil's, when Jenson said you two had loved each other forever..."

I nod. "Dead serious. And it's the same for him."

"So your marriages..." Sheldon starts to say but then stops himself.

"Yes," I say. "We tried to be normal like everybody else.

The problem is, we're not like everybody else, and we never were. We're freaks, I guess."

Sheldon's blue eyes narrow. "So you've been in love with him forever. I mean, it must have been..."

"Torture," I say, using the word Jenson and I use to describe it. "Yeah, it's been pretty much torture."

Sheldon runs his hand through his hair and tugs at the short strands. "Olive. Shit. I can't believe you kept this from me. Not because I'm a narcissistic asshole and I wanted to be in on a secret but because I can't imagine having to hide from you something that means that much to me." More hair tugging. "I feel like such an ass. All those times I teased you for your bad luck with men, and the things I said..."

I raise an eyebrow at him playfully. "Are you actually apologizing to me, Sheldon Graham?"

He nods seriously. "I am. And I can't believe I never saw the crazy ass chemistry between the two of you. Because once I started thinking about it, I realized it's always been obvious. Jenson's always looked at you like you're a goddess. And he treats you that way, too. Which makes me so damn happy to see my little sister finally be with a man she deserves."

I touch his leg. "Thank you for that."

"So what made you finally decide to go for it?"

"Last chances and all that. We were both finally single at the same time and both still wanted the exact same thing: each other. I guess we decided to stop worrying so much about everybody else and do what makes us happy. I have to follow my heart, no matter what Liberty Falls thinks." I make a face. "To be honest, I'm still working on that part."

Sheldon clears his throat. "You don't have to answer this, but when Jenson got married? I'm assuming the reason you skipped out was because..."

I nod. "Too painful." I look away from him and out the

window. Summer's nearly over, and I feel nostalgic for a moment, the way I always do when a season's coming to a close. My secret with Jenson is coming to a close. No more private rendezvous, no more nights out with Sheldon and Cara where Sheldon thinks we're just friends. That chapter is done and over with. And even though I called it torturous, it was such a part of my identity that I actually feel a sense of emptiness for the end. I'm so excited to turn the page, though, and I know it's beyond time.

Sheldon taps my leg, and I look back at him. "I'm happy for you, Olive. More than happy. I'm super stoked. Not that you need me to be, not that it matters..."

"It matters." I smile at him. "It does."

"Love you, baby sister," he says.

CHAPTER TWENTY-FIVE

When Jenson pulls into my driveway later that night, my stomach lurches as he gets out of the truck and I see his face.

Something's happened.

"Anxious?" he says as he gives me a kiss and walks inside. "It's okay. Nothing's going to be more stressful than what just happened, so I've decided to just sit back and see how the story unfolds. I highly recommend you do the same."

"What happened?" I say. "Because clearly something did."

"My mom and Dee have separated." He puts up his hand as I start to ask him why. "I'll fill you in. It's a bit tricky."

Jenson and I sit down on the living room floor with Bernie and get comfortable. Jenson tells me that after he talked to her about me, he told her he met Donald. Cindy then scheduled an emergency session with her pastor and said she felt at peace for the first time in years.

And she knew what she had to do. She went home and immediately talked to Dee. She told him about her affair with Donald and how she had Jenson tested when he was a baby to confirm who his father was. She even told him how she hid the amended birth certificate from him. And Dee was angry.

Very angry. And hurt. But he said that he was the one who raised Jenson, not Donald, and that Jenson is still his son, biological or not.

"That's good, right?" I say.

"But then..." Jenson begins. "They decided to separate."

"Oh, God."

Jenson shrugs. "They fight all the time although I never thought it meant they'd divorce. But they both want space. They've always seemed kind of distant, I guess. But it's all I've known."

"So where are they living?"

"My mom didn't want to stay in the house alone, so she's moving into the same apartment complex her sister's in, and Dee's staying in the house for now."

"This feels like dominoes. One truth comes out, and then another truth comes out, and then another until soon the entire landscape looks different."

"And speaking of that," Jenson says. "My mom was supportive of me telling Donald the truth. I've set up a meeting with him for next week."

"And he thinks this meeting's about real estate?" I say.

"Right."

"That should be interesting."

"Yeah," Jenson says. "Dee and I are...kind of weird. I don't know. He's very upset I knew about Donald for years and didn't say anything. He's angrier with my mom, and he knows she put me in an impossible spot, but he's just really upset."

"Of course. It was unfair to you from the beginning, and Dee should understand that."

"Donald was his best friend, and the betrayal has rocked him."

I lean my head back against the wall and close my eyes. "I feel like we had a choice to keep things the same or to detonate them completely, and we chose to detonate. And so did your mom."

"We had a choice to be together or to give up completely, and we chose us," Jenson says. "This is us. You and me, Olive."

Cindy calls in the morning and tells Jenson she's arranged for our family to meet at the banquet hall.

"No more secrets," she says to Jenson. "I'll see you and Olivia this Saturday at two o'clock. The hall had a last-minute cancellation, and I took it as a sign, a sign that it's time to tell the truth. Isn't that great?"

"Great," Jenson says as he looks over at me, and I feel the anxiety already building. "We'll be there."

I spend the week living in the mall with Hayley as I try to find the perfect outfit to wear on Saturday.

"Isn't this funny?" Hayley says to me. "It's like déjà-vu. You and I spent the week at the mall back in July before Auntie Sue's party. You were so afraid Jenson was going to show up." She laughs. "Guess he showed, huh?"

I smile. "Guess he did."

She pulls a pink top off the rack. "This may work. It's pretty."

I try on the top and decide it will work. Thank God because this is our fourth shopping trip, and I have to be at the hall in three hours.

"I haven't talked to my mother since her hypnosis class," I say to Hayley. "She left me a message, and I didn't have the strength to call her back. Now I'm regretting it because I'm scared she's going to scream to me from across the room about all the amazing sexual fantasies she discovered were lurking within her."

"I thought your Mom could hardly handle your naked sculpture being seen in public. What happened?"

"Apparently, that sculpture class set off fireworks within Mom. She went from that to sex yoga to this."

"So your mother's stopped worrying about others?" Hayley suggests. "Inspired by her daughter?"

I make a face. "I don't know about that. My mother's always been a bit of a wildflower inside. Kind of like Daphne, actually."

"You'd better go home and get ready," Hayley advises. "Let me know how the next big reveal goes. I really wish I could have witnessed the moment you and Jenson kissed in front of your families. Too bad no one videoed it."

"Just be glad you don't have to come to this thing," I say as I hug her good-bye and hurry to my car.

———

As Jenson and I walk into the banquet hall together, he grabs my hand just as we round the corner to face everybody. The air noticeably goes out of the room when our relatives look up and see us standing there as a couple. Patsy frowns and mutters something under her breath, and Matilda sighs so loudly I hear her even though her table is quite a distance away.

And Glenn is here with a cameraman.

"Reporters?" I murmur to Jenson.

"Mom said it was go big or go home," he says. "She couldn't be talked out of it. Your father knows something's going down. She had the good sense to warn him, but he doesn't know quite what it is."

Keeping my hand in his, Jenson walks with determination toward Sheldon and Cara's table. Daphne and Todd are sitting with Mom and Dad at an adjoining table, and I wave as we pass by. Before we make it to the table, Matilda calls out to my father to make sure his daughter "shows some manners."

I catch Dad's eye. He stands up and comes over to give me a kiss. He greets Jenson warmly, who says hi and lets go of my hand to sit down next to Sheldon.

I stop next to my father, knowing he wants to say something.

"I see it now, honey," he says to me quietly. "I see the love between the two of you. I'm just kicking myself I missed it. I suppose I should have realized..."

"Dad, no you shouldn't have. It's not exactly the first thing that would come to your mind."

I hear Matilda call out to my father again in a rude way, and I turn further away from her.

"Ignorance can hurt," he whispers in my ear. "But I know you and Jenson are stronger than that."

I look up at him. "We're working on it. But your campaign..."

"Means absolutely nothing compared to my daughter's happiness." He gives me a kiss and then turns to Matilda. "My daughter has delightful manners. If only everyone in this room had them, too, we may not be having any problems."

Matilda turns red and slumps back into her seat.

As I take my seat next to Jenson, Sheldon immediately starts talking about a fat ostrich in a zoo, "or maybe a neckless giraffe."

"What the hell are you talking about?" I say to him as I lean across Jenson. "If it were neckless, it wouldn't be a giraffe."

"I'm just saying that you guys are being ogled," he says.

I catch Cybil's eye. She harrumphs and turns away from me. I frown and try not to make eye contact with anyone outside of our table.

"Okay, I take that back," Sheldon says now. "I think you two are being ostracized more than ogled."

"Thank you, Sheldon." I clench my teeth. "Thanks for the dictionary lesson."

At the tap on my shoulder, I turn to face Daphne as she kneels next to me. "Hi, Daph," I say quickly.

"Hi. Look, I'm sorry I haven't called. I've been..."

"I know, busy," I say.

"Well, that's not really true," she says. "I just haven't known what to say because I don't think I understand the kind of love you and Jenson have for each other."

I did not expect that to come out of her mouth. "You've been married for years. And you love Todd."

"And yet I don't understand. You and Jenson are willing to risk being kicked out of the family and to suffer complete humiliation from Liberty Falls in order to be together. That's really big."

"Well...thanks, I think."

She gives me a hug. "I admire you," she says just as Mom calls across to me from her table.

I gesture that I'll be right over, but my mother apparently can't wait. She stands up and hustles over to me, practically knocking Daphne out of the way.

"See you later," Daphne says as she gives Mom a look and goes to sit down.

"Hi, Jenson." Mom moves over so that she can kneel in between the two of us.

He says hello to her, and then she turns to me. "Oh, Olivia, HypnoFantasy was fabulous!"

I close my eyes for a second, hoping when I open them,

my mother will have instantaneously vaporized back to her table.

But no such luck. Mom's still talking, and I open my eyes to see Jenson grinning at me.

"Sooo freeing," she says. "So invigorating. I found myself speaking out loud all these secret fantasies I've had for your father and never had the courage to act on!"

I resist the urging to cover her mouth. "That's great, Mom. Maybe we can talk more later..."

"I just wish you could have joined us," Mom says. "Bea said the same thing. All night she said, 'I wish Olivia was here, too. Imagine the years' worth of fantasies she's buried for Jenson!' And I told her I agreed. Honey, you must try some sexual fantasy evocation on your own." Mom turns to Jenson. "Don't you think that's a good idea, Jenson?"

"Absolutely," he says, and his eyes brighten on mine. "I'm glad you enjoyed the class, Nora."

"Mom, can this wait?" I say. "Today is awkward enough. Please, let's talk later."

Mom shushes herself and creeps back to her table just as Jenson's mother approaches the front of the hall and takes the microphone.

Cindy asks for our attention, and without any pausing or small talk, she immediately tells the room the truth about Jenson's conception and birth.

My head immediately turns to my father. His face is ashen.

Cindy's attention is also focused directly on Dad. "I never wanted to hurt either of them," she pleads to my father. "Please believe me."

My father's kind eyes are warm when he nods at her. "It will be okay, Cindy," he assures her. "No one's getting kicked out of this family. You, Dee, and Jenson are all part of the Grahams."

Not everyone has the same response. Gasps echo through the room, followed by calls for Dee, the "poor man who didn't know any better."

A raucous clamoring for Dee ensues with Cybil standing up and shouting as Patsy holds her by the elbow to keep her steady. Cybil cries loudly for Dee, begging somebody to please call him up and get him over here before he dies of loneliness.

Jenson finally holds up his phone to show that he has Dee on the line. "He's getting a haircut," Jenson announces to the room. "He'll stop by afterward."

Cindy returns to the microphone and says that she would also like to add, for clarity's sake, that Jenson and I are not related by blood, and therefore any children we have will not come from the same genes.

Patsy breathes a sigh of relief. "So it's the best of both. Jenson and Olivia are both in the family, but not in a gross way. So they're keeping it all in the family by being together."

Another silence before Cindy says, "Thank you for your input, Patsy. Let's eat, shall we?"

Dad steps to the microphone now. He recommends that everybody enjoy the meal Cindy organized "for all of us, and I suggest everyone take a moment to bow their heads and think about forgiveness and acceptance. Life isn't perfect, and neither are people," he adds. "Let's let Dee and Cindy work this out between the two of them."

The flash from the cameras is constant, and when I look over at Glenn, he gives me the thumbs-up.

"I think your dad just came up with his re-election theme," Jenson whispers in my ear.

I take Jenson's hand in mine. Our love is no longer a secret, and being able to fully live our story at last is the best part of all.

EPILOGUE

Six Weeks Later

Jenson and I haven't gotten officially engaged yet, not because we're delaying but because I keep changing my mind about the details. I tell him I don't want a fancy wedding or a lot of hoopla. But he thinks we need to do something official. He thinks it's important for us.

"Jenson's completely right about that," Hayley says when she and I meet for lunch at Bernie's. "Don't just go to the courthouse like Max and I did and forgo all tradition." She holds up her left hand, and I smile at the Native American ring on her left finger, a beautiful ring that's perfect for Hayley but looks nothing like a traditional wedding band. "It's different for you and Jenson."

"Why?" I say. "I don't care about those things, either, like big white, poofy dresses and old traditions people try to drag with them into the present."

"I know," she says. "But it's important for you guys to have a public ceremony to mark you officially becoming husband and wife. After all you've been through having to hide your love from your relatives, it makes sense."

"I guess so," I say. "I don't know if Matilda, Patsy, and

Cybil would even show up at our wedding. They don't know what to do with us now that they can't put us in a box. Some of the townspeople have been so supportive and excited about our romance, but others—well, let's just say it wasn't all warm and fuzzy."

"Oh, you know the naysayers," Hayley says. "They won't be able to stay away. Talking about your wedding will keep them busy till they die."

"That long? Matilda's only sixty or so."

"Olive, they could talk for over thirty years about yours and Jenson's love story," Hayley says. "That's part of what makes it great! Embrace it, for God's sake. Do something good with all the angst you two went through. Gossipers love to talk about forbidden love. It sounds so tantalizing."

"It does?"

"It's like the romance they wish they all had," she continues. "Full of passion and danger. You both risked everything that means anything to you in order to be together. They should be so lucky, and they know it too." Hayley looks at me confidently. "Deep inside, you know they know it."

I try to change the subject. "Jenson's birth father said that whenever we decide to tie the knot, he's going to come to our wedding. He already told Jenson he'd be there."

When Jenson told Donald he was his father, I have to say I was impressed by the man's response. He didn't miss a beat —sure, his face turned ghostly white, and he looked tempted to dash through the nearest exit, but he didn't. He stayed. He shook Jenson's hand and said he wanted to get to know his son.

And he's held firm to that promise. He and Jenson meet once a week for coffee. Sometimes Donald comes to Liberty Falls, and sometimes Jenson goes to Philadelphia. I've met with them a couple of times, and Donald's been really excited about our relationship.

And Dad? Well, his campaign for re-election, now heavily focused on the themes of forgiveness and family, is taking off. No attention is bad attention, as they say, and my father is a heavy favorite this fall to win. The healing has felt complete.

Hayley takes a sip of her soda. "Now what about Dee?"

Well, the healing has felt *almost* complete.

"Donald and Dee aren't on speaking terms yet, and I'm not sure Dee will ever forgive Donald for his betrayal. In terms of Jenson, once Dee and Cindy officially separated, he warmed up toward Jenson, but it's not all the way back yet." I shrug. "Maybe it never will be. Jenson wants it to be good between them again, but he's relieved that at least he doesn't feel like he's living a lie with Dee. Cindy says she was trying so hard to keep everything smooth that she never allowed herself to realize she wasn't happy. She says she was ashamed to admit the truth. She's happier now, actually. She really is." I smile at Hayley and stand up. "Anyway, I should get back to work. I'm so excited to be able to use my bonus from the deal I closed in Manhattan toward the down payment on whatever house Jenson and I decide to buy."

"I think it's awesome you decided to start fresh," she says. "A new beginning for both of you to finally have something to call your own."

Jenson

I grin as Olivia steps out of the bank with a wide smile on her face. It's the same smile she's had for the last six weeks. I'm sure it matches the dopey grin I wake up with every morning and go to sleep with at night. After what the two of us went through, working our way back to each other, any obstacle life throws at us right now feels easy to navigate.

Because we're finally able to be a united front and steer through any issues together.

"Hey!" I pick her up off the ground and swing her around.

She buries her face in my neck. "Hi, yourself."

I don't put her down like she no doubt assumes I will. Instead, I carry her down the sidewalk and then lift her into my truck.

"Where are we going?" She laughs as I jog around to the driver's side and turn the key in the ignition.

"Kyle and Connor are with Meghan, and Bernie's with my mom. So it's just you and me, babe."

I turn my gaze on her, and her gorgeous blue eyes light up. Olivia Graham's beauty still gives me chills. Being alone with her turns me on just as much as it did when we were being illicit. We still find ways to surprise each other, to make out in public places where no one can find us, and to be naughty when nobody has a clue.

Today, I take her to the town lake. "Nobody ever goes to the back side," she says even though she's said it a dozen times before.

I reach for her hand and lace her fingers through mine. "I know. That's why we're going there."

"We can't swim, though. It's too cold."

"We won't be swimming."

"So what..."

"Patience, Olive."

"I think I've proven I've got plenty of that, J. I waited for you for a long time. Years. You should get a medal in endurance too."

"What kind of endurance?"

Her cheeks flush. "The bedroom kind is definitely in the running. Although that's not what I meant."

I chuckle as I pull into the parking lot and drive around the lake. When I park, I hop out and then open the passenger door for Olivia. I help her down and tell her to stay right there. She puts her hands into the deep pockets of her winter coat and waits while I climb into the back of the truck.

"Okay." I come back to her with a big bag over my shoulder. "Let's go."

"What are we doing?" Her eyes narrow.

Olivia doesn't love surprises. I can't say I blame her after all the unplanned ups and downs our relationship has taken over the years. But she's going to like today's surprise.

I put my free hand on the small of her back and guide her down the wooded path. "You'll see, babe."

We walk for over a mile to a spot Olivia's never been before.

"And I thought I'd been everywhere in Liberty Falls," she says in a low tone. "But this, this is...an abandoned house?"

The farmhouse in front of us is dilapidated and has clearly seen better years. But it has a homey charm to it that I felt the first time I laid eyes on it.

Olivia seems to feel the same way. She starts walking toward it without hesitation.

The lake borders one side of the property, but the other side has miles of forest behind it.

"It's so beautiful I could cry," she says in nearly a whisper.

Living in suburbia has been choking her off. She's been wanting more land and more quiet. She told me all of this late one night, after hours of lovemaking, while we were lying tangled up in a mess of bed sheets and nothing else. I told her that I wanted that too. It felt like a confession of the heart, another secret we had been afraid to voice.

"I can't believe I've never seen this place before," she says.

I study her face. "I thought we could spend the night here together. Do you want to look inside?"

"Can we?"

"Sure. Nobody's living here right now." I lead her up the steps and turn the doorknob.

"Oh, I love this place inside, too!" She spins around, taking in the country kitchen, the awesome reading nook by the bay window, and the cozy living room with a picture window looking out at the lake. "This is amazing, J."

"I love it, too." My eyes find hers. "Do you want it to be ours?"

She gestures around the house. "This—is for sale?"

"Was. For Sale." I zero in on her blue eyes with my green ones. "I bought it. For us."

"You"—she shakes her head in confusion—"I don't understand. How could you afford it? And what about my bonus? I was planning to use it toward our down payment."

"You can use it to help with the renovations if you'd like. Clearly the place needs a little work before we move in." I drop to my knee, and Olivia covers her mouth with her hands. "I love you, Olivia Graham. This moment is something I've dreamed about my whole life. Will you marry me and live in this farmhouse with me?"

When I pull the little box out of my pocket and open the cover, the ring sparkles as brightly as the blue in Olivia's eyes. A sheen covers them as she swallows hard.

"Oh." She bites her beautiful plump lip. "I always held out hope, but I just never thought..."

"I know." I fight the emotion clogging my own throat. "Me, neither."

"It's beautiful, J." She gets on her knees across from me and touches the ring lightly with her finger. "But you didn't need to buy me this incredible house or this gorgeous ring to get me to say yes. I said yes to you a long time ago, and I've never changed my heart."

"I want to give you everything because that's what you deserve. And I've been thinking..."

"Oh, no." Her expression turns teasing.

I grin. "Nothing bad. I know we've gone back and forth on this, but I really do think that we should have a real wedding. In front of family and friends. It can be super casual, but I feel like an actual wedding is important for us. Maybe because of what we've been through."

She holds out her left hand. "Great minds think alike. Hayley and I were just coming to the same conclusion. Will you put the ring on me?"

I take the ring out of the box and slip it on her finger, right next to the one she already wears from me. "They fit together," I say.

Her eyes fill with tears. "I'm going to make this ring my wedding band," she says, pointing at the band. "They make a perfect match."

I bring her into my arms and put my mouth over hers. "Yes, they do."

For so long, I lived my life in a daze, missing Olivia and fearing the worst—that I'd lost her for good. I was lucky enough to get another chance to make her mine. And despite all our spin-outs and missed opportunities, here we are. Just the two of us, together forever. Olivia Graham is finally mine, and I'm never letting her go again.

BRAYDEN

What happens when you mix football and cowboy? You get BRAYDEN! He's the only Wild cousin still living in Montana, and he's also the most private, but he's about to find himself in the middle of a love triangle with a woman he never thought he'd see again. Available now!

Take a peek at BRAYDEN, a contemporary love triangle romance:

Leleila

Brayden Wild was my first kiss. The Montana football star with the cowboy boots and sexy tattoo. He salvaged my heart from a bad choice I wish I never made, on a night I wish I could forget.

But that was twelve years ago. And since then, I've been wise enough to play it safe. Certain. Risk-free.

Until I go to the store and spill granola all over...Brayden Wild. He's still rocking a wild mess of blond hair. He's still sexy as hell.

My smooth reaction? I trip and fall on him. And then I run off like a frightened deer.

Because I still WANT him.

But I'm getting married in a month.

Brayden

Leleila Wills. The bookish, teenage girl with the sad, beautiful eyes and killer body who electrified me at first sight—is now a grown woman living here in Mountainview. I finally know her name. I finally have a second chance to ask her out. But I can't.

Because I DON'T go after women who are taken. Ever.

I try to focus on coaching my football team and on taking care of things at the ranch. So why can't I get her the hell out of my head?

I tell myself it's because she needs a friend. I mean, what kind of tool stands up his wife-to-be before their wedding dance class? But the truth is...

I like Leleila's awkward, quirky personality. And I can't deny how my body's on fire whenever she's nearby.

I've got one month to get to know her the way I wanted to

twelve years ago, even if it's only as her friend. That will have to be enough.

So what the hell will I do if it's not?

READ BRAYDEN AND LELEILA'S STORY IN *BRAYDEN*, AVAILABLE NOW!

ALSO BY MELISSA BELLE

Boston Boys Series

BOSTON BILLIONAIRE

BOSTON LOVE

BOSTON ESCAPE

BOSTON ROOMIE

WILD MEN Series

WILD MAN

COLTON

DYLAN

AYDEN

JENSON

BRAYDEN

CAMERON

Sign up for Melissa's Newsletter to receive alerts and updates on upcoming book releases.

ACKNOWLEDGMENTS

Thank you so much as always to: Dawn for your eagle eyes; J. Hunter for your artistry and technical skills; and J.W. for your multiple talents.

And to my husband—thank you for your patience and unconditional love.

ABOUT THE AUTHOR

Melissa Belle writes contemporary romance novels in a style that's sexy, sweet, and steamy. She lives in New England with her family, and often works through her story ideas while hiking with her husband, or hanging out with her two rescue kitties.

When she's not writing love stories, Melissa Belle loves to travel. Her first novel was written while riding through Europe on the train.

To receive an email when Melissa releases a new book, sign up for her newsletter!